HEART

GHOST MOUNTAIN WOLF SHIFTERS BOOK 2

AUDREY FAYE

1

LISSA

I look down at Kelsey and grin. "How come you're not purple like everyone else, cutie?"

The small girl at my side just smiles sweetly and adds a handful of mountain berries to my bucket.

Myrna snorts. "It's because she's actually picking some along with eating them. The rest are just filling their bellies."

Rio laughs from the other side of the bush, where he's helping Braden extract himself from the brambles that caught his wolf when he stuck his head in too far chasing a particularly ripe berry. "They're growing pups. And these berries are really good."

They're some kind of relative to a huckleberry that only grows on the high south slopes of three local mountains. It was a climb to get here, but we filled the pups full of sausage and waffles before we left, and Rio, Shelley, and Kennedy have already ferried most of what we've picked back to the kitchen, where Kel swears he's guarding them with his life.

That might be a harder job when Ebony and Hayden get back from their run.

My wolf sulks. She wanted her alpha to come berry picking.

I sigh. We've had this conversation. A lot. He's a good man and a really sexy one, and this pack needs both of us focused on getting ready for the winter, not on things that might end up very complicated in a big hurry.

My wolf growls. She doesn't think it would be complicated at all.

She forgets so many things. All of our wolves do. Most of them have already embraced the wonder that is our new pack. It's our humans, far more sensitive to past and future, who are having trouble walking forward. I look over at the woman picking berries off the bush next to me. Eliza sits at the edge of the fire every night, watching the forest, sad that her boy hasn't come home. Even Kel is confused about that, but not a single dominant has so much as sniffed in the direction of the den, and it's been three long weeks since Banner Rock.

I guess their humans are having trouble walking forward, too.

I look up as a panting wolf comes over the rise, followed by a gamboling teenager who doesn't look winded at all. I shake my head. Kennedy has enough energy for six teenagers. I nod at the older wolf she chased up the mountain. "Hey, Shelley. There's water over by the pups." The ones we could convince to nap, at least. Braden's high on berries and won't nap for a week, and Kelsey has mostly grown out of sleeping during the day. Kel says she enjoys the quiet time with her pack's elders. Which I don't think he means as an insult.

Shelley shifts and grabs a pair of loose shorts and a t-shirt. "I'm fine. We stopped by the river on the way up."

Still trying to hoard precious resources for the pups, even though they're not scarce anymore. "Kennedy and Reilly lugged a whole lot of water up here, and they didn't do it so the pups could take a bath."

She snickers and looks at the sleeping pile of very sticky small wolves. "They could use one."

Robbie would howl mournfully if he heard her. Ever since swimming in the river became an option, he's objected strenuously to other forms of getting clean, aided and abetted by his alpha and both of his betas. Which is the stuff of healthy, normal packs, and it makes my heart ache every time it happens. Our days are so very good—and so many things are still broken. Living with both truths is a balancing act I haven't got remotely figured out yet.

I feed myself another small handful of berries and glance down at Kelsey, who's still quietly picking at my side. I've been taking a lot of cues from her lately. She's got an eerie patience and a way of seeing joy that calls to my wolf. "Are you going to make berry jam with Myrna when we get back?" The two of them are inseparable these days, partly due to one very large pink blanket they're crocheting.

She shakes her head. "Mellie."

Rio laughs. "She wants more hawk rides, does she?"

We've had three visits in the last two weeks from juvenile hawks who just happened to be in the area. They all ask Mellie if she wants a ride. She never says no. Which means the hawks won't stop dropping in anytime soon, especially when Myrna adds berry jam to our attractions. Fortunately, Miriam has mostly stopped having heart failure as her baby girl wheels around the sky in the claws of a teenage flying predator.

If I didn't know who Mellie's daddy is, I'd wonder if she were part bird.

Kelsey daintily eats a single berry. A very ripe, juicy one. She might be a judicious eater, but at least a dozen of the best berries in the patch have made it into her belly.

Rio shares a grin with me as Braden runs over to Shelley and the bag of snacks she's just pulled out. Knowing Shelley, there are cookies. And hopefully the eggs I dutifully hardboiled this morning in an attempt to balance out the impending sugar intake.

That's me, pack bookkeeper and purveyor of boring snacks.

Not that any of the pups complain. Even eggs are a treat when you've eaten as much rice and beans in your life as they have. Grocery delivery is a highlight of every week, even with Shelley in charge now instead of Rio. I start picking berries again, with more focus this time. The more foraged food we can add to our winter supplies, the less my heart will thump when I add up the grocery bills.

I know we can afford it—the math says so. My heart is still trying to catch up.

My wolf makes a pithy comment about my slowpoke heart that I ignore. I feed her berries instead. She needs to wait until after the new den arrives and we all settle in for the winter. Maybe then we'll think about what to do with our sexy alpha.

Until then, I need to stop feeling so restless and cranky and just breathe in the wonder of sitting on a mountainside in late July, picking berries and surrounded by pack, free of the fear that gnawed on us for six years, even in the happy moments.

I have no idea why that doesn't feel like enough.

RIO

These two are going to kill me. I catch Myrna rolling her eyes, so obviously she can hear the grinding in Lissa's head as loudly as I can.

The other half of this dumbass duo is off somewhere in the woods, running his betas into the ground and studiously ignoring what the rest of us can see coming from a hundred miles away. Which I would normally do something about, but my sentinel instincts agree with the noise in Lissa's head.

It's better to wait.

I grumble along with my wolf. It doesn't make sense. No matter how modern and evolved shifters have become, there are some realities that are damn hard to escape, and one of those is that mate bonds stabilize packs. Especially mate bonds at the top.

I remember how hard it shook Whistler Pack when Adrianna lost James. It devastated her and it ripped Hayden and Jules into tiny, forlorn, traumatized pieces, but the cracks it ran through the pack's foundations were legion—and brutally hard to heal. I learned a whole lot about being a sentinel in those years. And a whole lot about watching a strong woman remake herself so she could be the glue her pack needed.

I glance over at Lissa and wonder if that's why we're waiting. She's amazing, even now—but when she figures out what to do with her fear and her strength and her rage and her freedom, she's going to be jaw dropping.

Or so my wolf thinks. He might be biased. She's had him wrapped around her little finger ever since I set eyes on her, a terrified avenging goddess holding a great big stick. I'm not sure I would have wanted to be Samuel in that fight.

I smile at the grinding in my own head and get back to picking berries. I know how many of them I eat. If I want to keep eating them this winter, I have a more important job to do today than playing pack matchmaker.

Besides, if my paws are reading the earth right, someone else is coming to take care of that.

HAYDEN

I flop down on the warm ground between my two betas and wheeze. "You guys are evil." Thank fuck we're back at the den. If I die, at least the submissives will be kind to my remains.

Kel snorts. "She's evil. I'm just trying to keep up."

Ebony's wolf isn't the fastest in the pack—that would be Lissa. But she's got endurance that leaves the rest of us in the dust, and she just ran Kel into the ground. Which I didn't think could be done.

It also explains why I feel like I have an anvil sitting on my ribs.

A water bag lands on my chest with a thunk, freshly filled up from the river. One show-off beta, correctly figuring out that I can't move my ass enough to drink the easy way. I pull at the cap holding it shut and wheeze some more as cold water spills down my throat. Which is a combo that nearly drowns me, but it makes the anvil a little lighter.

I suck in another breath and glare at the woman sitting easily beside me. Her cheeks are pink, but other than that, she looks ready to head off on another lap. "Did we get the audience you were expecting?" I have to ask these questions carefully. Way too much shit in this pack is still on a need-to-know basis. I'm doing my damnedest to earn the right to know, but it's a painfully slow process. Today was about putting paws and fur where they could be seen and scented. Building a conversation with the various layers of ghosts in the woods. And apparently letting them watch their alpha get dusted by his betas.

Ebony shrugs and glances at Kel.

He shrugs back. "A couple dozen. One bigger grouping, a pair, and some lone wolves."

He'll know the exact count. I lost track somewhere around the time I punctured a lung. I did see the bigger grouping, though. Two I recognized as friends of Kennedy's. Which makes me wonder who's still in the trees guarding the den, but that's also need-to-know, especially when their fiercest member is up a mountain acting as chief berry sherpa.

I let my wolf's very real concerns about the safety of the den slide. All the most important treasures that need to be guarded are off picking berries, far away from anyone who might cause trouble. Kel was supposed to hang out at the den and hold the fort, but Ebony strolled in, told him the perimeter was covered, and issued a dare he couldn't resist.

Smart beta. She knew both of us needed a long run. Time away from things we can't make go any faster, at least not without trampling on the good things that are growing in the same dirt.

My wolf wants to protest, but he's too tired. He hates that teeth and claws can't all-the-way fix this, and some days he just wants to stalk into the woods and grab scruffs and drag his packmates home.

Unfortunately for him, he grew up in a pack where consent was the prime directive, and he took over a pack where it needs to be, in ways I'm only beginning to understand. Miriam kicked me out of the kitchen last night while I was washing dishes. She did it with her eyes down and a voice so quiet I could barely hear her, but she wasn't trembling and she snickered at my wolf when he whined in protest.

Which made him want to lick her. It shreds him when his wolves are scared of his teeth and claws.

Ice-cold water dumps over my head. I make a noise totally unbecoming a wolf and roll to my feet into a shambles of a fighting stance that sends Kel and Ebony into gales of laughter.

I glare at her, since she's the one holding the empty water bucket. "What was that for?"

She snorts. "I need a reason?"

Not in this pack. My immaturity has been wildly contagious. "That's cold, woman. Really cold." I edge my stance back toward the river. I may only have half a working lung, but nobody beats me in a water fight.

"Self-defense." She grins and plants her feet in a way that would worry any smart wolf. "Your brain was getting loud again."

Crap. "Sorry."

There's empathy in her eyes, along with the imminent-ass-kicking threat. "Give it time. It took us six years to fall apart. It's going to take more than a few weeks to put things back together."

She feints for my head, but I don't miss the point she's trying to make. Or the punch she throws at my gut. I use the fifty pounds I outweigh her by to drag her closer to the water before she shimmies out of my grip.

My wolf growls proudly. Slippery fighter. Good protector.

She dances in with a feint again, this time followed by a kick that misses my balls by little enough to make them wince. "There are other things you could be doing to occupy your time."

I know that tone in her voice. "I got banned from the knitting circle." Mostly. They offered me one ball of left-overs. The rest of the plane full of yarn delivered by Ronan's friend has been carefully doled out to people who actually pay attention to what their needles are doing.

She snickers. "That's not what I meant." This time the kick lands, and my ribs complain. Loudly. That's the lung that was half working.

I wheeze and move closer to the water. Never lose track of your primary objective. Besides, if she knocks me into the river, it won't hurt as much. "Half the pack is trying to play matchmaker. You guys need to knock it off. Lissa's been through a lot. She needs time and space and more evidence that I'm a decent guy and a good wolf." Things I tell myself every damn morning and repeat to my wolf hourly.

He's ready to gut me. He's caught her three tasty rabbits, and I haven't let him deliver a single one of them.

A kick to the back of my legs sweeps my feet out from under me and dumps me onto my ass.

Ebony rolls her eyes. "That, Alpha, is a load of bullshit."

I don't bother standing up. I pivot and catch her legs, which got too close while she was gloating, and toss her bodily toward the river. Which is an asshole move and one with no finesse, but she graduated from the kind of school where fights are fair a long time ago.

And it soothes both of our wolves when she does this.

Mine's never given a shit if people can hold their own with him. So long as they're on his team, he's even unduly chill about getting his ass beat. Something she figured out a couple of weeks ago and is having way too much fun pointing out to anyone in the pack she can get to watch.

But every damn time she does it, a submissive moves closer.

I sigh. There aren't any watching right now, which means she has a different point to make, and if I don't turn on my smart alpha brain and figure it out, my bruises are going to have bruises. But it's hard for me to be smart about a certain green-eyed wolf. "What happened to go slowly and be patient? If it's good for the pack, it's good for everything else, too."

My wolf growls. That's a really dumbass argument.

Ebony's eyes are focused and solemn. "That's the right answer most of the time. But there are times you're maybe too careful. This might be one of them."

My wolf preens. Smart beta.

I make my first offensive move in this fight, which just lands me on my ass again. Ebony giggles hard enough that she sounds just like Kennedy. I shake my head wryly.

"Sometimes moving too fast doesn't work out all that well, either."

She grins, and I realize I don't know where Kel is.

Which means I'm about to get my butt kicked. Again.

Then I hear a quiet laugh that isn't his—and shouldn't be in my woods. I spin around, staring at the woman who just walked out of the trees. "Mom?"

2

HAYDEN

I should have expected this. That's the only thought my brain can offer up as my mother dusts a stray leaf out of her hair and buttons her flannel shirt, a couple of the carry bags shifter wolves travel with slung over her shoulder.

She strides up to Kel, who doesn't seem at all surprised to see her, and kisses both his cheeks. "Your trackers aren't bad."

He scowls. "They didn't stop you."

She grins. "Most can't, sweetie. A couple of young ladies spied me, though. I invited them to join me."

Two teenagers step out of the trees. Kennedy, looking sheepish and carrying the baskets Rio rigged to carry berries, and someone bravely managing to not hide behind her—and nearly tripping over her own feet in awe. Someone I've never seen before, but her scent teases my nose.

My wolf remembers her. She was at Banner Rock.

They all look at me, because of course my mother has arranged to make her own entrance somehow secondary. Which shouldn't be a surprise. Wolves with PhDs in organizational psychology are tricky creatures. There's also no way she came here to destabilize my pack, although her version of help might not be all that comfortable.

I nod at the two teenagers, alpha to sharp-eyed perimeter guards.

They both straighten, their eyes proud.

My mom's lips twitch.

I manage not to snort as I look at Kennedy and carefully avoid making direct eye contact with her friend. "At last count, I think there were four people who've ever won Kel's bandana game. You managed to spy one of them sneaking into our territory."

The emotions that chase over Kennedy's face would be funny if my wolf weren't so thoroughly flummoxed. She elbows the lithe teenager beside her. "Ghost could have gotten that bandana, too. Probably better than me."

My wolf revels in the obvious show of loyalty—and skill. Good wolves. Strong pack.

I settle him down. Neither of these two have actually come back to the den yet, although Kennedy puts in regular appearances.

My mother smiles at both of them. "Good. Maybe

you can teach your alpha to make a little less noise when he bashes around in the woods."

Ghost's eyes fly up, and to my utter astonishment, there's anger in them. "He's not so bad. He just forgets to set his left foot down carefully sometimes. But being quiet isn't the most important thing. He's a really good alpha. He's kind and he knows how to make the pups feel squishy good inside and he leaves all his chocolate for the sentries."

I don't know who's most astonished by that speech, but Ghost and I are both really good candidates. The human part of me, anyhow. My wolf is seeing something far more important than the words she just said. She's a submissive wolf who can't quite manage to look the alpha of all alphas in the eyes—but not a hair of her is cowering.

I'm looking at a submissive who knows her worth.

"He must be doing a good job," says my mother, very quietly, "to have the loyalty of such a fine wolf."

Ghost nearly melts where she stands—and she dares to look up again. At me. "You are."

I'm getting past the shock of her words and into all the messages they contain. Including the fact that I've apparently had a very competent stalker. Which raises my respect for the young wolf in front of me a lot—and for whoever's leading the show in the woods.

My wolf quiets, thoughtful. There's been no alpha challenge, just protection of the den. But he would stand aside for one who can raise wolves like these two. I nod at Ghost. She's got warm brown eyes and milk-chocolate skin, just like Kelsey, and she tugs at me in much the same way. "Thank you." I phrase my next words really carefully. The last thing I want to do is divide her loyalties. "Since you watch so carefully, perhaps you can let me know when I'm missing something that could use my attention."

A job I'm pretty damn sure she does for someone else, but I don't see any hint of conflict in her eyes, only awe. She glances over at Ebony, who nods. Permission granted, through whatever shadow structures exist in this pack. Which grate on my wolf, but he won't drag them into the light.

Yet.

Ebony flicks her chin in the direction of the woods. "Go tell the berry pickers we have a visitor."

The teenagers are halfway to the trees before I can blink. I grin. Some of the power structure of this pack is plenty visible. I shake my head and walk over to the woman who has just turned my day upside down. She somehow manages to wrap me up in a hug that makes me feel like I'm Robbie's size again, even though I'm twice as big as she is. "You could have mentioned you were coming."

She chuckles. "And miss fresh berries? Not a chance."

She can try playing it that way. "How long are you here for?"

"Just until morning. I had Ames drop me off at the edge of your territory on her flight north. She'll pick me up again when she heads home."

Ames is a crazy-ass shifter who likes to spend most of

her time in her flying tin can, which would make most wolves nuts. She also likes visiting with the polar bears, and probably isn't above helping them torment their new residents.

I take the bags my mother is carrying. Her attention shifts from me to the rangy wolf standing on the edge of our reunion, looking uncomfortable and something else that makes me cringe.

My mom's eyes soften. "You did everything you could. Leroy told me so, and he's never gone soft on a dominant who shirked her duty in his life."

Ebony swallows hard. "I didn't do enough."

The alpha of all alphas walks over and puts her hands on two pale cheeks. "Says every loyal and courageous dominant in a situation too big to be fixed. You stayed to help innocents survive an outrage. Let go of the guilt, sweetheart. It doesn't serve your pack."

I shoot Kel an unhappy look. We've been working on that and I thought we were making some progress, but I can see the truth in Ebony's eyes.

She shakes her head. "He tortured pups while I watched. I didn't do nearly enough."

Adrianna Scott wraps the arms of a dominant who understands, absolutely, what it is to think you haven't done enough, around my beta. "Good. You have a big head. You'll need it to handle your new alpha."

Ebony snorts, but the anguish in her eyes dims as she steps away from comfort and back into the footprints of a warrior. "Careful. I like him almost as much as Ghost does."

My mother's laughter rings bright in the clearing. She looks over at me, her eyes dancing. "I like your wolves, Hayden. Very much."

I shoot Ebony a wry look. "They keep me in line just fine."

"So I saw."

Damn. I forgot she walked in on me literally getting my ass dumped into the river. Something she made sure happened to me on a regular basis, but still. "I hope you brought a sleeping bag. Our den's pretty rustic at the moment."

She laughs and glances at the bags on my shoulder. "I didn't have room, but I assume you have a pup pile I can join."

It might be the biggest pup pile in the short history of the new Ghost Mountain Pack. I have some idea how much our submissives worship the woman who just strolled in from the trees, and I bet I don't know the half of it.

Kel catches my attention with a quick hand signal. I listen. I can't hear them yet, but we have incoming. I contemplate how to play this and take the easy way out. "Let's wait here for a minute. I'd rather the submissives invited you into the den."

She inclines her head regally. "Of course."

I've watched my mother bounce back and forth between alpha and parent my whole life, and it still gives me whiplash on occasion. I lower my voice, which is pointless, because Kel and Ebony both hear like cats. "You've got some big fans here."

Her eyes soften. "I've been chatting with a couple of them on ShifterNet. Your pack is full of treasures, Hayden."

I shake my head. Of course she has.

Kennedy streaks out of the woods first, barefoot and pulling a t-shirt over her head as she runs. "They're coming. They were almost here, but a couple of the pups are sleeping so not everyone is furry." She skids to a halt in front of me, bouncing foot to foot. "I didn't tell them who our visitor is, but they know it's important because Ghost is stuttering and my wolf smells kind of excited."

I manage not to laugh. Teenage dominant egos can be fragile in some strange ways. "You want them all to be surprised, just like you were."

Her wolf settles. Her alpha approves of her judgment.

I brush her hair, not quite ruffling it like I do with Reilly, but close. No pup in this pack is going to grow up any faster than they already have if I can help it. Then I turn to face the sounds in the trees and wait for the summer that wasn't moving fast enough for my wolf to explode into a billion pieces.

LISSA

I have no idea why we're frenetically running back to the den. I know it's not an emergency—not the bad kind, anyhow. But Ghost is nearly shaking beside me, and her feelings are usually as quiet as she is. A visitor. That's all we know.

Myrna careens in beside me and we shift by the pile of clothes we left at the base of a convenient tree. She pulls on a pair of shorts that might be hers and a t-shirt that I'm pretty sure belongs to Reilly. I'm not doing a lot better, but unlike her, my eyes aren't as big as plates. Whoever's here, she knows who they are.

She grabs my elbow. "Let's go. We shouldn't keep her waiting."

My wolf forgot to sniff before I shifted back to human, but I can't smell hawk or cat or anyone else local. Just a wolf I don't know. I look down at the small girl who somehow kept up with us and scoop her up in my arms. "Let's go say hello to our new guest."

Kelsey nods solemnly, like that's something she knows how to do.

It hits me hard. In the four years of her life, I'm not sure we've had a single visitor. I swallow down the bitter taste of that. We have one now, and so long as she likes marshmallows, hot dogs, and berries, we can even offer her a lunch fit for a queen.

Hayden clears his throat, and I realize I've almost crossed over to where he's standing without looking up. Old habits, but ones that I know hurt his human and mystify his wolf. I bring my head up. I'm done hiding, even if old habits die hard. I smile at him—and then I read the pole-axed look in his eyes. My head swivels slowly toward the small woman in a flannel shirt as old and comfortable as mine, standing casually beside Ebony.

It takes me a minute. A real one, a whole sixty seconds for my brain to remember what it's seen on social media and who my alpha's mother is and to realize that my wolf has fainted dead away.

I open my mouth, but no sounds come out.

Adrianna Scott walks over to me, smiling and averting her eyes. A dominant being gentle with the spooked submissive. She looks straight at Kelsey, though. "Hello, sweetie. I came to see if maybe I could crochet a square for your blanket."

The abused, traumatized girl in my arms tilts her head, studying the most dominant wolf in North America. Then she holds out her arms.

My wolf tries to scramble to her feet.

"She's as safe with me as if she were my own." A steady, quiet voice speaking with absolute authority.

And telling me something I already know. There's no safer place on the planet for a submissive pup than Adrianna Scott's arms. I manage to take a breath. "I'm sorry. I know that. My wolf is just—you're so strong."

Myrna snorts beside me. "Of course she is. How do you think she bosses around all those misbehaving Whistler wolves?" She holds out her hand. "It's good to see you again. I don't expect you'll remember me, but we met once at a gathering. I'm Myrna."

Adrianna pulls her in for a quick side hug. "I remember you just fine. You've got three sons. Your oldest is down in Montana working on the wind-power project, yes? They're doing very good work. They're sending a contingent to us next year."

Myrna looks ready to die of embarrassed pride.

There's a scuffle at our feet. Adrianna squats down with Kelsey riding one hip. "Well, hello, tiny girl. Who might you be?"

Our pup who is scared of absolutely nothing beams and snuggles in alongside Kelsey, who happily makes room and volunteers an answer. "That's Mellie. She doesn't talk too much yet, but she likes it when Reilly splashes her."

I smile. It's a good thing someone in this pack can still manage to speak.

"Ah." Adrianna gracefully seats herself on the ground and arranges two pups in her lap. "You're the one who's getting all the rides from Kendra's hawks, then."

Mellie grins and makes a call that sounds impressively hawklike.

The wolf holding her chuckles and winks at Kelsey. "Are you sure she's got fur and not feathers?"

Kelsey's eyes shine, delighted to be in on the joke.

I could kiss the woman who's effortlessly making clear just how she thinks this visit should go.

Which is good, because the rest of us are utterly confused. I can hear the quiet, awed slinking behind me as the rest of the submissives try to get closer to their idol, even though their wolves are cowering. Her dominance is triggering us in a primal way, even though every single one of us has gone to sleep with her words as the only reason we were willing to get up again the next morning.

She's been our shield for six years against the crushing message that we don't matter.

I turn at a crashing sound, tumultuous in the scared, reverent silence. Reilly emerges from the trees, still in bear form, chasing a white streak headed straight for the woman sitting on the ground.

Adrianna moves at a speed that attests to the warrior that lurks inside her, tossing Mellie and Kelsey into waiting arms like they weigh nothing. Then she holds out her arms as my son bowls her over backward, laughing as his tongue slurps every part of her face it can reach.

"Robbie." It comes out sharper than I mean it to, but I've never seen him behave like this. Ever.

He utterly ignores me. So does the woman he just toppled.

A hand lands on my shoulder. Hayden, with nothing but amused kindness in his touch. "He's not a problem. She raised me, remember?"

Kel grins. "And if a dozen pups don't lick her face before breakfast, she gets cranky."

A giggle as Mellie squiggles out of Ebony's arms and shifts, heading straight for the fun new game on the ground.

Miriam squeaks behind me, but clearly she has no more idea what to do about this than I do.

Hayden hugs my awkward, tense body against his side. "Look with your eyes, Lissa. Not your fear."

I try, but that's my hero that my son is trying to maul.

Adrianna taps him on the nose as he grabs her shirt in his wolf teeth. "Careful, cutie. I didn't bring many of those."

Robbie lets go and licks her chin.

Braden is the next pup in, and he jumps onto the pile still human. The scariest wolf in North America picks up his wriggly, naked body and blows a raspberry against his sticky belly. "You must be the best berry eater in the pack."

He nods his head solemnly.

Reilly dashes up, neatly dressed in shorts and a t-shirt, his eyes worried and far too grown up. "I'm really sorry. Robbie started running as soon as we hit the perimeter and I couldn't stop him."

"He's a baby alpha," says Hayden quietly. "He'll be strongly drawn to her."

I try to hide my surreptitious look at Kennedy. We all have our suspicions. She's standing guard over by Ebony, way too self-controlled and grown up to join a pup pile-on, but she's leaning toward Adrianna like the woman has a planet's worth of gravitational pull.

Hayden snorts into my hair. "You can all stop trying to hide that particular cat. It's way out of the bag."

Reilly puzzles that one out faster than I do. "Kennedy will be mad if she hears you call her a cat."

Hayden ruffles his hair. "I know some awesome cats. And some awesome bears. You did exactly right chasing Robbie in here. Even the den isn't always safe, and I'm glad he had you ready to protect him."

Reilly flushes. "I ran into a tree. I tried to go between two of them and I didn't quite fit."

Hayden grins. "That happened to me all the time when I was growing up."

"It surely did," says a voice from the ground. Adrianna smiles at Reilly as she scratches Mellie's belly and somehow keeps Kelsey mostly clear of the rambunctious pile of dominant pups in her lap. "You must be Ronan's new best friend."

It's touch and go whether Reilly's legs are going to keep holding him up. "He told you about me?"

Adrianna snorts. "He brags about you every day at breakfast. I've heard about the fish you catch and how they taste much better than the ones in our rivers and that you know all the best bear jokes and you read so many books that Scotty had to send you more."

Reilly cringes, and my heart cracks.

Compassion flares in the eyes of the wolf watching him. She eases pups aside and gets to her feet, never taking her gaze off the young bear at Hayden's side.

Danielle whimpers behind me. Her cub didn't get the worst of Samuel's disdain—but he got enough.

Adrianna smiles at Reilly. "I'm thinking that your old alpha maybe didn't understand how special it is to have a smart bear in his pack."

Our sensitive, geeky, gentle bear's chin wobbles. "Ronan says it's good to be smart."

"He's right. He showed a good friend of mine some of the extra schoolwork you've been doing."

Reilly turns fourteen shades of pink.

My eyes flick to Ebony and Myrna and Shelley. They all look mystified. None of us knew this.

Ebony raises a wry eyebrow. "It's the middle of summer and you've been doing schoolwork?"

I know that voice. It's the one she uses when she's

prepared to embarrass the hell out of one of her pack-mates for their own good. My wolf whimpers in sympathy for Reilly—and cheers Ebony on.

Reilly squares his shoulders and nods. "ShifterNet has lots of cool stuff. It's all free and I've been getting my pack chores done and it's good for a bear to fill his head with useful things."

Adrianna tilts her head and studies him for a while. Then she walks over and sets her hand on Danielle's shoulder. "When it's time for him to go to university, you send him to me. We have a nice arrangement where our students go into the city once a week and professors come out for regular visits. We have a number of students from other packs. He'll be welcome."

Danielle squeaks.

Reilly squeaks louder.

My heart breaks. I had no idea he had such a wish.

I look at him, because this is a promise I know I can make and keep. "We'll save up the money, Reilly. If you want to go, we'll make sure it can happen." My brain is already offering up budget lines that can be shaved a little, and I can see determination in every set of eyes watching. We'll all do without. Whatever it takes. We might not be brave enough to make wishes yet—but if he is, we'll make it happen.

Adrianna scans us all, and none of us miss her faint, approving smile. Then she heads over to Reilly and ruffles his hair, just like Hayden does, in that rough way that his bear loves. "If you have half the brains and work ethic that Scotty thinks you do, he'll help you apply for scholarships. And we've always got an open job or two at Whistler Pack for shifters who learn quickly."

Hayden growls. "Mom."

She shoots him an innocent look. "What? It's true. Scotty's already making plans."

"He needs time to be a boy first."

Adrianna wraps her arm around Reilly's shoulders. "Of course he does. But boys have dreams, too." She looks straight at her son. "And sometimes they come true."

3

HAYDEN

There's probably a word for the level of chaos that just crashed into my life, but I don't know what it is. I look over at Kel and sigh. He's got lots of experience dealing with guerrilla attacks and hurricanes, and the arrival of Adrianna Scott probably falls into that general category. "Any bright ideas?"

He snorts. "Don't leave her alone with Kennedy for too long?"

I groan. My mother's exploits as a teenage dominant are still legendary. I look over at my pack, swarming our new arrival and fretting over what to feed her. She's blithely assuring them that she loves hot dogs, especially if they come with extra ketchup.

They'll learn soon enough that she means it. And that she eats ketchup on everything.

"She'll do no harm," says Kel quietly. "She'll make

sure of that. And she might create some interesting ripples."

Adrianna Scott always makes ripples. Any wolf as dominant as she is would, especially in a pack this uncertain of its own hierarchy—and where the bonds of loyalty to their new alpha are still so new. She's a thoroughly destabilizing force, and under any other circumstances, I'd be mad at her for messing with my fragile apple cart.

But I can't be mad, even a little, because she keeps sneaking glances at me, and it's not my alpha's eyes that are doing the looking. "My fight with Samuel scared her."

"No shit." Kel holds up four fingers, which is either the number of hot dogs he wants or some new pup sign language I haven't learned yet. "It scared the living crap out of me."

My wolf preens. He won. That's all that matters.

I shake my head. Sometimes he's a dumbass. Anything that can scare Adrianna Scott and Kelvin Nogues should have him quivering in his boots. "She came to check up on me, but that's still going to affect the pack."

"You think?"

I have the most ornery betas. "Quit being a jerk and help me figure out how to manage the unintended consequences." Kel is really big on those. He knows a lot of people who've ended up dead when they weren't managed. "The submissives adore her. Maybe there's an upside we can use." It pains me to think that way, but that's what alphas are damn well supposed to do.

"My advice?"

Finally, thank fuck. "Please."

"Treat her like your mom. Let her spoil the pups and eat hot dogs and tell embarrassing stories about when you were little, and then in the morning, load her on a plane and promise to send pictures."

I raise an eyebrow. "You think anyone's going to let it be that simple?"

He shakes his head. "No. But even when she's being meddlesome and irritating, she's a force for good. Let her be."

"She has really incomplete information." Even the best leaders can flail in those circumstances. I've been thrashing for weeks.

"It will come," says Kel quietly. He smiles at Kelsey, who's shyly making hand gestures at us. She loves the secret language he's teaching the pups. "You want four hot dogs or six?"

I hold up six fingers, which takes me a second to configure and makes Kelsey giggle. She turns to Reilly and Robbie and they confer. Reilly comes up with some number that makes both younger pups nod solemnly.

I grin. Pack math. It's how I learned.

Kel chuckles. "Mellie's going to straighten this all out for you. Watch."

I glance at him, puzzled, and then at the small girl who's ensconced in my mother's lap. She's looking up with a frown on her face, clearly thinking. Rio's watching her, and so are Ghost and Kelsey. Whatever's going on inside her toddler brain, it's got the attention of the pack psychics.

Mellie reaches up and pats my mom's cheek. "Gamma?"

The entire pack goes still. In one word, Mellie has just asked who this powerful wolf is in her life. A dominant, needing to know the hierarchy.

I wait for the quiet look my mom shoots my way. She doesn't need it, but asking for my permission will ease the wolves around her, and when it comes to comforting submissives, Adrianna Scott never misses a beat. I nod, offering my unnecessary blessing.

My mother smiles faintly. She looks over at Myrna and Shelley. "Does your pack have room for a visiting grandmother?"

Kel's quiet grunt is laced with approval. This is the stuff my mother does better than anyone. The most dominant wolf in North America entirely understands the power of asking for permission.

Myrna grins. "That depends. What's in the bags you brought?"

Adrianna Scott actually manages to look sheepish. "Treats."

Ebony snickers and looks over at me. "I think you're in trouble, Alpha."

She's not wrong about that. There's probably enough sugar in those bags to keep the pups speeding around until dark. My wolf just grins. He likes speedy pups, and he knows Mellie has neatly put my mother in the perfect place in the pack. One where she'll listen about as well as Myrna does and nobody will care. Which means he won't have to do dumb things to assert his dominance to keep his pack calm.

Smart pup.

My mother snuggles Mellie and looks over at Miriam. "Tell me more about your girl so I know how to properly spoil her."

My wolf glows when Miriam casts a careful look my way. I nod as gently as I can. There's no way Adrianna Scott will get this part wrong.

Miriam gulps, but she can't quite get the words out. Layla is inching up behind her, though, and her wolf doesn't smell like fear. She slides in close to Miriam and takes her hand. "Braden's mine. He's easy to spoil. Any kind of food will do."

My mother laughs and acts like two women holding hands while they chat with her happens every day. At Whistler Pack it does, but here, it's the first time they've been this obvious in broad daylight. My wolf wants to howl his approval.

My mom grins. "I have some experience with hungry boys."

Layla makes a wry face. "If you get him sticky, you have to give him a bath." She mock glares at Shelley and Myrna. "That goes for all of you."

Myrna shoots Adrianna a dirty look. "Oh, sure. You show up and suddenly we have rules for grandmas."

My wolf can't handle being this far away while his pack is being so brave. I roll in closer to Miriam as casually as I can and shoot her a grin. Her wolf is uneasy yet, even though her human is relaxing. "You better tell her the rules for flying with Mellie. She's got a lot of hawk friends."

Mellie claps her hands and makes hawk sounds again, which will probably have Kendra here by morning. My wolf snorts. The female alphas of British Columbia can't keep their hands off his pack.

I snort back at him. If he wants to sound truly disgruntled, he needs to work a lot harder at it.

He doesn't hear me. He's looking at the green-eyed wolf who just moved in closer with a sleepy boy in her arms.

Lissa looks at my mother and offers a soft smile. "This is Robbie. He's five and he loves swimming and being tickled and he's learning how to climb trees." Her wolf and her pride are both blazing in her eyes.

Adrianna Scott is anything but stupid. She looks straight at Robbie. "You picked yourself a very good mama, sweetie."

He did. One who didn't lead with an apology for his rambunctious behavior or his special needs, and my wolf might not understand what that means, but my human does.

The last three weeks haven't been nearly as useless as they've felt.

LISSA

It's probably not nice to be this amused by Hayden squirming, but I am. The whole time we've been eating dinner, he's been watching his mom like she might explode any minute. Which doesn't seem likely. She's been nothing but sweet and good to the pups, and she's beaming at Braden as he adds extra ketchup to her third hot dog.

He's found a kindred spirit. One who knows how to spit watermelon seeds and splash in the river and draw crayon flowers with Kelsey and fall over like Mellie in a grizzly bear's careful waves. It's hard to imagine she's the woman who single-handedly wrote the rules for how modern shifters live.

She grins as Braden misses her hot dog and ketchup lands on her knee. I snort at Layla, who's sitting beside me.

She rolls her eyes. "Awesome. He'll be forever known as the pup who made Adrianna Scott sticky."

Kel chuckles as he drops to the ground on Layla's other side, two Robbie-charred hot dogs in his hand. "He'll have to get in a long line. The pups of Whistler Pack all learn to feed themselves sitting in her lap."

Kelsey arrives at Adrianna's side with a napkin and a small bowl of berries. Braden reaches for them, his eyes happy—and then freezes, utterly astonished, as Kelsey taps his nose. "These are for our guest." Her little-girl voice rings loud and clear. "You can go ask Myrna for a bowl of your own."

Braden scampers off, casting wide-eyed looks at Kelsey as he goes.

Adrianna just nods solemnly, like the most submissive wolf in the pack gently chastising a pup is completely normal, and takes the berries. "Thank you, sweetie. Will you sit here and share them with me?"

Kelsey shakes her head. "Those are for you to eat while Reilly interviews you." She stumbles over the big word a little, but she manages. "He's a reporter. He tells the stories of our pack."

"I know. I read some of them. I saw the picture he took of your flowers."

"He wants to take a picture of you." Solemn four-year-old eyes. "Because you're important, too."

The alpha of all alphas nods, accepting the comparison to bedraggled wildflowers as the fierce compliment that it is. Then she looks over at Reilly, who's been clutching his tablet for an hour and watching her when he thinks no one is noticing.

He gulps and sits up straight.

She waits patiently—but it's no longer at all hard to believe she's the woman who re-wove the fabric of shifter society.

Somehow, that doesn't scare Reilly at all. He takes a deep breath, one that only wobbles a little. "Will you tell us about Hayden when he was a pup?"

Adrianna's eyes fill with delight.

Hayden's fill with astonishment.

My wolf wants to lick Reilly for asking exactly the right question, one that focuses on who *we* are and not on who she is. We're all so curious about our alpha, and none of us have dared ask much, because if we ask questions of him, he might ask them of us, and there are so many secrets still in the dark.

Adrianna winks at our resident reporter. "Would you like to know about the time he got stickier than Braden has ever been?"

Reilly sits up even straighter, a bear scenting a really good story. Hayden groans. "Mom."

Myrna cackles. Ebony shakes her head and slings her arm around his shoulders. "I'm never inviting my mom to come visit."

Reilly's eyes shine. "Did you get sticky when you were a pup, too?"

She shakes her head. "Never. I was the best-behaved pup in the history of wolf shifters."

Kennedy snorts from her seat over by Ghost. Robbie is sound asleep on their laps, probably because they ran him ragged in a game of river tag right before dinner.

Adrianna, who also played river tag and doesn't look at all worse for the wear, grins at the two teenagers. "I wasn't a well-behaved pup. In case you two ever need suggestions."

Ebony busts up laughing. "Those two do not need any help causing trouble."

Hayden's eyes fill with a strange sadness.

I know why. The smallest pups of our pack mostly act like pups, but the teenagers are still on their best behavior. Although if the careful, considering look in Ghost's eyes means anything, that might change soon.

My wolf hopes so. She was a teenager once. Not a

particularly troublesome one, but she enjoyed the mischief all the same.

Reilly clears his throat meaningfully.

Adrianna winks at him again. "The story goes like this. One day, a six-year-old wolf decided to disobey his mother and his alpha and go into the woods by himself."

Kel shoots her a sharp look.

She shoots one back. "Your sentries are better than mine ever were. No pup will get by them. Let me tell my story."

Ghost nearly explodes with pride. Kennedy, too. And I hear an owl hoot in the trees, which means we have even more listeners to carry the casually spoken words out to the woods. Bailey might pretend that a compliment from Adrianna Scott doesn't matter, but she'll be lying through her teeth.

Kel subsides with a grunt.

I roll my eyes. He probably won't sleep tonight, just in case a pup tries to be dumb like their alpha.

Adrianna looks back at Reilly. "His grandma read him a book that said he could find honey in big holes in tree trunks, so he decided to go find some."

Reilly shakes his head ruefully, a wise bear who knows where you find honey in a Canadian wilderness.

She chuckles. "Exactly. Unfortunately for him, it was spring and the pine sap was running and he kept trying to climb the pine trees to find honey. Eventually, he got stuck to one."

Reilly winces. "That stuff is really sticky."

Adrianna nods. "I know. His father had to use scissors to get him down. I think there's still some yellow wolf fur stuck to that tree."

Reilly's eyes are dancing. "Was his dad mad?"

"No." A glint of something that might be sadness in Adrianna's eyes. "James rarely got mad. He thought it was funny. He helped Hayden shave a fancy pattern into his fur so that his wolf didn't look so silly while it grew back."

"He sounds really special." Reilly's voice is wistful. "Like a really good dad."

Nothing about Adrianna noticeably shifts or changes —but somehow I know that every inch of her is paying sharp attention.

"He died, right?" Reilly looks unfathomably sad.

It's history we all know. It shook the biggest pack on the continent, and we all felt the tremors. But sitting here, with the remnants of charred hot dog in my belly, I can feel the echoes of the smaller, more potent quakes. The ones that hit the woman with ketchup on her knee and the son and daughter she raised alone.

Adrianna nods gently. "He did. Thank you for letting me tell a story that helps remember him."

Reilly eyes her solemnly. "I'll do a really good job of writing it up."

She smiles. "Ronan is right. You're a very special bear."

He is—but he's not listening to the woman who just paid him a huge compliment. He's looking at Hayden, and there's dawning wonder and fierce compassion in his eyes. "Maybe that's one of the reasons you came to be our alpha. Because you know what it's like not to have a dad."

The pain in Hayden's eyes has my wolf moving in an instant.

He shutters it before I get there, tucking it away someplace alphas put things that might hurt their fragile pack. But I saw it. The pain of a small boy who still misses his father—and sharper than that, the pain caused by a pack that still thinks our secrets belong in the dark. We've asked him to be the alpha of six pups without even talking about something as simple as who their fathers are.

I can't fix all of that, but I can fix some of it. I clear my throat and speak as calmly as I can. "I'm not sure who Robbie's father is." I have some guesses, but they won't ever see the light of day. Robbie is mine.

His hands make fists in his lap. He looks at me and nods.

The gratitude in his eyes scrapes me raw.

"My dad is a bear, but he didn't know how to be a good dad, so we came to live in my mom's pack instead." Reilly tries to sound casual, but the wistfulness hasn't left his words. My heart aches for him. It left him so open to the garbage the male dominants dished out. Reilly's bear kept him physically safe, but guarding his tender heart is something we failed at miserably.

Danielle comes up behind him, wrapping her arms around him. I don't need to see her face to know it's awash in guilt. She brought her baby boy to a pack that had four decent years—and then hell found them again.

The sudden growl beside me yanks my attention back to Hayden.

He turns it off, but all eyes are on him, including Adrianna's—and hers are full of surprise.

My wolf isn't surprised. Her alpha is so very done with his wolves feeling guilty.

Hayden shoots us all an apologetic look and then turns his gaze back on Reilly. "I had a really good dad for a while. That made it easy to grow up to be a good man and a decent wolf."

It takes Reilly a moment to understand the compliment—and the challenge. When he does, his eyes shine. "My mom tells me a lot of stuff about how to be a good bear. And Ronan says he can help, too. For the things my mom maybe doesn't know about."

Danielle's head pops up over her son's shoulder, her eyebrows high.

Hayden offers her a wry look. "If you have a chat with my mother before she leaves, she might be able to exert some influence on Ronan and what he considers to be an appropriate bear education."

Adrianna snorts.

Danielle shakes her head wryly and loosens her hold on her son. "Bears."

Layla grins. "I'll trade you. One really sticky wolf pup for one smart, well-behaved bear."

Kennedy grins. "Riles, we need to get you in more trouble."

He looks delighted by that thought. Which makes everyone laugh, even his mom.

"You picked a good mom." Adrianna smiles at Reilly. Then she looks down at the pup in her lap. "And you, cutie, have two moms. Which makes you a very lucky pup."

Layla and Miriam both turn several shades of embarrassed, pleased pink.

I see the hand squeeze between them. Miriam casts a careful look at Hayden. "Mellie and Braden are siblings. They have the same dad."

He smiles slowly, his eyes those of the wolf who howled in delight when he recognized their mate bond. Then they turn haunted.

Layla shakes her head fiercely. "No. No one from the pack. I left, and I met Miriam after that. We were going to have a family and stay far away." She shrugs, her eyes dropping to her knees. "I grew up here, but I didn't feel welcome. Even before."

Secrets, pulling each other out of the dark. My wolf wants to wiggle in shame. This one, we can't blame on Samuel.

"We were idiots," says Myrna flatly. "We weren't willing to look the obvious in the face. Love matters."

Layla looks up and smiles. "You looked."

"Eventually. After that bastard dragged you back here."

I see Hayden stiffen, and I know the worst hasn't landed yet. This next part is going to be hard for him to hear. My wolf scratches at me from the inside. I inch forward on the grass.

Layla clears her throat. She's looking down at her

knees again, but her words are crystal clear. "We lived in town, and sometimes pack friends would stay in our spare room. Evan was one of them. He had a thing going on with someone else, but after Braden was born, Eamon got it into his head that Evan was Braden's father. Evan said it was true. So Eamon showed up with half a dozen lieutenants and made me come back."

She squeezes the hand clutching hers and looks up, her eyes fierce. "Miriam snuck in to try to get us out and Eamon caught her. Kenny got in Eamon's face and said Mellie was his. To protect her, but it trapped us here even more."

Hayden's wolf quivers under my hand. I don't know when I put it on his back.

So much pack pain and shame. Evan was a teenager when Samuel took over. A decent kid with a baby face who got reshaped by evil. Kenny tried and got reshaped by his failures. The rest of us didn't do enough to make a packmate feel like she belonged—and then we didn't help her run far enough away.

Hayden looks at the two of them and then at each one of us. Mellie watches solemnly, with a dominant's instincts for shifts in the power running through her pack. Kelsey, snuggling in Rio's lap, is watching just as closely. It's silent, but I can feel the air practically crackling with something that isn't quite dominance. It takes me a minute to figure out what it is.

Approval. Gratitude. And an alpha's fierce pride.

He's not talking to our humans.

He's talking to our wolves.

ADRIANNA

It was a mistake to come. I knew that when I climbed into Ames's plane, but I did it anyhow, because I needed to lay eyes on my son before my wolf shredded me.

It was a mistake—and it let me be present for this.

He's magnificent, and so is his pack, and the quiet woman with green eyes and a hand on his back has earned herself my undying teeth and claws and anything else she might ever need.

Hayden's eyes are fully wolf, something I've only seen once in his adult life. Whatever has gone wrong in this pack, and my nose says it's a lot more than even the high court understands, there is strength here, and resilience, and tattered remains that refused to die and are instead acting as the nurse logs of a pack that's going to be stunning.

And Hayden is rising up to be the alpha they need, the alpha they trust—and the alpha they love.

James would be so very proud.

The small girl in my lap reaches up a hand to touch my cheek. I lean into her warm fingers and let them gently stroke my grief and sadness and the singing in my heart.

Sometimes mistakes lead you to life's very best parts.

4

LISSA

I pick up a stack of dishes and fall into step beside Myrna. We're being visited by wolf royalty—and somehow she's not the most important event of the day.

I shake my head. Mellie sneezed and Reilly giggled and the sacred moment with our alpha ended, and now we're having a regular pack night with an extra grand-mother to read stories as we try to herd the pups in the general direction of sleep.

"What do you think of Hayden's mom?"

I look at the woman beside me. She tried to make her question sound innocent. It's not. She's head of the not-at-all-secret matchmaking brigade. "She's not what I expected."

Myrna smirks. "She never is. She waltzes in and applies her charm in carefully chosen places and a few hours later she's part of the pack and everyone loves her and nobody remembers that she could chew most of them up and spit them out without even trying hard."

That sounds vaguely underhanded, but my wolf is impressed. Most dominants don't know how to be subtle. "She did really well with Reilly." He's busy writing up his article for the pack newspaper and sneaking peeks at the university's website while he does it.

Myrna rolls her eyes. "She's brilliant, remember? She understands the psychology of pack and how to work it in her favor better than anyone alive. We're just lucky she's on our side."

That's not wrong, but it's not all the way right, either. "She's on Hayden's side."

Myrna's eyes soften. "Yes. She came to see how her boy's doing."

A visit the woman beside me hasn't been able to make nearly often enough. She rarely dared—we might not have been in one piece when she got back. "You could go on a trip soon. Visit your sons."

Or have them come here, which is a dizzying thought.

A flicker of a smile. "I will. In a bit. I don't want to miss the good stuff."

We need her here to help make it happen. She remembers healthy pack better than most of us do.

"I can take those."

Adrianna walks out of the dark and smiles at Myrna, reaching for the plates in her hands. "Reilly has some photos he'd like to put online. I'd appreciate it if you can make sure they don't all have me filling my face with berries, or half of Whistler Pack will find some excuse to come visit by morning."

Myrna gives her a look that says the berry photos will stay private and she's not at all fooled by the casual attempt to send her away.

I study Adrianna. She doesn't look like a sneaky wolf or smell like one, but Myrna's practically never wrong. "If you want to talk with me, you'll have to dry dishes while you do it."

She shoots me an approving look. "Good. You're not a pushover. You'll need that to stay one step ahead of Robbie. He's a cutie, but he's not quite figured out his own strength yet."

She's not talking about his muscles. I mutter something mostly incoherent as Myrna abandons me to a conversation I've equally dreamed about and feared over the years. I never expected it to take place here. "We're working on his manners. I'm really sorry he tackled you."

"So you've said, at least half a dozen times." Adrianna pushes open the kitchen door with her hip and turns on the temporary overhead lanterns Rio set up for us because apparently none of the wiring that came with this place can be trusted. "Some advice from a mom who's raised a baby alpha? Stop apologizing for him. He's his own person and his own wolf, and he won't thank you for trying to smooth his way in the world."

That makes my human angry and my wolf sad. "He's just a pup."

Adrianna sets down her dishes and wraps an easy arm around my shoulders. "Sssh, now. That wasn't a criticism. You've held this pack together with nothing but the strength of your will and wisps of hope, and you've raised a wonderful boy in the midst of hell. You did exactly right. I wasn't talking about the past. I was talking about his future. Which is just me being a pushy grandmother, so you're absolutely right to growl and hand me a dish towel."

I manage a watery laugh and push away from comfort my wolf desperately wants. "Adopting all of our pups, are you?"

She smiles. "If you want to think of it that way."

I shush my wolf. We're not playing word games with a woman who has a PhD in them. Instead, I run hot water into the sink and look out the small window Kelsey carefully cleans to a shine every day. The pups are so proud of their chores. Including Robbie. "You're right. My instincts are still to hide him, to try to keep him small. I need to work on that."

Adrianna starts shuffling dishes closer to the sink. Glasses first, like she does this on a regular basis. "You'll be fighting that instinct his whole life."

It takes one mama wolf to understand another. "You came to make sure Hayden is okay."

She nods ruefully. "Yes. I was hoping it wasn't quite that obvious."

I shift bubbles around in the sink. There are piles of them, another small luxury in my life. "Myrna knows. I don't know if Hayden does. He might think you're here for the submissives."

A quiet chuckle. "It sounds like you know my son very well."

My wolf sits up and begs.

I hush her and stick my hands in warm, soapy water, pouncing on the first glass I find. "We all try. He's an easy alpha to like."

"That's all he's ever wanted," she says softly. "To be the teeth and claws of a family worth protecting."

I look at her sharply. "You knew he was going to leave Whistler?"

"Yes." She takes the wet glass out of my hands. "He worked hard to be happy and to stay, but his heart has always wanted his own pack. Keeping shifters with alpha instincts content is a challenge in a large pack, and one Whistler does very well at, but he's wanted this since he was a pup no older than Mellie. In many ways, he formed his own pack at ten years old."

It takes me a moment. "Kel and Rio."

"Yes." A smile, hazed with remembrance. "Rio gave in reasonably quickly, but it took Kel a long time."

I have a pretty good idea just how deep Kel's loyalty runs now. "Because Hayden was so young?"

"No." Adrianna's voice is steeped in sadness. "Because Kel had forgotten how to believe in pack. Hayden brought him back from that. Nobody else could have done it."

I've heard some of this, but clearly not all of it. "That's not the way Hayden tells the story."

A chuckle. "It's not the way he sees it. Whatever his

faults are, my son has never had a big head." A pause. "Which sometimes means it's up to those around him to remember his value. You're doing that beautifully here. Thank you."

She saw us at our best. We need to do that more often. "Sometimes we forget."

"Oh, I think you'll have plenty of reminders."

I raise an eyebrow, caught by the odd hint of amusement in her voice. "What happened?"

She flashes me a grin that reminds me very much of her son. "About two minutes after I got here, I said something a wee bit disparaging about Hayden's stealth in the woods. A feisty young woman named Ghost read me the riot act."

I blink. Ghost rarely uses two words when one will suffice, but she can be fierce for the right cause. It warms me somewhere really interesting that she considers Hayden worthy. "She's not usually chatty with strangers."

Adrianna laughs. "You didn't apologize for her. Well done."

I shake my head ruefully. "Does anyone ever win a conversation with you?"

Amusement still tinges her words. "Only if they're right."

I like her, very much. I expected to be in awe. She's not letting me be. I take a deep breath and find a new glass to scrub. "It's hurting his wolf that the pack's not all here." That's as much as I can say, and even that much feels like treason. But if anyone might understand how to heal the structure of a complicated, broken pack, it would be the woman calmly drying a drinking glass.

She nods. "Alpha instincts. His have always been strong. What do yours say?"

I blink.

She snorts and takes the next glass from me. "I imagine my son has asked as well. He's not dumb enough to ignore the wisdom in his pack."

He asks all the time, for small opinions and large ones. It embarrasses me and pleases me and confuses my wolf to no end. "It's so big I don't even know where to start."

Adrianna dries her glass meditatively, like the stack of dishes beside me doesn't have to rush us at all. "Tonight, I saw a simple question from a ten-year-old bear cause something really important to happen." She sets the dry glass up on one of the shelves above the sink that appeared with no fanfare one morning. "A small action that had big consequences."

I think about what Myrna said, and about a canny mother who told a story about honey and missing dads. "You picked the story you told Reilly on purpose."

She chuckles. "I did. It didn't go where I expected it to, though. Sometimes small actions have different consequences than you expect."

My wolf niggles me. This time I let her speak. "I'm very sorry you lost a man you obviously loved very much."

She lets out a soft, sad breath. "It was a big mess of a snowstorm. He pulled over to the side of the road and got out of his truck to help a stranded family. He was hit by a van that lost control."

I lean into her, my wolf offering comfort the only way she knows how. I know it happened almost twenty-five years ago, but the pain in Adrianna's voice is fresh and fierce.

The alpha of all alphas lays her head on my shoulder. "He was ten minutes from home."

My wolf shudders at all the layers of horror in her words, but most especially at one of them. Alphas have incredibly strong pack sense. There's no way she doesn't. "You felt it."

She lifts her head, her eyes full of unfathomable sadness. "So did Hayden."

5

HAYDEN

I raise a wry eyebrow at my mom, who has a strange fondness for the crack of dawn. And at Ames, who nearly cracked up her plane trying to land in a clearing barely big enough for a helicopter before the sun was up. "Next time, come and stay for a while." I glare at Ames. "Not you."

She snickers and throws my mom's bags into the back of the plane. "Your troublemakers aren't very imaginative. The polar bears are bored."

I hope they stay that way. "Don't give them any ideas."

She smirks. "The wolves or the bears?"

Either. I toss a container at her. "Berries for the road."

Her eyes gleam. "Thanks." She shoots a look at my mother as she hops up into the cockpit. "Five minutes on the pre-flight check. Don't keep me waiting."

Most shifters who talked to Adrianna Scott in that particular tone of voice would meet up with a sharp attitude adjustment. Ames has gotten away with it my whole life. Comes with being the Whistler Pack alpha's favorite aunt.

We stroll far enough away from the plane to be able to hear ourselves think. I can see eyes in the trees, but Ebony and Kel laid down the law, so none of them are close enough to hear. "Got any words of wisdom for me? I'm really new at this alpha gig."

My mother smiles. "You aren't the kind of alpha I am."

I'm not sure whether that's wisdom or just an observation. "Maybe one day."

She shakes her head. "No. I was never sure what kind of alpha you would be, because you're a wolf with the capacity to become the leader your people need."

This is why I never got away with shit as a teenager. "That sounds ominous."

She chuckles. "You're adaptable. It's always been your greatest strength."

I grin and pull her in for a hug. "I thought those were my good looks and lovable immaturity."

She snorts. "Those, too."

She stays leaned into my chest, looking up at the dawning sun. "You're going to be the kind of leader your father was, Hayden. It makes my heart ache to see."

She's always talked about him—and always, there's been the sadness of a mate bond that broke far too soon. Or maybe one that didn't. Jules is the family mystic. I'm just a wolf who loves his mom. "He always insisted you were the alpha and he was just your trusty sidekick."

She smiles. "Your Lissa is trying to argue that same thing."

I groan. I never should have left the two of them alone. "What did you do?"

She flashes me a grin. "Nothing at all."

I don't believe that for a hot minute.

She touches my cheek. "I was the leader of Whistler Pack. James was its soul, its heart. Lissa is the heart of this one."

My wolf has always known that. "Yeah."

She stretches up and drops a light kiss where her fingers just were. "Hearts get ready in their own time. I think hers will be worth waiting for."

I watch my mother's back as she walks away, her long wolf strides carrying her toward a battered plane that has more lives than a cat. Those weren't the words of wisdom I was asking for—but they're good ones, all the same.

LISSA

I look at the faces I dragged into the forest with me. We don't have long. I don't want Hayden to know about this meeting. Not unless we actually manage to deliver. And I figure we have even less time than that before Kel smells something happening in his woods and comes to investigate.

Ghost sits down on the log next to Kennedy and eyes me. Then they both eye Shelley.

She shrugs. "I have no more idea than you do." She looks at me and smiles. "What's up, boss?"

I make a face. I'm not a boss. I'm just a wolf with a burr in her paw, and I need help getting it out. "We're making a mistake." Three sets of eyes widen. "We have some big problems in this pack, right?"

Three heads nod. Duh.

"The biggest, though, is that we're not all together."

I hold up a hand as Kennedy's mouth opens. "I know. There are some good reasons for that. And some bad ones, but we can't fix the big stuff. Not yet, anyhow."

Ghost snorts. "Too many stubborn wolves."

They have reasons, but she's not wrong. And I know better than to try to out-stubborn either Bailey or Kenny. "That's just it. We've been waiting on the stubborn ones. Or waiting for our alpha to win some kind of stupid staring contest with wolves he can't even see."

That gets under Ghost's skin.

I hold up my other hand and hope Shelley doesn't protest, too. I'm out of hands, and I can still hear the plane engine, but I don't think it will be here much longer. "We're going to stop waiting for someone else to fix this. We're going to take some small actions and see what happens."

Kennedy wrinkles her nose suspiciously. "What kind of small actions?"

I laugh. Dominants don't like being subtle. "We're

going to be smart about this. We're going to drop pebbles in a pond."

She wrinkles her nose some more. Ghost and Shelley are eyeing me curiously, though. They're both experts at subtle. Which is why they're here. I need Kennedy for a trip only a dominant can make without hurting her wolf, but I'm sending her to the king of sneaky and subtle. Or bombastic, depending on his mood. Sometimes small actions have different consequences than you plan for.

"I have a job for each of you. A pebble for each of you to toss." Ones that I hope will make ripples that help build the kinds of foundations good packs need. Because Adriana's visit reminded me of so many things that are part of normal, healthy packs. Visitors, and stories, and moments of truth.

Somewhere in the middle of the night, that remembering lit a mission in my soul. I'm done trying to be safe. I want this pack to be whole. Because Robbie deserves it, and Mellie, and Ghost, and Miriam, and everyone else, including a really good man who felt his father die when he was eight years old.

Ten minutes from home.

I spent all night thinking about those four words, because there are way too many wolves in this pack who are ten minutes from home, and we can all feel every last one of them. I look at the three faces on the log and list the tasks I sorted out in the hours before dawn. Then I wait for protests, or nose wrinkles, or flat-out refusals.

Kennedy slowly smiles. Shelley's eyes get fierce. Ghost just vanishes.

6

HAYDEN

I cast a hard look at my two betas. "Do I need to be at all concerned that half my pack has vanished?"

Kel gives me a sunny smile. "Nope."

I side-eye him. That's a really scary smile.

Ebony shoots him a look. "What do you know that I don't?"

He shrugs.

She glares at him.

A beta pissing contest is not what I need right now. "Have pity, you two. My mother just left. I'm sure I know less than either of you, but I do know that Rio headed into town in his truck with Shelley and Lissa. It's not grocery day and Lissa never leaves Robbie. Ever."

"He's protected," says Kel quietly.

I roll my eyes. Reilly is practically sitting on Robbie, and Myrna's watching both of them like she can cast imprisonment spells with her eyes. Which is entirely possible. "I know that. Now tell me what's so dang important that Lissa left to go do it."

"I don't know." Ebony clears her throat and looks a little sheepish. "I tried to corner Shelley, but she just told me it was important and I should mind my own business."

Wonderful. "So the submissives are staging a coup and Rio's helping them?"

Kel gives me that disturbing, sunny smile again. "Yup."

I sigh. "Does my mom have anything to do with this?"

"Good question." He nods, like I've finally done something useful with the brain I was born with. "I don't think so, other than her usual stirring of the pot. I'm pretty sure that whatever this is, Lissa's the mastermind."

Ebony sulks. "How'd you figure that out?"

He grins at her. "I'm sneakier than you."

She sticks out her tongue. "You are not."

I roll my eyes at the sky. Now is not a good time for them to act like their alpha. "Kennedy's gone, too. And Ghost."

"Ghost was just here for a visit." Ebony glowers. "She leaves the den all the time."

I stare her down. Ghost is up to something, same as the rest of them, and I'm not taking any more shit for knowing a few scraps about the wolves of my pack.

Kel crosses his arms over his chest. "She didn't head out the way she usually does."

Ebony growls at him. "You're not supposed to be tracking the sentries."

"I'm not. She stopped by to make sure I kept an extra watch on the south perimeter."

Ebony's eyebrows fly up.

Kel watches her. My wolf does, too. Waiting to see what happens when the shadow-pack hierarchy is challenged.

She nods slowly. "Good. You have it covered?"

The faintest of smiles from Kel—and an almost invisible whiff of relief. "Yeah. Eliza's out there."

This pack is so desperately short of teeth and claws, at least the kind that won't instinctively cower if a dumbass dominant throws his weight around. Which means three sets of them shouldn't be sitting here trying to figure out what loyal pack members are up to. "I'll go hang out with Eliza for a while." She's still getting used to my wolf.

Ebony clears her throat. "I know which way Kennedy headed."

Kel rolls his eyes. "I'm glad someone does. She led me on a merry chase up a stream until I decided her sorry ass can hang in the wind if she wants it to."

Which means he couldn't smell any danger, she was dragging him too far away from the den, and he absolutely trusts Kennedy to handle herself.

There are days he still doesn't trust *me* to do that.

Ebony smirks. "You do smell like damp wolf."

I growl, which gets their attention. Mostly. "Did she head in any direction I need to worry about?"

"She'll be fine." Something odd comes into Ebony's eyes. "But if I'm right about where she's going, and why, I have two things to say. First, Lissa's doing exactly what we need her to do, and if you chew on her, I will figure out how to beat your ass into the ground."

Kel grunts. "I'll help."

Now they team up. "I don't chew on wolves who act with the best interests of the pack in mind." I may have no idea what Lissa is up to, but I don't doubt her motivations at all. And I never chew on submissives unless their name is Kelvin Nogues. "What's the second thing?"

Ebony's grin is almost as evil as Kel's. "You might want to buckle up."

LISSA

This is crazy. I look over at Rio, who has asked exactly zero questions. He's chattered about recipes with Shelley and told us funny stories from when he and Hayden were kids and talked about what Scotty and Reilly are up to on ShifterNet.

Apparently we have a pack genius.

Which is good, because we might also have two pack idiots. Or criminals. Depending on how this goes.

Rio pulls over where Shelley tells him to. He eyes the bank outside his truck window and looks at us, his eyebrows raised. "If you two need a getaway car, I should probably fill up with gas first."

If it gets that far, we'll both faint dead away from sheer terror. "We just need to make a withdrawal. It might take a minute."

He shrugs and pulls one of the pack e-readers out of his pocket. "No problem. This book's just getting good."

Shelley eyes him. "You're not just reading to make Reilly feel good?"

I hide a grin. That's why Shelley is reading. Or it was until Danielle mentioned a historical romance with a hot guy in a kilt.

Rio snorts and bumps her shoulder. "Go. Take a really long time if you like. Get a pedicure."

She laughs. "I don't think the bank runs to those."

He waves a hand vaguely at the rest of the town.

I huff out a laugh and drag her out of the car. If we manage to pull this off, our feet will be shaking too hard for nail polish to land anywhere near our toes. I propel us inside the door and stop. "Are you sure about this?"

I don't say any specifics. We've talked them through, and I'm pretty sure banks have cameras. We aren't committing any crimes, but we're definitely thinking some. And I'm not entirely sure about the first part, despite spending half the night running Google searches and scrutinizing all the pack paperwork I could find.

Shelley nods. "It's our money. Let's do this."

I close my eyes and try to feel like a marauding warrior reclaiming what's hers instead of like a meek bookkeeper. I pull the meek-bookkeeper paperwork out of my bag, though. Google was at least helpful on that part. "After you."

Shelley walks up to the counter and smiles politely at the young man perched on a stool. "I'm Shelley Martins. My husband passed away a few weeks ago. I want to withdraw the funds in our joint account."

This is the tricky part. We talked about transferring them into an account solely in her name, which is what would usually happen, but Shelley is almost as stubborn as Bailey. These are pack funds, and she flatly refuses to have them in her name.

The young man looks honestly saddened. "I'm very sorry to hear that, Mrs. Martins."

She winces at the name. "Call me Shelley, please."

An older woman with a very competent manner walks over, summoned by a discreet call button or the panicked looks on our faces. "Is everything all right, Jordie?"

He looks at her, relief in his eyes. "This lovely lady has lost her husband, and she wants to withdraw the funds in her account."

"Ah." Honest sympathy again, which raises my opinion of Samuel's bank considerably, even if they tolerated him as a client. "I'm Ally Yazzan, bank manager. Why don't we have Jordie pull up the account files? Do you want to withdraw the funds or transfer them? We'd be happy to keep your business."

Shelley turns a little pale. Even a hint of conflict is still so very hard for all of us. "I'd like to take them out. Please."

I hold up my file folder. One meek bookkeeper,

trying her best to be a worthy sidekick. "I have all the paperwork here if you need it."

Ally scans the screen Jordie pulled up. "There's no need. Shelley is a signatory on the account, so she has the right to remove funds at any time." Her eyes widen a little. "This is a substantial amount of money. Would you perhaps like a cashier's check or a bank draft?"

This battle, I won. Mostly.

Shelley nods. "Yes, please. But I'd like a thousand dollars in cash. In small bills, please. And coins. A big pile of them." She smiles. "For the grandchildren."

Ally's eyes soften. "Of course. I'll go dig out the new-issue coins so they're nice and shiny."

I manage not to tear up as Shelley nearly wilts with relief beside me. This shouldn't be shiny money, not at all—but it's somehow exactly right that it will be.

RIO

I make the turn onto the dirt road that starts our trek into the backcountry. I carefully don't look at my two passengers, both of whom are still occasionally hyperventilating.

My wolf is bemused. He thought he knew which way the wind was blowing, but now he's less sure. What he does know is that it's very, very good. Most days, even for sentinels, are pretty ordinary, and I like it that way just fine. Today, I'm holding the capes of superheroes.

I wait for Shelley's breathing to settle again. She came out of the bank looking like she'd seen a dozen ghosts—and kicked the asses of at least a couple of them. I'm taking notes. The pack is going to want to hear this story over and over again. I don't know why yet, but I will soon enough.

My wolf lives for moments like this. Especially when they come with big, clanking bags of loot in the back of the truck. They each came out with one. The bank manager waved goodbye as she ushered them out the front door, so I don't think any official robberies happened.

Maybe an unofficial one, though.

My wolf grins. He really hopes so.

LISSA

All of me is shaking. I climb out of the truck that Rio parked in the neat, hidden clearing off a dirt road that's barely more than two tracks. One mile to go.

Then I'll know just how well my new alpha deals with his authority being totally undermined. I somehow didn't realize just how much trouble this is going to cause for him until we were leaving the bank.

Shelley takes my hand fiercely. "We did the right thing. Don't you dare go thinking otherwise. Our pack can handle whatever happens."

It felt right in the dark of night when I hatched this plan. Fifteen minutes away from looking into Hayden's eyes and telling him what we did, I'm not nearly so sure.

Rio hauls two bright green, clanking cloth bags out of the truck bed. Ally gave us the prettiest ones she could find and tied them up tight with some cheerful yellow nylon rope. He holds one out to each of us. "I assume you two ladies want to deliver these."

I don't. In the middle of the night, this felt like a pebble that a bookkeeper and a woman who needs to reclaim herself from the pain and anguish of being mated to evil could throw, but walking into the den with these bags is not a small action. It's not even close. I can't believe I did this, and I talked Shelley into it, too, and she's still working so hard on getting up in the morning and not letting us see the tears she cried while we were sleeping.

A hand lands on my shoulder. Rio's. Shelley's already heading down the trail to the kitchen, the one we walk every week with the groceries. He looks me square in the eyes. "Don't. Whatever's going on inside you right now, it's trying to push the good away. Don't let it win."

I blink. "Are sentinels mind readers?"

He snorts. "That would be damn handy, but no."

I sigh. "I think maybe I made a big mistake."

He shrugs. "Maybe. If you did, own it and know that your alpha will be damn happy that his pack did something daring, even if you failed."

That just makes me blink faster.

Rio herds me down the path. "Remember that he's a guy who once stuck himself to a tree with pine sap."

That story is going to be funny for a long time. "Was it really that bad?"

He chuckles. "Yeah. He smelled like tree for a week."

I look over at him. My wolf is curious again, which is better than feeling like I'm about to puke. "You knew him back then, but you two weren't close yet, right?"

"Whistler's a big pack. He was a year or two older than Robbie, and I was a teenage wolf who was way too cool to hang around with little dipshits who got stuck in trees."

I've never heard that word used with quite so much affection. "What changed?"

He snorts. "About four years later, he just started following me around and wouldn't go away."

There are ways to make anyone go away. "You let him stay."

Another shrug. "He grew on me. Then we got assigned to Kel and persistent dipshit was the right medicine to save him."

I close my eyes. The love between these three men is so vast. My heart dares to hope that Reilly and Robbie might feel that way about each other someday.

That thought somehow eases the angst inside of me. I'm allowed to have dreams like that now. I'm allowed a lot of things that I thought were impossible just a few short weeks ago. I hoist the bag of money higher on my shoulder. Maybe I'm about to stick myself to a tree, but I don't think so.

I just accidentally tossed a boulder instead of a pebble.

HAYDEN

I stare as coins tumble out of Shelley's bag onto the ground at my feet. A lot of coins. Really shiny ones. "What did you do, rob a bank?"

Rio shoots me grin from behind Lissa. "That was my first question, too."

It better not have been his last. However, that's not my next line. This is clearly a grand entrance, and I can feel Lissa's determination and worry from here. I look pointedly at the bag in her hands. "Please tell me that one has doughnuts in it."

Braden squeals.

Rio laughs as Lissa empties her bag out on top of Shelley's. "Sorry, buddy. No baked goods."

Reilly, frantically moving around taking photos of the money pile, grins. "Myrna made banana muffins with chocolate chips in them."

"I did. Which nobody is getting until someone tells me why this field is covered in money." Myrna arrives from the kitchen on the double and stares at Lissa and Shelley like they've grown horns. "What did you two do?"

Shelley looks at Lissa. Lissa looks at Shelley. Shelley finally shrugs and looks sheepish. "That's all the money from Samuel's account. We took it out. It belongs to the pack."

I stare, the implications of what she just said staggering my wolf. A mountain of coins probably isn't that much money. It doesn't matter. It matters that two of the most cautious wolves in my pack just poked a stick in a hornet's nest without their alpha's permission, and I need to get this next part absolutely, blazingly right. "How did you get it?"

"It was a joint account." Shelley swallows. "That's the way it was set up, because Samuel wanted control of the pack money instead of having a financial officer like Lissa. I couldn't take money out before, though. There are four bank cards. The lieutenants have them."

Kel's flashing hand signals, but I don't need them. "This was the account that the dominants used to pay their beer tab while the rest of you did odd jobs and went without to feed the pups." I've been picking up scraps from Ebony. They make me want to kill Samuel again.

Shelley looks surprised, but she nods quietly. "Yes. Lissa kept our little bits of money somewhere else. She didn't tell me where. It was safer that way."

There is so much horror in those last two sentences. I need to never forget just how brave these women are.

Lissa reaches into a file folder and hands me a slip of paper. "This is a bank draft for the rest of it." She looks over at Myrna with sad eyes. "I went digging through pack records to figure out why they haven't run out of beer money yet. Samuel sold your daddy's house in town. There's not much left. I'm sorry."

The sum on the bank draft is surprisingly large. Not house-in-town large, but not the spare change I figured they had. No wonder the guys in the woods haven't come back to the den. This is enough beer money for years.

I kick myself for not thinking of this, and I can feel my two betas radiating the same consternation, but none of us are bookkeepers. It took a green-eyed wolf who's good with numbers to figure this out.

My wolf can't decide if he wants to lick her or bring her a tasty rabbit snack first. I grab him by the scruff of the neck and remind him he's got a job to do. Several of them, starting with the one right in front of his nose, because this isn't a stick in a hornet's nest, it's a hand grenade—and every single person staring at Shelley and Lissa knows it.

The two of them stare at my feet and start shrinking where they stand.

My betas step forward as a unit. A single, sharp sign from Rio stops them.

Myrna puts her hands on her hips. "Let me get this straight. You two waltzed into a bank and took out all the money the assholes in the woods can access?"

Lissa nods slowly.

Myrna, bless her, isn't done. "And it's right here in this field?"

Shelley squares her shoulders. "Yes."

My turn. I keep my voice as quiet as I can, which isn't easy. My wolf is beside himself. "What were you thinking to do with it?"

Another moment of shrinking—and then two wolves decide they're done getting smaller. Both sets of shoulders square. Shelley meets my gaze. "Well, Lissa's our financial officer. But I say we spend it so they can't take it back."

I don't say anything. I just let a fraction of what my wolf is feeling show in my eyes.

The glee that dawns on Myrna's face as she reads my wolf's message is a sight for the ages. One Reilly captures for posterity. Then he starts madly snapping photos of the rest of the pack as they bombard Shelley with questions and congratulations and laughing wonder.

I shake my head at our young reporter. He's a very smart bear, but he's taking pictures of the wrong wolves.

The real story is the quiet pride in Lissa's eyes.

7

HAYDEN

I set down my fork, entirely content after three plates of breakfast. I didn't get to eat much of the first one, but the other two came piled high with pancakes and extra sausages for the ravenous pups who have figured out their alpha is a soft touch.

The rest of me is at least as happy as my belly. The pups are all furry this morning, gamboling in the still-cool air while the adults talk about boring stuff. Like how to spend more money than most of them have seen in six years.

There was talk of saving it, maybe for a tuition fund, but Shelley put a firm stop to that. Money that's spent can't be threatened or stolen or used to pay off beer debts. Wisdom she earned the really hard way, but she's smiling this morning. She reclaimed a lot more yesterday than money.

"I think we should get couches." Miriam casts a careful look at me, but she's an active participant in this conversation, which is fantastic. She's not the most submissive wolf in the pack, but she's usually the quietest, especially while I'm around.

My wolf is happy to keep the quiet seat warm this morning. He doesn't care how we spend the money. He only cares that his pack smells like happiness.

Layla grins at her mate. "Really big, squishy ones."

Ebony snorts. "You two just want to cuddle."

They both turn wildly pink, but Miriam manages to stick her tongue out at her beta's easy teasing. Rio elbows Ebony, but he's not remotely trying to shut her down. He knows just how important pack banter is for healing. He's also not talking any more than I am this morning, but Kelsey, who shared her breakfast with him, has hopped up twice now to go whisper things in Myrna's ears.

A sentinel, planting seeds.

Lissa smiles at the den's only mated pair. "We won't have beds for a while, so squishy couches could double as a place for some people to sleep."

More than one quick look gets cast my way.

I borrow Miriam's shorthand and stick my tongue out. Anyone who thinks the dominants of this pack will be sleeping on couches while there are elders or submissives on the floor clearly hasn't been paying attention.

Danielle giggles and slaps her hand over her mouth.

Myrna winks at me. "He'll be fine on the floor. We're making him a really big blanket."

I've seen it. It's possibly the most garish blanket in the

history of shifters, and I thought Ronan had that award sewn up for eternity. It's for the very best of reasons, though. It's being made from the leftovers of the yarn going into all the other pack blankets. My wolf will probably blubber when he finally gets to sleep with it.

I fix Myrna with a firm stare. "You would be one of the people who gets to sleep on a couch. Just in case you were planning on arguing."

She sniffs. "We'll see about that."

We will. I'll use all the mean, nasty, alpha tricks at my disposal. "Since Danielle has the new table all squared away, I think couches are a great idea."

She looks down, but not before I see the surprised pleasure in her eyes. Reilly's are gleaming, too. He's proud of his mom, and rightly so. In the long discussions about our new den, the logistics of how to sit everyone down to eat turned into a sticky issue, both literally and emotionally. Good chairs and tables are expensive, and this pack has a history of them being used to bludgeon submissives and their self-worth.

A few days ago, Danielle came up with the brilliant idea that fixed both of those problems. Instead of raising wolves up on chairs, the table could be lowered. Which, a lot of scribbling and consultation with Rio and Eliza later, turned into a design for a river-rock-embedded, polished-concrete table, supported by short, fat legs. It will go on a raised platform in front of a big bank of windows in the new den, surrounded by cushion seating Eliza and Cori are already busy making.

Cheap, beautiful, insanely practical for life with pups, and unique.

Or it was for five minutes, until Jules started drooling and building them in as an option on all future Home-Wild designs. Which means I'll be arm-wrestling my sister at some point in the near future. The talented people in my pack need to stay right where they are.

Lissa looks up from her laptop, taking a break from exercising her spreadsheet superpowers. "I'm chatting with the bear who makes the couches you suggested, Rio. I don't think he's giving us a fair price."

Rio glowers.

She snickers. "Not that kind of unfair. There's a Reilly discount in his quote that's almost as big as the bill. And the delivery charge is in buckets of fish."

Rio relaxes, and Phil the furniture-making bear gets to live another day. "Take whatever terms he gives you. He's plenty rich enough to afford it."

Every submissive in the pack glares at him.

He smirks. "Fine. Go ahead and argue with a polar bear."

Lissa's chin firms. "He makes beds, too. I'll tell him that we'll take this as an introductory price for the couches, but we're paying regular price for the beds when we're ready to order them or Reilly won't catch him any fish."

Reilly looks stricken until Kel winks at him.

Rio makes a thoughtful face and nods at Lissa. "That might work."

My wolf wriggles happily. Smart pack. Good pack. Happy pack.

LISSA

Being a bank robber is really good for my self-confidence. I send the nice bear on the other end of my chat window a firm message. We have money to spend, and I intend to spend it before anyone tries to get it back. They're welcome to try to extract it from a polar bear if they want.

I grin. I've learned a few tricks from our new alpha.

Shelley sets a platter of still-warm muffins on the flat rock in the middle of our very informal meeting. "If there's enough money, I'd like some for paint for the den murals."

I had a chat with the nice artist lady in Whistler Pack before breakfast. "I heard there are some specialty paints that are good for murals. And brushes."

Shelley looks horrified. "I can use the regular kind."

On cue, the entire pack glares at her. We're getting really good at this ganging-up stuff. And we're maybe a little high on coin fumes. Reilly helped the other pups make them into nice, neat piles this morning, which we all regularly walk over to admire, and I saw Shelley tuck a stray coin into her pocket.

Symbols of freedom take so many forms.

I grin at everyone in my pack who's within earshot. "Who's in favor of fancy paints for our mural?"

Hands go up, including a couple of furry paws from pups who don't have any idea what they're voting for.

Kel snorts. "Since when did this become a spending democracy?"

I smirk at him. "I'm a benevolent dictator." Who is definitely high on coin fumes. I grin at Reilly. "I think we need a TV screen, too. One big enough to see from our enormous couches."

He somehow manages to look delighted and wildly uncertain at the same time. "Maybe we should vote on that."

He's such an adorably innocent bear cub. I keep a straight face, mostly. "Fair enough. All in favor of a really big screen where we can watch lots of movies with kissing and flowers, raise your hands."

Reilly and Robbie look at each other, shrug, and stick up their hands. Kel grins and sticks his up, too. Rio and Hayden vote with two hands each. The submissives mostly manage to stop laughing long enough to cast a vote.

I make a wry face. I keep forgetting that my pack isn't full of sexist idiots anymore. "Done. Couches from a bear, and he's going to coordinate with Rio and Jules to make sure they fit in our den. It sounds like we're going to build around them. We'll have to cut the den in half if we ever need to take them out."

Hayden grins. "Perfect. They'll be really old, ratty couches one day. Just the way I like them."

Those are probably fighting words to the polar bear I'm chatting with. "Jules is going to order the media screen and add it to our bill, and she promises to charge us the actual price. Something about shareholders who will complain if she loses money." Which I don't believe for a minute. I know who HomeWild's key shareholders are, and one of them is a big bear with dreadlocks and an obsession with knitting who thinks fish are perfectly reasonable currency. The other one is going to be sleeping on a couch when she comes to visit, which is a battle that's already making my wolf giggle, because she isn't going to be the one who has to fight it.

I look up from my screen and soak in all the happy faces looking back at me. It isn't the money, although that definitely helps. It's the possibilities. A pile of wolves, cozy on our big couches with hand-knit blankets, hanging out in our new den in the middle of winter. A scene of pure, unfettered happiness.

A shared dream.

We're allowed to have those now.

I clear my throat. Time to wrap up this meeting. "That's all. We're basically out of money except for the coins, which I think we should split between the pups and take them shopping in town." They never get to buy anything new.

Layla squeals quietly, which is kind of how I feel, too. We never get to *take* the pups to buy anything new, either.

I duck my head, but I can't stop smiling. This is a really good day to be the pack's financial officer.

An arm lands on my shoulders. Hayden takes a seat

on the grass beside me and cuddles me in, something he does all the time, but this feels different. "Thank you."

My wolf sighs happily. "Thank you for not being too mad. I know this stirs up trouble with the dominants."

He snorts. "They're seven pathetic guys who just ran out of beer money. I'm pretty sure Kennedy can take care of them all by herself."

That would require a teleporter. "She's kind of busy with something else."

A long pause. "Are you going to tell me what that is?"

I do what Rio suggested. I check in with my wolf. She's got a clear answer—and a surprising one. "I will if you pull rank. But otherwise, no."

He chuckles and nuzzles my neck, which sends shivers right down to my toes. "Feisty wolf."

This is so not how I expected this conversation to go. "You're not mad at all, are you?"

"No." Another long pause. "Just so you know, my wolf wants to bring you tasty rabbit snacks. He thinks you did this for the pack, but he also thinks you did it for me."

I try very hard not to turn into gelatinous goop. I'm not very successful. "You're not at the top of the list."

A quiet growl that doesn't help the state of my bones at all. "Good."

My wolf yanks for my throat. "But you're on it."

A consternated groan. "I shouldn't be."

"That," I tell him, in my best meek-bookkeeper voice, "is not your choice to make."

"Are they going to kiss now?"

Our heads fly up.

Ebony claps her hand over Reilly's mouth and grins like a loon. "Don't let us stop you." Reilly's eyes dance merrily above her fingers. The rest of the pack watches us like an egg that might hatch any minute.

I put on a bright-red shirt this morning. It felt like the color of victory. Right now, I'm pretty sure I match it.

Hayden chuckles in my ear.

My wolf preens. She likes rabbit snacks. The rest of me can't remember my very good list of reasons why all that needs to wait.

This is so not what I expected when I robbed a bank.

ADRIANNA

I push away from my computer screen, still laughing. Reilly sent me a link to his latest story. It's a great article, one about bank robbers and the long arc of justice, and it says just as much about the reporter who wrote it as it does about his pack. The photo at the top of the story is going to be seen by every shifter on the planet by dinner time. It's not every day you see wolf pups cavorting in piles of money.

The photo he sent me privately, the one he captured of my son and his green-eyed wolf, is even better.

I do like that bear cub.

Jules walks in and shoots me a suspicious look. "Mom, what trouble are you causing?"

I already caused it. "Nothing."

She snorts. "Really? Because Phil just got a thirty-thousand-dollar furniture order from some formerly law-abiding bank robbers. Which means three of my client orders got bumped, because mine aren't for the world's most adorable bear. I don't suppose you had anything to do with that?"

She's about as mad as a sunny day. "Not really."

I pull up the other photo on my screen. The one that will go up on my wall as soon as I can sweet-talk Ronan into making me a frame. I swivel my screen so Jules can see it.

Her eyes go soft and dewy in a heartbeat. She studies the image for a long time. Then she looks at me, every drop of love she has for her big brother written all over her face. "Does she know how soft Hayden's heart is?"

I think of green eyes, standing over a sink full of suds and dishes, when I told her of a man ten minutes from home. "Yes, I do believe she does." And far more importantly, if I'm reading the bank-robber story correctly—she intends to protect it.

8

LISSA

Ebony tosses me a shirt out of the small bag of clothes she was carrying. Robbie, who hasn't bothered to shift out of his fur, sits quietly, waiting to see if she pulls out anything that resembles a snack.

She grins and tosses him some jerky, which he catches in mid-air before he crashes into her legs.

She chuckles as she rights him. "Still not thinking about landings before you take off, cutie?"

His wolf-pup eyes manage to look sheepish.

She scratches behind his ears. "It will come. You haven't had your fur long." She hangs a small strap with a canteen on each side over his shoulders. "Take those down to the river and fill them for us?"

He puffs up with pride and trots off, jerky still in his teeth.

I smile. It's all of a hundred feet to the river and he'll

need to shift to deal with the canteen lids, but he's a wolf providing for his pack. One who happily ran the whole way here. I stretch, delighting in the new strength in my own muscles. Daily pack runs have done wonders for my endurance. Which I'm clearly going to need to keep up with my son.

"We should be out to Bailey by noon." Ebony shoots me a casual look as she digs more snacks out of her bag. "I assume that's where we're headed?"

There's not much else out this way. "Yes." I don't need a reason for that—Bailey's been my best friend since both of us could walk. But that's not why I'm headed to see her this time, and I'm not surprised Ebony knows. I'm also not sure it's good timing. There are a lot of ripples from the last boulder I tossed that haven't happened yet. "Maybe we should head back and do this in a few days."

She snorts. "After the dominants throw their tantrum?"

I nod. "You're important for keeping the den defended."

"The den's locked down. It was before, but after your bank-robbing stunt, Kel got creative. An invisible mouse couldn't sneak in now."

There's a hint of awe in her voice that makes my wolf snarl. "He's not better than you." I know exactly how many nights she stalked the woods the last six years keeping us safe.

She smiles. "He is, and I'm glad for it. I was just a foot soldier in the war games we both played. He was a guy who led foot soldiers into impossible situations and got us out alive. Our pack's better with him in it."

It wasn't her pack, once. She was only here for a visit when Samuel challenged our old alpha. She stayed so we didn't go through hell alone. She deserves, so much, to see us walk all the way out of it. Which I can't tell her, because Ebony tolerates gratitude about as well as she handles poison ivy.

I hand her a piece of the new jerky instead. Shelley's making fancy kinds with spices. This batch tastes like Chinese food.

Ebony gnaws on the end as she looks down at the river. Robbie, still furry, is sitting on his haunches, trying to open a canteen with his paws and teeth. "Stubborn little wolf, just like his mama."

I'm a meek bookkeeper. "He did not get that from me. Maybe from Myrna." They're not genetically related, but that doesn't matter much in a wolf pack.

Robbie backs away from the canteens and growls at them. I manage not to laugh. Typical dominant pup, trying to intimidate something that isn't going his way. So not the boy I thought I was raising.

Ebony hands me a container of trail mix. "It's the adult version."

That means it's only half marshmallows and chocolate chips. I pop the lid off of one of the cute little snack containers that came home with Shelley on the last grocery run. It took me almost thirty minutes to convince her they were a reasonable use of pack funds. Watching her lead the fight yesterday to spend thirty thousand dollars on couches was priceless.

I won't let her see the bill for the special mural paints, though. I take a handful of snack mix and remind myself that pebble turned out well enough, even if it was more like a mid-sized boulder.

The size of this next one really isn't up to me. "Any suggestions?"

"Eat the marshmallows first. They're the fastest sugar hit."

I throw one at her head. "I'm not talking about snack mix, smartypants."

She picks it up off the moss, dusts it on her shorts, and eats it. "You mean do I have any advice on how you might handle our mutual friend Bailey when you try to convince her to do something wild and crazy like actually come meet her new alpha?"

That isn't the only thing on my list, but it would be a good start. "She isn't at the den. She doesn't really know how much things have changed." She gets reports, but it's not the same as being there. I don't know how open she's going to be to what I have to say, though. For good reason. Lives are in her hands. They have been for six years, and she's done an amazing job.

I take a deep breath. "How do you convince a soldier that maybe her war is over and it's safe to come home?"

Ebony blows out a long, slow breath. "I don't know." Her hand squeezes my shoulder. "But you're the right person to try."

I make a wry face. "She's never listened to me all that well."

"She doesn't listen to anyone all that well." Ebony's tone is as dry as dust. She nods her head at the river. "But eventually, even the most stubborn dominants give in."

Robbie, naked and human, is grinning at the canteen he's finally uncapped. He looks up at us, waits for the special hand signal Kel and Ebony have taught all the pups, and heads over to the river's edge. I laugh as he splashes happily, getting far more water on his body than in the canteen.

"He's one of your secret weapons," says Ebony quietly. "All the pups are. Bailey isn't seeing as much of them as she used to, and I bet it's killing her."

That seems like an awful card to play, but I will if I have to. "I'm hoping the call of pack is enough."

"It would be for her."

I think so, too. Neither of us says the rest. She won't come in until the others do. Or at least that's her current line in the sand. One I'm hoping I can budge a little.

Which is kind of like nicely asking to comb Medusa's hair.

"You have two more weapons."

I know one of them. "She loves me. Trusts me."

Ebony nods.

I think for a minute and shake my head. "I don't know the other one."

She smiles. "You might not—but Bailey will."

HAYDEN

Kel slides into the second form of the martial art he learned from some shifter who grew up in Nepal. Given how bloody hard it is, I'm assuming the guy had a prehensile tail.

I teeter as I move into a low lunge, which just makes Kel smirk.

I ignore him. Most people who try this particular art form tie themselves in a knot before they even manage a bow to their teacher. He reserved it as a form of torture for a select few of us in Whistler Pack. "Are you teaching this to Ebony?" She has balance like a cat.

"Yes." He drops into a crouching toe balance from an arm stand. "And Shelley's watching from the woods. I wanted to check in with you before I started showing her some moves."

I stare at him, which means my arm balance ends up using my head for ballast. "Why? Teach her every damn thing."

He aims a pointed look at my arm. "If you're going to bend your elbow like that, you might as well just hold it out so your assailant can lop it off."

I fix my elbow. "I hear that some betas show respect for their alphas."

He shrugs, which is damn hard to do while leaping through the air. "Haven't heard that."

Jerk. My leap is way less graceful than his. "I'm missing something. Why wouldn't you teach Shelley?"

"Sometimes fighting isn't the best way to deal with wounds and scars."

Ah. The single point on which Kel sometimes doesn't trust his own judgment. Sadly for him, I do. "You and Rio are the experts on that. Unless he thinks it's a bad idea, I say do whatever Shelley wants."

He sweeps a leg around in a three-quarter circle and knocks me on my ass. Which isn't part of the form, but I'm smart enough not to complain.

I get back on my feet and avoid the second sweep he aims at me just in case I've fallen asleep. It's a lazy effort, so I haven't fucked up too much yet. I scan the woods as I drop into my own sweep. Habit, and wishful thinking. There should be dominants lurking, trying to learn fighting skills. It's how I learned most of mine. Kel spent years flatly refusing to teach me and Rio anything.

I shoot him a look. He can be as patient as a mountain, but I'm betting this isn't one of those times. "When is Lissa back?" She took Robbie for a woods walk this morning. That's code for visiting the wolves I don't officially know about.

He raises an eyebrow. "I think they took overnight gear. Ebony has a phone on her, said she'd check in later. Why?"

Because I'm missing my green-eyed wolf and looking for dumbass excuses to make her come home. I sigh. She's off doing something that matters, even if it really is just a visit. "I want to poke at the guys in the woods. Let them know their beer money is gone."

He grins. "They'll find out on Friday night. Some guy

in town challenged Colin to a rematch. Apparently he's good at playing pool while he's drunk."

I consider that intel as he hits the final movement in the form. "Is it overkill to sneak into their camp tonight and steal the loose change out of everyone's pockets?"

"What makes you think I haven't already done that?" He rises out of the last stance and moves into one of the stretches he does for the knee that sometimes has the nerve to ail him.

I study his face. He has very few tells, and he's more than capable of petty theft for a good cause. "My entire pack is turning to criminal activity."

He grins. "I left the change. I just made sure nobody had a stash of money under their bedroll."

I'd make a crappy criminal. I didn't even think of that. "Do you need me to take an extra shift tonight with Ebony gone?"

"Nope." He picks up two water bottles and tosses me one.

That's way too casual for a guy who knows there's an imminent threat to the pack, even if it's a mostly incompetent one. "Do I want to know what you've done?"

He laughs. "I don't think it's a felony."

That's not exactly reassuring.

He eyes me as he opens his water. "What did your mom say?"

I make a face at his choice of subject change. "To me, or to Lissa?"

He snorts. "To you. Lissa's not talking."

That he tried to find out and failed says plenty. "That

I'm not the same kind of alpha she is. I'm more like my dad."

He whistles quietly. "So much for my plans to keep you humble. That must have felt good."

"Her sun still rises and sets on him, so yeah."

He contemplates me as he takes a long swig of water. "I can see it. You're bolder than James, but if I overlay bossy wolf on top of who he was, I can see it just fine. He led from kindness. You're doing a good job of that."

It's so much easier to take when he comments on my weak elbows and sloppy feet. "Mostly I'm getting my ass kicked by my betas while the rest of the pack does my job for me."

He smiles slowly. "No, I think that's exactly what Adrianna meant. She considers fixing things her job. James held everyone's capes while they did the fixing. You're doing this the way he would have done it."

"I don't really remember him as a leader." I remember the dad who laughed and steadied and played and loved with every breath.

He snorts. "Nobody does. He liked it that way. It's harder to hold capes when people expect you to be wearing one. He had Adrianna as cover. It won't be so easy for you." He shrugs. "Or maybe it will. Lissa seems pretty fond of her new superpowers."

I drink my water and ignore him.

Smart betas are a definite pain in the ass.

GHOST

I butt my head against a tree trunk and scratch my nose. Wolves aren't supposed to sweat, but it's really hot out here and it's been a long run since the last stream.

Which is why the wolf I'm trying to hunt down is probably sleeping in the shade somewhere. I'm doing like Bailey taught me and borrowing tricks from other kinds of shifters. Traveling hard in the heat of the day is just like climbing trees—the less we act like wolves, the more often we can surprise them.

I don't know if I actually need to surprise this one. I hope he just listens. I can find him, but Kennedy or Lissa would do a way better job of explaining things. I'm not a very chatty wolf. I mostly just think a lot inside my own head. Bailey says she likes that about me, but Lissa didn't send me out on this mission to be quiet.

My wolf growls softly. We're out here doing something big and important for pack, and she's mad at my human for making it complicated. It isn't.

I grin wryly and scratch the other side of my nose against the cool bark. There's a nice stream about an hour away if we keep heading this way. The trail is a faint one. I'm getting closer, but the wolf I'm following is really careful. He doesn't want to be found.

I don't blame him. They got me out before anything really bad happened. These woods are full of wolves who weren't that lucky.

I move away from the tree and scent the air. I mostly smell dry grass and pine needles, but there's an owl nest in one of the trees ahead and really fresh mouse trail criss-crossing in front of me. Mice are silly. Darting around like that just makes them easier to scent. This one was probably more worried about the owl, though.

I hope the mouse got away.

My wolf snorts.

I keep moving, my paws landing soundlessly on the forest floor. My wolf is used to my human and all her strange, mouse-loving ways. Even Bailey eventually decided I was going to starve if she kept trying to make me catch one. But she never lets anyone else tease me for being a vegetarian wolf, and sometimes the other pups copy me and she quietly goes off and finds us more nuts to eat or trades with the rogue cats for cheese.

I love cheese, but I don't like it when she uses up trade goods that could feed the pups. There's lots of cheese coming in the new baskets that Ebony and Kennedy bring us, though. My belly has been weirdly full for three whole weeks. Except for when I'm on long treks trying to find a stubborn wolf who doesn't want to be found.

I laugh quietly inside my head. My wolf's a little bit of a complainer, but she doesn't really mean it. She feels free out here. Like she could be a lone wolf and like it, except that's not really true because she likes cheese and she loves pups and she would die before she made Bailey sad.

There are so many wolves who are too broken to stay.

I pick up a stronger scent trail and speed up. This stretch of forest is really pretty, and the wolf I'm following got lazy for a bit. That's what happens when you think you aren't important. I check to make sure the light breeze that's teasing my fur is still upslope. It will blow my scent into the treetops, and the owls don't care about lone teenage wolves and their silly missions. They just get cranky when we borrow their calls for sentry duty. Especially Hoot. She can confuse even the full-grown owls.

My human heart feels sad as I run. Hoot wants to live at the den with the new alpha who likes girls who can climb trees. She even yelled at Bailey a few days ago, which isn't fair, because Bailey has to make harder choices than any of us, and we make it worse when we fight with her. But Hoot doesn't really understand that, because her wolf has a short temper and likes to fight.

She loves the best of all of us, though. And even the wolves who are really broken try to love her back.

I'm not like Hoot, either, but I'll do my best. Lissa sent me out here because she knows I can find anyone and Bailey always says that getting the job done isn't about our skills or our courage. It's simpler than that. We have to do it. There's no one else.

We have to be enough.

9

LISSA

She comes out of the trees as we round the bend in the river, a lethal streak of red fur and flying paws and radiating dominance.

She skids to a halt at Robbie's feet and nuzzles him.

I wince and shift. "Dial it down, B. You're making my wolf bleed."

Bailey shifts and smirks at me as she picks up Robbie and tosses him into the air. "Yours, maybe. This little guy has some serious balls."

His wolf doesn't have any experience with that kind of dominance being used as a weapon. "Our new alpha doesn't let anyone blast bossy juice in the den."

She snorts, and then laughs as Robbie's wolf licks her nose, trying to figure out where the strange sound came from. "Sounds like a good reason to avoid the den."

I walked right into that one, but it's hard to think clearly when my wolf is anxious and jittery. The last red wolf who charged my son wanted to kill him. Which is precisely why Bailey did it. She's big into desensitization. It's not exactly gentle, but the wolves who live out here with her can all handle a big, bad wolf running at them with fangs bared.

Something I failed at miserably the day my old alpha decided my son needed to die.

Bailey's watching my face like she can hear everything in my head. Which she probably can. She's been my friend since the dawn of time, and I've never had anything remotely resembling a poker face.

She rubs her nose against Robbie's. "Want to go play with Tara and Stinky, kiddo?"

I laugh. "Are you ever going to let him ditch that nickname?" The skunk who sprayed the rangy, good-natured eight-year-old probably has great-grandbabies by now.

"Nope." Ebony gives Bailey a casual hug and scoops Robbie out of her arms. "Come on, cutie. Let's go find playmates and see how much trouble we can cause."

Robbie's not usually the instigator of trouble, but Ebony has plenty of skills in that direction. So does Stinky. Nobody messes with Tara, though. She's old and crotchety and she hates everyone in equal measure—except for the pups. Those, she guards with her life.

One of Bailey's finest achievements has been keeping Tara alive for the last six years.

Ebony shifts back to furry, and my white ball of fluff

heads off into the trees, following her lithe dapple-gray form. He has the audacity to try to nip at her heels, which makes Bailey laugh. She turns back to me, her eyes happier than I've seen in a long time. "You got snacks in those bags?"

She's still too thin. Which means all the bounty we've been sending out here is feeding pups and lone wolves and probably skunk great-grandbabies. I rummage in the bags we brought and toss a container her way. "I sent Kennedy off on a short trip, but she should be out here with more food soon. If you need it faster, I can bring a load out." My wolf isn't the best at hauling a lot of weight, but she's happy to carry the hot, heavy bags if it helps her pack.

Bailey's eyes soften. "We're good. It's summer. You'll just make us soft."

That will happen shortly after the world ends. "You need to eat some of what we send."

Her eyes harden. "Keep it for the pups at the den."

She really, truly doesn't understand. I face her, needing her to hear and see and smell my truth. "We just bought five really enormous couches from a bear named Phil. They cost enough to feed all the pups for two years."

Fury lands, hot and ready to rumble.

I grab her arm a split second before she goes ballistic. "It wasn't Hayden's idea. It was Shelley's, and I authorized the spending. We had the funds. We won't have them again for a while, but every pup in this pack has so much food to eat, I promise you. I would never buy couches if that weren't true."

She stares at me with those eyes of hers that see everything. "You're not shitting me. For real?"

I nod slowly. "I'm guessing you didn't read Reilly's latest story."

She shakes her head. "No reception here. That new hookup is really great, but it doesn't work this side of Moss Rock."

Moss Rock is more like a small mountain, but one with good berry picking on the western slopes, and it's likely getting in the way of whatever magic Danielle and Rio cooked up so that the wolves out here can use the den's satellite internet connection. I'll let Danielle know. Maybe she can apply more of her chewing gum and duct tape and convince a mountain to play nice.

In the meantime, I give Bailey the short and relatively accurate version of the bank-robbery story, which isn't what she'll get online. Reilly's article holds some resemblance to the truth. The versions in the ShifterNet forums are rapidly becoming the stuff of forest legend.

I hope no one in Kenny's camp has reception, either.

Bailey slides down the trunk of a tree, laughing as I finish my tale. "That's insane. I can't believe you did that. And then spent all the money. That must have made your cheapskate heart break in two."

I snort. She loves my cheapskate heart. It's always managed to find a little money tucked away somewhere when we needed it most. "We had to spend it before the guys in the woods tried to retrieve it. I figure they won't try if a polar bear has it in his paws."

She snickers. "Not those losers."

Those losers have caused her plenty of heartache. Mostly because her hands have always been tied by love and loyalty and needs far greater than vengeance.

Needs I'm out here to ask her to consider giving up.

I sober. She needs to know the part I didn't tell anyone else. The couches weren't a frivolous purchase, but they weren't the only really important one we could have made. "I considered asking the pack to use the money to buy one of the HomeWild portable dens." It would have made her winter a lot easier. In a move of defiance I still don't totally understand, it's an idea I never spoke out loud.

I don't miss the anger that flashes in Bailey's eyes. "Trying to make my choices for me?"

She's never been slow. "The pack would be weaker with two dens."

Which is the right answer, but it's one that will kill me if there are pups shivering out here this winter. I try to have faith in what my gut so firmly believes. This pack needs to be whole. I look at my best friend in all the world, who holds a bunch of the keys to making that happen. She's still cranky, but she's not disagreeing with me. I try to take that as a sign of progress. "Maybe you can come and meet him."

She raises a dubious eyebrow. "No, thanks. I haven't decided if I'm going to challenge him, yet. I don't want him getting a read on me until I decide."

She's got an excellent poker face, but I've known her since she punched a pup six years older than she was in the nose because he was teasing me. Which wasn't easy—she was barely big enough to reach his nose. "I call bullshit. If you were going to challenge, you wouldn't wait for him to consolidate his power."

Her eyebrows rise a little higher.

I snort. "I listen when you talk, you big idiot."

She smiles a little. "I guess you do."

Always. The war with Samuel and his lieutenants didn't give any of us a choice. "Eamon got his tail eaten." A tidbit Hayden somehow kept out of the pack gossip column, but Bailey deserves to know. She stopped herself from killing him more times than I can count. "He taunted his parole officer's daughter."

Glee wars in her eyes with something darker.

I will the glee to win. I need that Bailey back. I've missed her so darn much. The pack needed her to be a warrior queen, and she rose up and became who we needed. But the cost has been so very high.

I pick through the other tidbits of gossip lying around in my brain. "Braden spilled an entire container of maple syrup in Hayden's lap the other day."

She rolls her eyes. "I heard. My sentries think he walks on water."

None of them were at that breakfast, which means the pack gossip chain is alive and well and climbing trees. "You haven't pulled the sentries back."

She shrugs. "I don't need them."

Needing and loving are two really different things. "It's good to have them close by."

She smirks. "Especially since you went and riled up the dominants, huh?"

I did some sleuthing before I left. "They'll likely find out Friday night. Colin's playing pool." Which will probably make enough money to cover the beer tab—if he wins. If he doesn't, those guys might finally have to wash some dishes. Either way, there's going to be big drama back at the den.

Bailey eyes me. "That's a good bribe. Well set up, well played."

I smile wryly. She loves seeing mischief land. She's also about as easy to manipulate as gravity. "It won't be as good as watching Kennedy stroll in with the red bandana." Something Bailey absolutely denies having instigated, but I'll believe that when the sky starts raining squishy pink gumdrops.

She sighs quietly.

I lean against the tree trunk beside her, angling in until our shoulders touch. "We're building something really good, B. We need you to come home."

"Maybe." A shrug. "Not until the others do."

"They won't come in if you stay out here." Bailey might not want to be alpha, but for the lost souls, she basically is.

"They might. A few, at least."

I'm working on that, but I came out here to toss a different pebble. Or a handful of them. I reach into my pocket for the next one. "The older pups are starting school in the fall. There's a ShifterNet co-op where the packs all help teach each other. Reilly and Scotty are doing a unit on the science of living in a space colony."

She scowls at me. "Who the hell is Scotty?"

I smile. Weapon number four—Bailey's a terrible gossip. One who likes to have her finger on the pulse of everything. "He's a guy in Whistler Pack who's helping Reilly get the kind of learning materials he needs."

"Good." Bailey sighs again, letting me hear the regret she hides from everyone else. "He's such a smart kid. We didn't do nearly enough for him."

I balked at buying her a den. It's not in me to withhold more. "We could get you hooked up to the co-op portal. Maybe have the pups here get together with the ones in the den for classes sometimes. You could teach woodcraft."

She shoots me a disgruntled look. "I already teach them that."

"Not often enough."

She growls. "Damn you, I'm doing my best."

That's the marvel of who she is—and the problem. "You don't need to carry so much. Not anymore. Come in and bring whoever will come with you, and then let the whole pack figure out how to help the rest."

She's quiet for a long time. "It's not that simple. I know you mean well, and I'm coming around to the idea that the new guys don't suck, but there's only so much all of you can do. Hell, you can't even get seven idiots who can't find their way through the forest on a full moon to come home."

My wolf wants to growl. "They might have been the center of this pack for the last six years, but the rest of us are done with being expendable asteroids."

That gets me a reluctant, amused snort. "You've been hanging out with Reilly too much."

He's a hard bear to resist. "If you don't listen to me, I'm sending him out here next."

"That's playing dirty."

I'll do whatever it takes. Somewhere on the run out here, I got really clear on that. "We have a sentinel, B. He's a really good guy. He can help with the wolves who are hurting."

She grimaces. "He already is."

I glance over at her carefully. "Are you okay with that?"

"He didn't ask permission."

She's given it, or he would have found himself on the receiving end of a world of furry red hurt.

She huffs out a breath. "He's careful. And respectful. He very neatly skirts where we are, almost like someone drew him a map."

It wasn't me, but that doesn't matter. I'd have made him one if he asked. "Ebony, probably."

Another long silence. "Do you trust him as much as she does?"

The answer rises from my wolf, simple and clear. "Yes."

Her eyes fill with surprise.

We should have had this talk weeks ago. This is the first time we've been alone, but that's a feeble excuse. I let myself get stuck thinking that loyalty to my friend and loyalty to my pack were different. They're not. "That day when Samuel tried to kill us? Rio put his body between me and the fight and Robbie between his front legs. My wolf was almost gone, and he stood there and protected both of us."

The sheen in her eyes as she stares off at the trees nearly guts me. "I'm so sorry. I should have been there."

She would have bled out right beside us. She wasn't ever sick enough or cruel enough to match Samuel's dominance. "I should have left earlier."

She lets her head rest on my shoulder. "You should have. I told you that every damn day for six years."

She did, and her head on my shoulder is the biggest reason I never went. It would have taken too much of the fight out of my best friend—and too much of what's left of her softness. "And yet somehow I'm still here."

She snorts. "Yes, you are. Causing trouble and trying to convince me that the den has transformed into some kind of fairy tale that won't turn into a pumpkin at midnight."

Rio discovered Shelley's pies last week, so I can't actually make any definitive promises where pumpkins are concerned. "We have a smart alpha who thinks submissives and women matter. He made Ebony beta and he regularly lets her dump him in the dirt while half the den is watching. He called Kelsey's wolf out of her in just a few days, and Eliza walks with her head up, and the sentries get more chocolate than can possibly be good for any teenager."

All of which I'm sure she already knows, but she's always been willing to listen to my heart. "He's a good man." He's not the whole pack, but we're wolves. The ones at the top really matter. She knows that better than anyone.

She rolls her eyes. "You're as gooey-eyed as my sentries. No guy is that perfect."

I turn to face her. "He's not. He's got flaws. He's teaching the pups way too many swear words and he doesn't eat his vegetables and he's scared to wield his authority as often as he maybe should and he's letting his pack hurt him because he doesn't want to say that he matters as much as we do."

She stares at me, her jaw literally hanging open. "You *like* him."

She always sees. Always. I wrinkle my nose. "What are we, fourteen again?"

She completely ignores my pathetic attempt to distract her. "Is your wolf gone on him, too?"

She's never believed in fairy tales—except for one. "No magical mate bond dropped out of the sky and made me start pining for his puppies."

"You like him."

"He's a good man who saved my life and Robbie's, and he's making and guarding space for our pack to rebuild itself. Those are plenty of reasons to like him a whole lot."

The dawning glee in her eyes is terrifying. "You're totally gone on him."

She's been my best friend forever. I sigh and tell her the truth I'm not really ready to see. "I might be."

She laughs softly. "Then why are you out here talking to me instead of wooing your alpha?"

I clap a hand over my wolf's mouth. "We need to make the pack safe and whole, first."

She snorts. "It doesn't work that way."

I give her a wry look. "And you know this because?" She's been a monk for the last six years, but before that I was the trusty sidekick of a woman who thought relationships that lasted longer than a week were boring.

She smiles. "You're not me. You were always going to do this. It was just a matter of finding the right wolf." Mischief gleams in her eyes. "Although you always did have a thing about wanting to kiss a frog and see if he turned into a prince."

Like skunks, some childhood exploits can never be lived down. "I only did that once. And Hayden isn't a frog. Come meet him, or at least come skulk in the trees with the sentries and spy on him."

She raises an eyebrow. "What makes you think I haven't already done that?"

Sheer gut instinct. She's too easy about staying out here to have laid eyes on the wrecking ball to certainty that is Hayden Scott. "If you'd been watching, you'd know that my wolf has been slobbering all over him."

My wolf sticks out her tongue. There hasn't been nearly enough slobbering.

Bailey reaches out her hand and tugs on my curls,

soothing both of the beings who share my soul. "Your human has always been harder to convince."

Hardly. I tried to resist being Bailey's friend when she rescued two-year-old me, mostly out of embarrassed, dented pride. I made it all of ten minutes. "I've got good reasons to be careful."

She nods slowly. "We both do."

Arguing head on with Bailey has never worked, but I'm out here because I believe that we both have good reasons to maybe not be so careful, too. "I robbed a bank and poked a stick at one of Hayden's biggest headaches and he's proud of me."

Her eyes are a jumbled mix of sad and wistful and softly happy. A whole bunch of things she never lets anyone else see. "Good. You deserve someone who knows exactly how wonderful you are."

I'm pretty sure my eyes look just like hers. "I've always had someone. I need her beside me to make sure my wolf doesn't do anything stupid."

She leans her forehead into mine. "I might have to come check him out."

Sometimes the best reason isn't nearly as important as the one that works. I know that Bailey won't walk into our den for a long time yet—she's about as fast to change direction as Moss Rock. But skulking in a tree will let her watch, and when she watches, she sees the truth. "Let me know when you come. I'll steal some chocolate and come hide out with you."

She smirks. "One of your sneaky betas will follow you and then my cover will be blown."

One of them has always known where Bailey can be found, but this isn't about facts. It's about what lives in scarred and tough and terrified hearts. I hug her as tightly as she'll allow. "Would that really be such a bad thing?"

Her answer is in her silence.

I remind myself that's exactly how pebbles sound just after they land.

10

LISSA

Kel holds up a pair of pants that are almost entirely missing the knees. "Make shorts out of these?"

Cori and Eliza are refusing to relinquish the sewing machine on loan from Whistler Pack, but they've agreed that we can submit a basket of clothing for repairs. Which isn't nearly as much fun as making pillows out of all the pretty fabric that came on the plane, but given how fast this pack goes through clothes and how little any of us ever want to sew by hand again, something has to give.

I study the gray pants in Kel's hands. They're a drab color, but the fabric is sturdy. "Sure. Let's hem them, and maybe Cori can use some of the pillow leftovers to add a couple of patches." Reilly's the pup they'll fit next, and his eyes shine whenever he gets something colorful to wear.

Kel snorts. "It's hard to sneak through the woods when you're wearing rainbow patches on your clothes."

I let the pain brush against me and move on by. It's the only way I know to give it less power. "That's why so much of what we have is gray and brown and green." Sneaking was a way of life these last six years.

A long silence. "When I came back after my tours, I wore nothing but black and gray for three months. One day I walked into my room and two little punks had switched out all my shirts. The most sedate one they left behind was a lime green that would make your eyes bleed."

I'm pretty sure I know those two punks, and I'm not sure they were ever little. I also know Kel doesn't easily share some parts of his past. I try to hold this one gently. "Did you wear it?"

He grunts. "Yeah. Every damn day."

I lean against him and run my hand down his back, soothing him just like I would Robbie. "Do you still have it?"

He makes a wry face. "If you wear them long enough, they fade to something pretty close to gray."

I shake my head. He's a wolf who plays the long game, always. But he's not the only one, and I'm guessing two grown-up punks will never be done making sure he stays in the color and the light. "How often do they steal your shirts these days?"

He glances suspiciously at the pile of clothes we're sorting. "We'll see how many of them we find in there."

I shake my head, laughing. "Is that why you volunteered to help with this?"

His grin is that of a small boy very pleased with himself. "Yes."

I elbow him, but it's hard to be stern while I'm giggling. "You can put all the gray ones in the pile headed out to the woods." I wasn't shy about creating one. I might not be ready to lift all the veils of secrecy in this pack, but I can darn well let some of them blow in the breeze a little. It will do the wolves in the woods good to wear something that smells of pack.

Kel eyes me just a hair too casually. "Can I talk you into telling me when the other shoe is dropping?"

Tossing pebbles is kind of like wearing rainbow patches on your pants. It's awfully hard to sneak. "I'm not sure." It's the truth. All the pebbles have left my hands. "There might be more than one."

He folds a flannel shirt that might have been blue once and sets it on the pile headed out to Bailey. "Any idea what's in them?"

I shoot him a wry look. "Obviously you've set a few things in motion in your time."

He chuckles. "We used to say that no plan survived engagement with the enemy."

In this pack, our biggest enemy is fear. It tries to eat everything good about who we are and who we can be. And it turns even the smallest pebbles into boulders.

I hold up a torn t-shirt that's too small for any of our pups, but all of them have worn, and add it to the special scraps pile. Cori and Eliza have a plan. Something about sewing our good memories into a pillow to live in the den. And maybe some of our not-so-good ones, too. So that we don't forget where we've come from.

I glance over at Kel, because I'm quite sure any attempt to protect his faded t-shirt collection is secondary to his real reason for sitting beside me this morning. "Am I doing the wrong thing, going around Hayden like this?"

He puts a ragged pair of pants covered in berry hand-prints on the special scraps pile. "You're not going around him."

That's not the answer I expected. "What am I doing?"

"That's a really good question. One you need to answer for yourself."

There are easy answers and far trickier ones, and most of them make me squirm. "I'm not sure all my reasons for doing this are good ones."

He sets a hand on my knee. "They never are. People are complicated, and those of us with animals inside us are more complicated than most."

He's not wrong about that. I take a pair of pants that used to be mine until they somehow shrank and add them to the pile that might fit Kennedy or Ghost or one of the sentries.

Kel tosses another t-shirt onto Bailey's pile and makes a face. "Shit. I swore I wasn't going to do this, but apparently I am." He turns so that he's looking me straight in the eyes, which gets my wolf's attention. "Hayden is one of those complicated people. He's a patient guy, and a strong one, and he'll give you all the space and time you need, both personally and as alpha of this pack."

I stare at him. Kel never makes frontal attacks.

He sighs. "Which is where I should stop." He looks down at the flannel shirt in his hands. "But as his friend? Don't make him wait too long."

The breath whooshes out of my lungs. "It's not only up to me."

A small smile. "He won't make the first move. He's Adrianna Scott's son and you're a wolf who's spent the last six years surviving hell."

My wolf sits up, frustrated and mad. She isn't traumatized.

He chuckles quietly and strokes my hair, petting my wolf. "Let him see you, sweetheart. Lissa here is hiding you pretty damn well."

I scowl. If she had her way, we'd be drooling over our alpha all day long.

"Good grief, you too?" Rio plunks down on one of the sorting piles and shakes his head at Kel. "This pack does not need more matchmakers."

I've seen these two work together too often to be fooled. This isn't an unplanned interruption. It's their version of good wolf, bad wolf. One to rock me a little, the other to steady me again.

"Maybe we do. We're kind of short on mated pairs around here." Kel flashes him a grin. "Isn't helping with that a sentinel's job?"

Rio looks moderately horrified.

I laugh. They're adorable, even when they're being as

obvious as Robbie when he's trying to get my last slice of bacon. I look at Kel, because even if my skills are a little rusty, I know that the best way to fight this particular kind of fire is with more fire. "You're single."

He snorts. "This pack doesn't exactly have a big supply of decent men to choose from."

Rio grins. "I'm decent."

"You're straight. You're also sitting on the sorting piles."

Rio moves over, which just sits him on top of another pile. "Picky, picky." He holds up a bright orange shirt that's at least five sizes too small for an adult. "This would be a good color on you."

I hide a grin. Softies, all of them. Tricky, loyal, scheming softies.

Rio shoots me a look as he puts the orange shirt on the pile for mending. "Kel's an annoying nuisance, but he's not wrong. About Hayden."

Good wolf, bad wolf, back on task. I pick up a set of green fleece pants that were Robbie's favorites. He wore them until they were practically up to his knees. "I know Hayden's more vulnerable than he looks. His mom already had that conversation with me."

Rio shakes his head at Kel. "She always gets there first."

I already knew. She just helped me look a little more closely. "I like her. She's not scary like I expected."

Rio snorts and takes the green pants out of my hands. "Adrianna and Kel are the scariest wolves I know and nobody's ever scared of them."

I snicker. "Says the big black wolf of death."

Rio looks honestly confused. "When did you see him?"

Kel punches his shoulder. "The day we met, dumbass."

Rio grins. "That was the big black wolf of do-not-fuck-with-a-pup. He's actually a pretty nice guy."

"He's not. Lissa here is nice. You alternate between scary wolf and wise old man and candy thief. None of those are nice."

Rio throws a companionable arm over my shoulders. "Lissa is plenty scary."

Kel contemplates me and nods. "You have a point."

Goofballs. I elbow Rio. "Get to work, wise old man. I want a swim, and that doesn't happen until these clothes are sorted. So make yourself useful or get your big, scary self off my piles."

He grins at Kel as he rolls off our rag-tag collection of pack scraps and hand-me-downs. "That's his job. I'll go give our alpha more practice dealing with bossypants wolves. Seems like he might need it sometime soon."

His tone is joking—but the careful look he sends me isn't. A sentinel and a very good man, making sure he isn't actually pushing me where I don't want to go.

I smile quietly. This pack is full of complicated layers and soft hearts, and a lot of them have rips and tears and holes in them, including mine. But there are so very many reasons to do the mending.

HAYDEN

Watching Lissa giggle and hold her own with two of my best friends is good for my wolf. Or at least that's the story I'm telling myself. It sounds better than any alternative explanation for why I'm sitting where I can watch her, pretending to deal with the paperwork involved in getting our pups enrolled in school.

Shifter forms are easy. The provincial requirements are a pain in the butt. Especially when they want things we don't have, like birth certificates and health records. All of which can be handled with exemptions, but every last one of them requires the pack alpha's blessing.

I can't be the first alpha to think that's ridiculous, but humans have strange ideas of how shifter packs work.

My wolf yips inside my head.

I scowl at the tablet in my lap. He hates paperwork, too.

He yips again, sharper this time.

I look up, using my human nose and eyes to read the situation, even though they're crap at figuring out what's got him stirred up. My wolf isn't alarmed, though. Just sitting up straight, his eyes glued to the woods.

There are so many things that could be.

Kel's on his feet, but he eases back when Ebony slips out of the trees, giving the all-clear hand signal. And one to stay where we are.

Not one of the dominants, then. She'd want us meeting him with our claws and teeth on display.

A moment later, Kennedy waltzes out of the trees, a

nonchalant grin on her face and amusement she can't hide in her eyes. Two owls hoot behind her, a very belated warning of an incoming friendly. Kel and Ebony exchange the kind of glance that says there's going to be a little chat about perimeter security later. One where their bark is going to be a whole lot more serious than their bite, but where an important lesson will be handed out all the same.

My wolf would normally be pretty interested in that conversation, but he's thoroughly distracted. Not by Kennedy. A teenager whose pack loyalty outweighs her is no threat. He's far more interested in the look on Lissa's face as Kennedy heads over to the crew sorting clothing.

Lissa's trying hard to hide it, but she's profoundly relieved.

That pulls me to my feet. Time to see just what else my chief financial officer has lobbed into a calm, sunny day.

Lissa and Kennedy both glance my way as I arrive, but it doesn't interrupt the silent conversation running between them. One that doesn't have any hand signals, but they don't seem to need them.

My human growls. This pack has entirely too much practice at keeping things under their alpha's radar. Which I'm intending to say something about, but my wolf grabs my throat. He doesn't give a shit what they're trying to hide. The heart of his pack is beating stronger, feeding on tasty rabbit snacks—and the green-eyed wolf is the lead hunter.

I blink.

Kennedy plunks down next to Kel, right on top of a pile of clothes. "Can I help?"

Ebony raises an eyebrow. "You disappear for three days without saying a word to your alpha or your betas and that's all you think you need to say when you get back?"

"I sent her." Lissa's eyes are stern, and it's very clear that if we want to ride Kennedy's ass, we'll need to go through her. Which has Kennedy grinning. Troublesome teenager.

My wolf keeps his eye on the ball that matters most. "You're pack leadership. If you gave her a job to do, that's fine by me. I'd appreciate knowing what it is, however."

I wince at the bossy alpha in those words, but my wolf is looking at her eyes. He has no doubts at all. She can handle this.

She makes a wry face. "Same deal as before. I'll tell you if you pull rank. Otherwise, I'd like to wait."

Kel blinks, which is his version of utterly astonished.

Ebony looks thoroughly impressed.

It isn't either of them who has my wolf's attention, though. He's too busy gaping at Kennedy. She hasn't shifted, but she's in a crouch, the kind that could attack at any moment, silently bristling at me. From *behind* Lissa.

He's entirely confused. Every line of her is screaming dominant challenge—and she's using a submissive wolf as a shield.

I pat him on the head. Somebody's been studying the tactics of Adrianna Scott, and it clearly isn't him. This is exactly the kind of stunt my mother would pull.

Lissa's eyes are as wide as platters as she turns so that she can see the teenager behind her. Kennedy isn't leaking dominance, which is a very nice demonstration of control, given how riled she is. But the message in her eyes communicates just fine. One baby alpha, putting me sharply on notice.

I need to get this right.

I look at Lissa and say several things I should have said out loud long before this. "There are some people around here who think I'm supposed to be the savior of this pack. They're wrong. I'm an immigrant, just like Kel and Rio."

My green-eyed wolf isn't blinking. At all.

My wolf wants to growl at Kennedy, who has somehow managed to ratchet up her fierceness, but I keep my eyes on Lissa. "We're useful immigrants, and loyal ones, and we'll fight as hard as anyone here for this pack to be everything it wants to be, but I have no intention of standing in the way of the people who are going to get us there. I don't know the details of what you're doing. I don't need to know. I can see where it's headed."

Her breath lets out all at once. "Thank you."

Rio waits a beat and then nudges Kennedy with his shoulder. "I think we can let him live."

She smirks at him, letting go of her lightning in a bottle as fast as she picked it up.

Lissa hasn't. She's still watching me. Waiting. She doesn't bristle like Kennedy, but her message is just as clear. I need to get this right, too.

I roll my eyes. "What, you think I'm going to eat

Kennedy for breakfast? Have you tasted teenage wolf paws?"

Kennedy snickers first, but Lissa is right behind her.

Ebony and Kel huff out the long-suffering sighs of betas stuck with an alpha who's managed to retain most of his maturity issues.

Rio wraps his arm around Kennedy's head. "I don't know. We could add ketchup."

She manages to squiggle out of his hold and springs backward in a way that would break me, giggling and ready to rumble.

Time for an alpha with maturity issues to do his job. I shoot Lissa a grin. "Let me take these troublemakers out of your hair. It looks like it's time for another session of beat-up-the-alpha."

Kennedy's eyes widen. Up until now, that's been a game for betas only.

Rio snorts. "I'll stay here and fold clothes, since I sat on at least half of them. Kel can come and make sure the girls don't beat you up too badly."

My wolf catches the look Kennedy and Ebony exchange and yanks for my skin. I let him have it. I kick my shorts off as the two of them tear into the woods. I have good, important alpha work to do, stabilizing the dominant hierarchy in my pack, and I'm going to go do it.

It's either that or break a really important promise I made to myself. One that involves waiting on a woman who still has far too much caution in her green eyes.

Because the last ten minutes were a case study on why that promise matters. Every time Lissa faces me down or wires ridiculous amounts of money to a polar bear or sends wolves in the pack off to do her bidding, who she is stands a little taller. Runs a little faster. Beats a little stronger.

I won't let anyone get in the way of that. Including me.

LISSA

I slip into the trees, casting one last look behind me as I go. Robbie's white fur is visible in the firelight. The dark background behind him is Ebony, lounging in her fur as three pups snore in a pile, tucked in against her. She won't let anything happen to him.

I'm not alone. There's a second black wolf in the forest with me. Not close—Rio somehow understands that I need to run alone tonight. But he's there, his paws touching the earth as he shadows me to make sure I stay safe.

My wolf wants to lunge against the restraints. She doesn't need a babysitter. She's fast. No one will ever catch her.

I put the energy of her frustration into my legs, into the breath pushing in and out of my lungs. I'm rebelling enough as it is. My pack doesn't need me breaking rules that need to be absolute. Not when I'm the one poking sticks at what might try to attack us in the night.

The ink-dark wolf moves further away. Letting me have more space. More freedom.

My wolf dances her paws on the earth. She might not be big and strong, but she's a smart wolf. A wily wolf. The answer beats back from the earth. She is worthy. So worthy. Her pack needs her. Loves her. Respects her.

Her resistance quiets. The big black wolf of darkness never lies.

Laughter from the earth. *Time to play, small, wily wolf.*

She zooms between two trees that would snag a bigger wolf. She wants high ridge lines tonight. The ones up past Banner Rock will do nicely. She leaps over the strewn branches of a new nurse log and scents another predator. Kennedy, her trail cool and old.

Silly teenager. She took three days to do a job that a fast, wily wolf could do in one.

My human murmurs from somewhere deep inside my wolf. She knows better than to ignore the very smug look a certain teenager was wearing, even before she managed to drop her alpha with a leg sweep.

My wolf snorts. He made her pay for that. Strong alpha. Good alpha. One who picked a grinning Kennedy up out of the dirt and complained about all the underhanded tricks she's learning from her betas.

He's right—and the most important ones have nothing to do with fighting. She's learning to be silly. To lead from behind. To trust.

We all are.

The trees break suddenly. My wolf makes her way

nimbly up the steep goat trail to the top. She can't feel the black wolf of shadow and wisdom and protection any longer, but it doesn't matter. He's out there somewhere, and nothing will catch her up here except maybe a goat, and they know to get out of her way.

So much energy, and she needs to leave it all on the mountain so she can go back and be who her pack needs her to be instead of a fountain of restlessness.

I offer her what little apology I can. I didn't know the hardest part of throwing pebbles is the silence after they land.

11

HAYDEN

Myrna shoots me the kind of grin only pack elders can get away with. "It's not much further."

That's what they always say. I shake my head at Ebony and Shelley, who are draped in just as many chairs, bags, towels, and random kitchen implements as I am. Neither of them has watermelons, though. Apparently carrying those is a sacred alpha duty.

Reilly grins as he pops up between us, a smiling, excited kid with a furry white wolf at his heels. "Myrna's not just saying that this time. We're really close and it's the best surprise and she even had Rio come and test it just in case the laws of physics don't work the way they did when she was in school."

I raise an eyebrow at my sentinel, who's walking between Lissa and Danielle and looking entirely too innocent. "You knew about this?"

He catches a blanket that's trying to slither off his shoulders, probably because Braden is wrapped inside it, and grins. "Nope. Just one small part, and Myrna swore me to secrecy. No cookie privileges for a year if I talked."

Mellie claps her hands on the top of Kel's head. "'ookie!"

Her two moms roll their eyes in unison and shoot Rio long-suffering looks.

I grin. They bug me about eating my vegetables, too. I'm happy to set a good example for our pups, but it's just never going to involve zucchini.

Cori and Eliza, walking off to the side, swing Jade between them. Her giggles wash over the pack, dusting us with infectious, small-girl sunshine. Mellie bangs on Kel's head again. She wants to swing, too.

They're killing me, all of them. Myrna dragged us out of our sleeping bags bright and early this morning for a day of fun, but she refused to give us any details. She just issued orders and got us all ready and now we're rambling through the forest carrying ninety percent of the den with us, and my pack is so stinking happy I can literally feel it soaking into my skin.

I cast a quick glance at Lissa. Rio looked damn tired after the two of them came back from a run that lasted deep into the night, but she's as full of the same bright energy as everyone else. And was just as surprised as the rest of us this morning. Whatever Myrna's up to, my green-eyed wolf wasn't one of her accomplices.

Lissa smiles at me, and my wolf rolls over with happiness inside my chest. I turn to face forward again so that I don't accidentally squish a pup or run my backpack full of watermelons into a tree, but it's probably a good thing I have so much gear holding me down. Gravity feels really light today.

There's an all-clear hoot from the trees ahead. Ebony, scouting to make sure nothing in the forest is trying to surprise us.

A hoot sounds from much closer by.

I carefully don't look at the two slim figures shadowing us in the woods. One of them is Kennedy, but the other I only know as a smell I trust. She isn't any taller than Reilly, but my wolf knows that's deceiving. When the sentries are hooting, she's their leader.

He's good with that. Small but mighty is a lesson he learned long ago.

A small hand reaches up for mine. I look down at Kelsey, who's been dancing the whole walk, touching flowers and friends and smiling at them all. "Hi, cutie."

She beams up at me. "I like watermelon."

I laugh. "That's good, because I think I'm carrying twenty of them." Either that or Kel tossed a couple of rocks in my backpack for good measure.

Kelsey looks over at the figures in the woods. "Hoot is my friend."

If Kelsey ever decides she wants to run this pack, my wolf will roll over and offer her his belly. "I'm glad she came to play with us today."

A small smile. "She helped Myrna with the surprise."

Myrna's eyebrows fly up as she turns around and

walks backward. "Just how do you know that, young lady?"

Kelsey grins. "Kel showed me how to be sneaky. We watched."

I hear his snorting chuckle from behind us.

Myrna shakes a finger at him. "You're a bad, bad wolf."

Kelsey shakes her head adamantly. "He's a good wolf. He knows how to do bad things, but he wants to do good things. They make his heart feel better."

Kel's eyes close. When he opens them again, the look in them nearly tears me in two. "You're exactly right about that, sweetie. Thank you. You take really good care of my heart."

She smiles at him and swings my hand in hers. Just another day in the life of the pack's most submissive wolf, laying a scent trail for the rest of the pack to follow. And they do. Shelley closes in beside Kel and wraps an arm around him, leaning her head on his shoulder as they walk. Robbie brings Kelsey a pretty rock and drops it into her outstretched hand, bounding away again as Lissa tries to toss him a shirt to put on.

I grin. If we're headed where I think we're headed, trying to keep naked pups dressed is going to be a lost cause.

LISSA

My wolf can smell where we're going, and she's excited. Faint hints of water and moss and the deeper, earthy smell of a place that only sees full sun a few days of the year.

But on those days, it's glorious.

I haven't been there in six years. It's too close to the den for us to have been able to relax, and this place won't permit anything else.

Miriam and Layla catch up to me, doling out apple slices to pups and adults alike. I glance over to make sure Kelsey got some, and take the handful of cool, crisp slices I'm offered.

Accepting the look in their eyes is harder. Word got out fast about what Hayden said, even though there weren't very many witnesses. My pack is looking at me differently today. Not in a bad way—but it's harder to look back at them and keep believing I'm just a meek bookkeeper.

They don't believe that anymore, even if I do.

I guess that's what I get for robbing banks, but I'm not the only one throwing pebbles. Today wasn't my idea, and other people are using it as a springboard. I look over at the two teenagers in the woods. Kennedy showed up with Hoot at the crack of dawn, which means that trail I scented last night was a certain teenage baby alpha off to ask Bailey's permission to break the rules.

And Bailey granted it.

Small actions, beginning to have consequences. I like this one a lot. Hoot wants to be here so badly her teeth ache with it. And while Hayden isn't nearly perfect, he gets quiet, sensitive girls down to the ground. The four-year-old holding his hand and singing a song she's making up as she walks is more than enough proof of that.

I grin at the two of them as he tries to sing along with her and intentionally gets it wrong. He's got a talent for making us underestimate him.

My wolf sniffs. She sees exactly who he is.

I roll my eyes. Her persistence is noted.

Rio winks at me. I'm not the only one noticing my wolf's antics.

Fair enough. She led him on a merry chase last night.

Robbie runs through the woods to my left, followed by a bear in human form. Cori and Eliza swing Jade up just high enough for a fuzzy white streak to dash underneath. I exhale happily as toddler giggles fill the forest. More magic of this day. Eliza misses her son, still sitting off in the woods sulking with the other dominants. Jade's good medicine for that, and Eliza's good at bringing Cori in from the periphery. They've been friends for a long time, but we hid those connections these last six years. They offered too much leverage to those who watched.

Subtle changes, but such fiercely important ones.

Myrna turns around at the head of the pack.

Even human noses can smell where we are now, but that doesn't dim the delight in her eyes the slightest bit. "All the adults need to close their eyes and hold a pup's hand."

Layla takes Braden's hand, already laughing. "That's just going to get us all concussions."

Probably, but we'll do it anyway. I look around for

Robbie and spy him headed straight for me with Rio in tow. The big man grins and adds Reilly and Ebony to a growing chain. The rest of the pups promptly reach for two hands each. Hayden shakes his head and looks down at the hand he's holding. "Kelsey love, you wouldn't walk me straight into a tree, would you?"

She shakes her head, her eyes twinkling.

Kel snorts and grins at me. "I notice he didn't ask the pup holding his other hand."

Mellie squeals happily, not at all sure what she's being accused of, but always happy to be the center of attention.

"Fine. If you're going to be wimps about it, change of plans." Myrna walks over and takes Mellie's other hand. "Anyone under the age of sixteen needs to close their eyes."

I wink at Hoot, who's next to Kennedy, right at the end of the line. Tricky Myrna. Hoot's sixteenth birthday was less than a month ago, and she never gets included with the adults.

She smiles and shrugs, looking mostly embarrassed, but I can feel her wolf. Delighted. Proud.

My human is less submissive than my wolf, just like Kelsey. Hoot has the opposite challenge. She's a shy, careful sixteen-year-old with a scrappy animal inside her. Myrna just managed to honor both parts of Hoot's shifter soul in one casual sentence that wasn't even obviously pointed at our not-quite-acknowledged visitor.

I'm a pebble-tossing amateur by comparison.

Robbie tugs on my hand. The line is moving, and he's

totally impatient to get to the surprise. It isn't him I watch as we clear the line of trees, though. I'm too busy taking in the small waterfall and the big, mostly shallow swimming hole, and the brand-new rope swing hanging off a tree limb that looks like it grew just to give pups a way to fly.

If it's strong enough to hold Rio, today is going to be the kind of fun my wolf barely remembers.

I realize I'm dancing in place, jiggling nearly as much as my son. And my alpha is grinning at me.

My cheeks flush.

His eyes change. Sorrow. He wasn't trying to dampen my joy.

I stand entirely still, my son's hand in mine, here in this place of rocks and moss and hidden forest waterfalls, and look into kind, intent, hungry brown eyes as that sinks in.

He wasn't trying to dampen my joy.

HAYDEN

I know I should stop looking at her. Our pack is basically erupting around us, the lure of water and rope swing far too strong to hold them still even for a moment that feels like it's changing who I am.

I have no idea what just happened—but I know I won't ever forget it.

Lissa staggers and looks down as Robbie tackles her, a

wildly excited ball of white fluff who doesn't nearly know his own strength yet. She laughs and casts me a rueful look as she taps her pup's nose.

I grin. She's not going to get his attention that way even if she uses a two-by-four. And moments that change us at the cellular level don't ever go away, even if we spend the rest of the day teaching pups the fine art of letting go of a rope swing at the right time.

I stride over and gather her into my arms, and her rambunctious pup too, because what lives in me absolutely needs to hold them for a moment. Then I kiss the top of her head and toss a wriggly pup high and far into Ebony's waiting arms. Robbie shifts in mid-air, so the catch is trickier than I intended, but just like my other beta, she always has my back.

Lissa laughs beside me, and it's a sound as pure as the water of this place.

"Alpha."

We both turn at Myrna's call.

She holds up the end of the rope. "Will you take the first swing?"

I snort. "Will you promise to sleep on a couch?"

She looks like I just stabbed her with a rusty sword. "No."

I grin. "Then not a chance. I say you swing first."

Lissa chortles quietly. The pups beam in unison. That's a solution they can all support.

Myrna scowls and holds the rope toward Reilly. "Bears should be good at this. You go first."

He doesn't even bother to glance at an adult to

double check his instincts. "I think I need to see a good example first. From someone who's done this really a lot."

Smart pup. Generous, loyal pup.

Myrna scans the other pups, looking for one less wise to the ways of the world.

Lissa glows as Robbie tucks himself in behind Reilly, shaking his head even though his eagerness is practically splitting him in two.

I let my chin rest on top of her head. "He understands the important things just fine."

She softens in my arms. Then I feel her gather herself in like she always does—but this time, she doesn't slip away. She just solidifies somehow. She lays her hand over my heart and pats it twice. Then she tips her head back, her eyes full of mischief. "Last one in has to wash all the dishes."

I stare at her. "We didn't bring dishes." I hope. My pack was pretty damn heavy.

She grins. "Fine. Be a rotten egg, then."

My wolf objects fiercely that my feet aren't moving. He knows a challenge when he hears one, and the green-eyed wolf has just thrown down a gauntlet.

My human thinks she might have tossed down more than one.

LISSA

I hit the water, flailing and yelling and trying not to belly flop as I run into chaos—and away from disorder of a totally different kind. I apparently lied to Bailey. My wolf is entirely ready to have his pups, and she's kind of in charge right now.

I turn to face him and cup my hands in motions long forgotten.

He reverses course with impressive alacrity, a huge grin splitting his face. "I'll remind you, I learned how to water fight from a bear."

My wolf is completely delighted with him. "What makes you think I didn't?"

Reilly whoops from the shore.

Hayden squirts a nifty fountain of water my way. I dodge. He's going to have to do a lot better than that if he wants to catch my wily wolf.

"A dozen cookies for the winner!"

I laugh at Myrna as she tucks the rope between her knees. "Whose side are you on?"

She cackles. "I'm not sure. But you two better get out of my way. I'm aiming straight for your heads."

I grin and backpedal into deeper waters, which works fine until I trip over a mountain of fur. Reilly shifts and surfaces behind me, an abashed grin on his face. "Sorry. My bear's a little excited. He came to be on your team."

Hayden wraps an arm around his neck. "I'm the underdog here, silly."

Reilly snickers as they topple over sideways into the water. Robbie charges in on top of them, totally willing to play for any team that will take him.

I duck as Myrna flies past, shrieking like the teenage hoyden she once was. The whole pack stops long enough to watch her land.

I grin. She's not pebble-sized. It's a really impressive entrance.

An enormous shoulder tackles me from behind, taking us both underwater. I come up in Hayden's arms, my wolf not sure whether to nip him or kiss him.

He grins. "Reilly made me do it. He's in charge."

I look over at a giggling bear. "I thought you were on my team."

"Nope." He grins and swims backward, fast. "Hayden says it's boys against girls, and we're gonna lose so we have to be smart right at the beginning."

I laugh as Ebony tosses a bucket of water on his head. Kennedy whoops behind her, swinging out on the rope with Kelsey in her arms. They land with enough of a splash to drown everyone.

Kelsey comes up giggling so hard she can barely breathe.

I glance over at the shore, where the littlest pups are getting loaded up onto adult shoulders. Hoot rope-catapults into the water just behind Kennedy. She swings the rope back for Cori and Eliza and looks at me expectantly. I fire a look at Ebony, but she just shrugs and waits. I grab the bucket and help her toss some more water at the assembling guys. Or that's where we aim, anyhow. "How come I'm the general of this war?"

She grins at me. "Because you started it?"

I flail helplessly as Reilly's bear swamps us with a wave. "That's totally different from finishing it."

"I know," she says, winking.

My wolf shakes the water out of her eyes. This so wasn't what she was trying to accomplish.

I laugh at her, even as we get hit by the next wave. Small actions sometimes have unintended consequences. And if I don't deal with these, we're all going to drown.

12

LISSA

I grin over at my son, who literally fell asleep with his face in his plate. He's not the only one passed out. All the smaller pups except Kelsey are close or gone, full of sunshine and water and watermelon and the energy of a pack drunk on goofy joy.

Kelsey is sitting between Hoot and Kennedy, who are happily including her in their ongoing celebration. We won an overwhelming victory in the water fight to end all water fights, or at least the best one I've been a part of in a really long time, and the three of them had a whole lot to do with it.

Rio ruffles their heads as he walks by, followed by a bear who does exactly the same. Kennedy swats at Reilly's hand with exactly the right amount of menace to make him giggle, and orders up another slice of watermelon.

I somehow won us the war. They decided the price of defeat.

Reilly makes a wry face that doesn't quite hide his delight and heads off for the much-diminished pile of watermelon slices. Hayden and Rio and Kel have been casually, effortlessly modeling just how to lose gracefully, and a young bear has paid careful attention. He brings back a slice for Kelsey, too.

Mellie follows his movements with sleepy, adoring eyes. She's already eaten her body weight in watermelon, even though she decided she was a boy and hopped up on Rio's shoulders while we were still figuring out how to deal with Reilly's fearsome bear paws. Which was a major factor in their defeat. Braden followed suit and that meant Layla and Miriam got to lead the underwater shark attacks, which are hard to fend off when you have to keep your head and shoulders out of the water so you don't drown a pup.

It was Hoot and Kennedy who delivered the sneakiest blow, though. They used Bailey's home-grown hand signals to communicate a secret plan. One Kel thought he had intercepted and understood—and one he pulled a bear out of position to defend. Which is when the real plan happened. Myrna and Shelley swung in on the rope as Ebony and I tossed Kelsey at Hayden and the submissive shark squad took out every last man and boy at the knees.

Winning a fight when you outnumber the other side by at least two to one probably isn't all that impressive, but we've spent six years on the losing side of everything.

Which I suspect our alpha knew when he set up the teams, but logic isn't dimming any of the joy of this day.

Kel shakes his head as he sits down beside me. He wraps his hand around mine and guides my slice of watermelon so he can steal a bite. He shoots Kennedy and Hoot a wry look. "I can't believe I fell for that. Oldest trick in the book."

Reilly grins and licks sticky fingers. "I guess that means you need to read more."

Rio gives him a bear-sized nudge. "Whose side are you on, punk?"

Reilly snickers. "Next time I'm gonna stay on Lissa's team. She's really smart."

Rio casts me a sidelong look. "Yes, she is. She figured out how to use our instincts against us. She knew we'd protect the pups. We didn't realize she was using them as her secret weapons."

Kelsey beams.

As she should. When Ebony and I tossed her, she threw her limbs around like a tumbleweed. On purpose. Best alpha distraction ever. Which we needed. Reilly's bear is really effective in water fights because of how much water he can move, but Hayden is tricky and sneaky and swims like a fish. It took two sharks to take him out, even with Kelsey doing her best to act like a human windmill.

Miriam and Eliza grin at each other. They were the sharks.

Hayden shakes his head at them ruefully.

They turn pink, but they don't look scared anymore.

Probably because he's been shaking his head at them all afternoon. A job I accidentally dumped in his lap, because I didn't even think when I sent them off on an underwater attack to take out their alpha. Pebbles tossed in the heat of the moment are frighteningly potent.

Myrna lifts the lid off the old, cranky, cast-iron frying pan that caused a lot of laughs when it emerged out of Hayden's backpack after the water fight. I know why she brought it, though. It's well seasoned from years of cook-outs back when her daddy was alpha. Good pack karma. She glances at me. "More steak?"

The pups had burgers for lunch. So did Rio, who has the stomach of a five-year-old boy. The rest of the adults and a shy, pleased Hoot got marinated steak and crispy hash browns that are being delivered one frying-pan load at a time.

I smile and shake my head. I already ate one heaping plateful, and then my wolf made me eat another, and there's not a stitch of room left in my belly for more food.

Myrna casts a sardonic look at Hayden. "In that case, I think it's safe for you to eat more, now."

He hasn't starved, but I'm pretty sure he's mostly eaten hash browns. The pups kept stealing bites of his steak.

He offers her an easy grin as he sits down beside me. "I'm good. Try Hoot. I think she's got three stomachs, and they might not all be full yet."

Hoot turns quietly pink as Kennedy guffaws and nearly pushes her over.

Myrna snorts and starts filling two plates. I imagine

one of them will be heading for our alpha, probably delivered by Kelsey so she can kiss the war wound on his face again. I touch the small bruise delivered by her heel so that she doesn't feel the need to come over and tend to it right this minute.

Hayden grins at me and wraps his arm around my shoulders. "I'm going to let the girls of the pack beat up on me more often. You're really nice to me after. Kel's just mean."

Kennedy and Ebony snort in unison.

Hayden rolls his eyes at them. "Sorry. You two aren't nice at all. You're very mean. Is that better?"

Kennedy grins. "Yes."

I can feel his wolf delighting in her, just like he does when Kelsey comes over to touch his cheek or Braden shares a sticky, mostly eaten watermelon rind. An alpha who knows and appreciates all the ways in which his pack loves him.

I snuggle in a little closer. Watching him love our pups the way they need to be loved makes my wolf feel all mushy inside. He spent a very patient hour this afternoon swinging Robbie on the rope through a bear-generated waterfall. A game they invented when my son couldn't figure out the timing to let go of the rope.

He's so very easy with letting people be who they are.

Ebony chuckles as my wolf rubs her cheek against his arm. "Lissa, stop being nice to him. You'll give him ideas."

I tuck my head down and try to hide my pink cheeks. I'm pretty sure he already has ideas. My wolf surely does, and on days like today, her simple needs rise very close to my surface.

Myrna rattles the lid of the frying pan a lot louder than she needs to. "I have food that's getting cold here. Hoot, eat up. Alpha's orders. Kelsey darling, I bet you know where this other plate needs to go."

I silently bless her for the interruption. And for making sure Hoot is as full as we can make her. It's not an entirely altruistic move—Myrna's more than tricky enough to use food as a bribe to bring our lost ones home. But she's also always been solid earth under the paws of the pack's fledgling adults.

Even when their pack just fell into hell. She helped me get up the next morning more times than I can count.

Hoot holds out her new mountain of food to Kennedy, who reaches for a strip of steak with her fingers. She looks around before she eats it, though. Making sure no suddenly hungry toddler pup has arisen from the depths of sleep.

I hide a smile. Being a graceful loser isn't all that's getting modeled today.

A shadow crosses in front of me. Kelsey, delivering a plate—but she doesn't hand it to Hayden. She gives it to me. Which momentarily confuses my human, until I figure out why. Then it's all I can do not to dump marinated steak and hash browns into the lap of the man with his arm around my shoulders.

HAYDEN

I sit and I watch and I wait for the bomb to explode. Or my human does. My wolf doesn't understand why we have a problem.

He's not paying enough attention to the woman in my arms.

Or the small, worried girl standing in front of us.

Kelsey's wolf reads the ley lines of pack as well as anyone—and she just delivered a meal to her alphas. An act of pure, innocent instinct.

And a potent, ticking dare.

I can feel the eyes on us. The pack has been orienting all day, responding to the echoes of whatever happened this morning when we arrived in this place of timeless joy. Wolves, reacting as they always do to the presence of a new magnetic force inside the pack.

Which feels good and simple and right to my wolf.

The rest of me knows it's a lot more complicated. My pack isn't shards of metal. They're beating hearts, human ones as well as wolf, and the woman sitting absolutely still under my arm is already making herself into one kind of pack magnet and might not ever want to be the other kind.

She's stepping into who she is and who she wants to be, and my wolf is orienting toward her just like every other wolf in this pack, asking her to be the center, the heart of who we are. But no matter what a tired little girl just did, wolf instincts don't get to dictate all the terms, especially the kind that try to tie up leadership and mate bonds and pack structure in a nice, neat bow.

I am Adrianna Scott's son. I believe that modern shifters need to have choices, always, and I'll use my teeth and claws to make sure Lissa has hers, no matter what my wolf wants, or hers, or every orienting wolf in this pack.

But I can't say that. I can't say anything at all.

Because a four-year-old didn't put the plate in my hands.

LISSA

The tugs are so strong, and not just the ones coming from a bunch of wolves I can't look at. The other tugs. The ones that attach to the moment this morning when I looked in Hayden's eyes and felt a pebble land inside me.

I take a shallow breath, inhaling the aromas of sweet and salt and sticky pup and sunshine. I'm not ready yet. It's not about my pack—they've just been a handy excuse. I can feel the answer to that in the tugging. They're ready.

I'm not, and as I sit here with a plate of food not meant for me in my hands, I know just how important it is to give myself the time. I've been getting braver, picking up pebbles and tossing them, but I haven't looked squarely at the ooze still living inside me, feeding my doubt and worry and shame and insidious fear. I've tried to stand on the edge and throw stones because it's far too scary to be in the water.

Today, in this place where the sun only shines three days a year and standing in the water brought nothing but joy, I can see the ooze. Feel it.

It won't ever go away. I've been watching Kel, and I know that. Ooze doesn't get washed away and it doesn't get neatly managed and it takes a really special kind of strength to know that and choose to walk forward anyhow.

I smile. I'm headed the right way, finding that strength. Today I can see that, too. But I need to wait for more of my pebbles to land, the ones I've tossed and the ones the rest of my pack are tossing and a bunch I probably don't know about yet. They're changing my pack, and I need to let them change me.

So that I can maybe become someone who might one day be worthy of this plate.

But knowing I'm on a journey and pretending I don't know where I'm hoping to go are two really different things. I tip my head down and pitch my voice for Hayden's ears only. "I need some time."

His words are a quiet whisper against my ear. "I know."

13

KENNEDY

The shadows beside me are too empty. No Hoot. She's gone, headed back to Bailey with the big container of steak Myrna snuck into her bag and her heart full of stories to tell about our new den.

I know she needed to go, but today I felt like a little kid and Hoot felt like my sister and I didn't want her to leave. I want them all to come home. That's probably selfish and immature and me just being a sucky brat, but I don't care. My sleeping bag is still out with Bailey, but it doesn't feel like that's where I live anymore. My wolf has chosen and my human knows it.

I think Hoot's wolf chose today, too.

Adrianna says that modern shifters need to balance the needs of their humans and their wolves, but sometimes we need to let one have a veto or they won't be able to breathe and grow and that causes a kind of damage that never goes away. I don't know what Hoot will do if her wolf tries to veto. Her animal is pretty fierce, and she maybe doesn't understand why Hoot loves Bailey so much.

I need to figure out how to help instead of pouting like Braden did when he didn't get the last slice of watermelon.

I sneak a look over at Lissa. She's walking by Hayden, who's got Kelsey cuddled up in his arms. Adrianna says to watch the smart submissives. That's different from what Bailey does. She trusts the submissives, respects them—but she doesn't learn from them. She leads from the front.

Hayden is different, and I think Adrianna is mostly different too, even if her wolf is so strong she nearly gave mine heart failure.

That hasn't happened in a really long time.

My wolf growls. She doesn't like it when I think too hard.

I growl back. She's not the boss of me. She can't be. We'd be dead a hundred times over, and then I couldn't be a baby alpha who can maybe help my pack if I can just figure out how to be smart about it. Which means I need to think.

She quiets, mollified. She likes our new pack. It doesn't underestimate people. Nobody underestimated Hoot today. She's not a submissive wolf, but she's small and her human is quiet and for a lot of people, that's the same thing. But Hayden and Kel and Rio all treated her with respect. Not the same way they respect me, or Reilly, or Kelsey. The kind of respect that fits Hoot.

My wolf really liked that.

I hear an owl that sounds real, and a few more calling back to it. Hoot, passing by the sentries. She probably left them some steak. They couldn't all come today, mostly because Bailey put her foot down. She said it was about perimeter security, but it only takes one sentry to keep an eye on the stupid-ass dominants and we all know it.

I think Bailey's scared that too many wolves will choose before she's ready to come home.

I take a deep breath and let it out slowly. I know what Bailey would do, but I think maybe that's not the kind of leader who can fix this. I need to help from the back. I'm not so good at that, because I have a big mouth and my teeth and claws have always been needed at the front, but when I growled at Hayden from behind Lissa yesterday, everyone gave me those looks that said they were really proud of me and Hayden even let me beat him up a little.

So maybe I got it at least a little right.

Then Lissa led our team today, and I got to see how submissives win, and it was pretty awesome. What happened after that was pretty awesome, too. And what came before, because my wolf thinks Lissa maybe started that water fight so she didn't kiss Hayden. Which I'm kind of sad about. The pack feels more solid when they get all cuddly, kind of like a fighting stance that's found its center.

"I don't know what you're planning, but maybe give us a chance to sleep and wash some clothes, first?"

I flash Lissa a grin and try not to look too guilty. "Washing clothes is boring."

She snorts. "Says the person who seems to magically disappear whenever it's time to hang stuff out on the drying line."

That's Kelsey's special job, the one she does with Rio, and nobody in the pack would dare take it away because it makes his wolf all mushy and hers strong and glad. Which Lissa knows, so she's just teasing me because that's what happens in good packs. "I have important work to do. Like coming up with a new set of hand signals for the sentries so we can annoy Kel for a few days." I can't believe how fast he learned the last ones. The guy is some kind of genius.

A kind I hope I don't ever have to be.

Lissa pushes against me with her shoulder. That's new, too. Her wolf is pretty submissive. She used to be too scared to touch me without getting all tense inside. "That was a great idea you and Hoot had. Kel didn't see it coming at all."

I shrug. "You figured out the big parts. We just helped a little."

She grins. "You surprised Kelvin Nogues. That's more than a little help."

Kinda, but leading from the back means not saying things like that. "The shark attack was the best part." It was. They were fast and they were fierce. My wolf was really impressed. A bunch of submissives who aren't nearly so scared of big, bad dominants anymore. The super-nice ones, anyhow. Hayden worked really hard to calm Miriam's wolf down after she took him out at the knees. "It was cool to see how submissives fight."

A careful look my way. "Sounds like you've been reading the words of a wise female leader."

My wolf squirms. She thinks I need to keep my big baby-alpha thoughts to myself. "Maybe."

A longer pause, and I can practically hear Lissa's brain whirring. "She would be happy to talk to you, I bet. If you wanted some ideas on how to be a fourteen-year-old leader in a complicated pack."

I feel like Ebony just landed one of her hard kicks on my ribs. "Adrianna Scott has way better things to do than to talk to me."

Lissa chuckles quietly. "I bet she wouldn't agree with you."

Probably not. She was really nice when she came to visit. Not at all like I expected. Even if her wolf could gobble mine for breakfast. "I have lots of people I can learn from here. Ebony and Kel and Hayden and Bailey and you."

She makes a face.

I make one right back. I have a rep to maintain.

She laughs and wraps an arm around my waist. "Would you like me to ask if she'd mind having the occasional chat with a baby alpha?"

I can't believe people are saying that out loud. I've always known—and always known it made me dangerous. Hayden acts like it's no big deal, or maybe even a good thing. Which means listening to his mom is maybe a pretty smart move. "That would be really great. I promise not to be a stupidhead."

Lissa grins at me. "Neither of us should make any promises we can't keep."

My wolf tries hard to be insulted, but she's too full of watermelon for it to stick. And too full of something I don't have a name for. I just know that it's good.

HAYDEN

Kennedy tips her head against Lissa's shoulder, a teenage dominant taking a rare moment of comfort. I shake my head. "Think I need to be worried about those two?"

Kel snorts beside me. "If you weren't worried days ago, there's no hope for you."

He's not telling me anything I don't already know. Rio's sentinel is practically drunk on whatever's in motion right now, and those two are right in the thick of it. They might not be the most likely duo to terraform a pack, but I'm not betting against them.

I am a little surprised and a lot impressed that Kennedy's letting Lissa take the lead, though. Which is maybe safe ground to talk about. My green-eyed wolf is guaranteed conversational quicksand. "Kennedy's a lot smarter than I was at her age."

Kel doesn't bother to snort this time. "Duh."

"I was worried she was going to try some dumb stunts on her own."

Kel's lips twitch.

I sigh. "How many of them have you and Ebony run off at the pass?"

He shrugs the shoulder that sometimes pains him. "Fewer than I expected. She's got a good head on her shoulders. And she's watching you."

My watermelon-soaked brain struggles to engage. "I haven't done anything really dumb for days."

He punches my arm with the kind of force he needs to save for our bear cub. "She's watching your alpha moves, knucklehead. Did you notice how much she quietly did in the background today?"

Maybe. "I saw her follow Ebony's lead and make the submissives captain the water fight."

Kel just shakes his head and appeals silently to the cantankerous gods in the sky who tasked him with watching over one such as me.

I smirk at his theatrics. It's an act he's been putting on since I was ten years old, so it's lost most of its power. "What did I miss?"

"It wasn't Ebony's idea. It was Kennedy's. She also convinced Reilly to come lose with us so the teams weren't hopelessly lopsided and the moms would have to step up, and she settled Cori down in about ten seconds after they took Rio out."

That, I didn't entirely miss. The submissive shark attack was genius, but it shook a lot of their wolves. Which was hidden by adrenaline until we all came up spluttering and Rio didn't get a lid on the retaliatory intent in his eyes quite fast enough.

He's way too used to getting dunked by me.

I know Lissa did some of the calming, and Myrna, but I was busy with Miriam, who hit me with an impressive underwater tackle, and with Kelsey, who apparently didn't intend to kick me in the head with her ninja-warrior moves. "I can't believe they went on the offensive like that." It's an act of profound trust for the submissives in a pack to play that way. Especially when we're holding their pups.

"Yeah." One exhaled word, steeped in quiet, heartfelt pleasure.

He's put in a lot of the hours to get us to this day. But he'll take credit for that shortly after the world ends. "They got proud of themselves fast. Kennedy definitely helped with that."

Kel grins. "She's got a mouth on her. She even got Reilly going."

Teaching a meek bear the fine art of respectful trash talk isn't all that easy. Fortunately for him, he's got a lot of teachers. "He needs more guy-bonding time."

A careful look. "He's worried about what will happen when the assholes in the woods show up."

I'm not. My wolf has a plan for that. "He's worth more than all of them."

"He doesn't know that yet."

He will, because I'll shred anyone who disrespects that kid, and I suspect I'll have to get in line. One that starts with Myrna and her mammoth cast-iron frying pan. "You getting any sleep these days?"

He shrugs. "Some."

It's more of an answer than I expected. Getting under

Kel's guard is about as easy as sneaking off with one of his red bandanas. "We have a couple of nights." It's not Friday yet. The dominants aren't going to boil over until their bank cards start bouncing. And when they do, I need my betas sharp.

Not that I would ever dare say so. I don't know exactly how long Kel can go without sleep, but it's measured in months, not days. That's not going to stop me from expending all my ammunition, though. "Kelsey wakes up more when you're not sleeping."

He sighs. "That's a low blow."

I don't care. It landed, and it needed to. "You're allowed to take care of yourself. You'd kick the ass of anyone else in this pack who ran themselves this ragged."

"I don't get ragged."

He doesn't. He just turns into honed steel. The kind that sometimes has a hard time finding its way back to real life. I might not have been watching Kennedy closely enough today, but I was watching Kel. Today was the kind of game he lives and breathes for, and he wasn't all the way present. He fakes it better than anyone I know, and he had a good time, but I've had twenty-two years of practice annoying the hell out of that place he goes—the one where he thinks his pack needs his warrior and not the rest of him. "We've got this. We've got plenty of teeth and claws on hand and those guys just aren't that big a threat."

He exhales slowly. "Yeah. I know."

He's always seen shit in the shadows that the rest of us can't even imagine. My job has always been to make him join the damn water fight anyhow. "Don't make me send Kelsey and Kennedy to double team you."

He snorts, and something in his wolf lightens. "That bad, huh?"

I toss an arm over his shoulders. "Nah. You had a few dark moments today. You know the rules. When I call you on it, you sleep, you hang out with the pups, and you wear the lime-green t-shirt until I say you can stop."

He rolls his eyes. "Fine. I'll let Kennedy take my shift tonight."

I grin. "That only counts if you wear the t-shirt and cuddle with Kelsey while you sleep."

He growls.

My wolf growls back. I'll go furry on his ass over this and he knows it.

He exhales slowly. "Sorry. I don't know what's got me in a twist. It was a really good day."

It was. And sometimes those can twist his wolf up more than anything.

I ignore the small voice that knows my wolf got pretty twisted up today, too. Lissa asked for time. She'll get every second of it she needs. Even if I'm so far gone I'll be sleeping in this shirt tonight because it smells like her.

Kel glances at me. "She thinks she's the one who needs time to be ready."

Even when he's having an off day, he doesn't miss anything. I smirk at him. "I know I'm not ready." Life never seems to wait for me to grow up.

He grins, and the shadows in his eyes recede a little further. "Just checking that you know."

I do. But I also know something he has trouble believing. Happiness and love and belonging aren't things you earn. They're gifts that get bestowed on you, deserving or not, and you just have to do your damn best to be worthy.

LISSA

The problem with pups who fall asleep in their dinner plates is that they rise in the night as vampires who pretend they've never heard of sleep. I sigh as Robbie dashes past me in wolf form. Clearly he's not walking calmly with Gramma Shelley while she tells him a story.

Which means the force is strong in him tonight. He loves Shelley's stories.

I pull my hoodie off over my head and hand it to Kennedy. "Mind carrying this for me? I have to go chase a vampire pup."

She giggles, which is a really good sound. Today might have pushed on me in some very grown-up ways, but it let our kids absolutely be kids, even the ones who've had to grow up way too fast.

Kennedy carefully collects the rest of my clothes as I strip out of them. Old habits. A good one to keep in this case. A couple of truckloads of stuff from the thrift store mean our pack has more things to wear than we know what to do with, but that doesn't mean we have to get reckless.

Besides, I really like that hoodie. Especially when it smells like Hayden.

I shiver as my wolf takes my skin, and it's not from the night cold. My senses sharpen, and so does my need to act and stop listening to that annoying caution from my human.

I tell her to focus. We have a pup to track.

She snorts. Robbie is about as hard to find as a herd of elephants. He practically glows in the dark. Silly moon pup.

I grin as I run. White is definitely not a practical color for a wolf who wants to stay hidden. Already, I can see flashes of him in the trees ahead, and the shadow shapes of the much bigger, darker wolves who are tracking his gamboling run through the trees.

My wolf veers left. She's fast. She'll circle ahead of him and chase her silly boy back to Shelley and stories and pup piles. After she runs with him awhile first. He's fast, just like she is, and his paws are getting bigger.

I chuckle. He's trying to grow big and strong like his friend Reilly.

Her feet tap the earth, amused. Robbie's going to be really surprised when he discovers he's not a bear. Maybe Reilly will find his wolf instead. Some pups can shift to the animals of both their parents, and it's safe to be a submissive wolf, now.

My human heart aches at how deeply she believes that. It's as true to her as the scent of the forest and her love for her silly moon pup.

I jump, clearing a nurse log that wasn't there the last

time I ran this way, and skirting a boulder that was. Then I angle back toward my pup—and cross a scent trail.

A fresh one.

Wolf.

Kenny.

Heading toward the den.

A warning.

My wolf flies, pushing every ounce of my panic into her feet.

A gray wolf joins my run, and I can feel his fierceness. Kel smelled the intruder, too. We both head straight for the pups. I seek Robbie first, until I see his scruff in Ebony's teeth. We veer toward the others.

Kennedy hoots. *All safe.*

My wolf doesn't relax a hair.

She did this. She stirred up men who spent six years punishing brave behavior. She tried to make her pack better, but maybe she just made it less safe.

She shivers as she runs.

14

HAYDEN

Kel and Lissa arrive, running hard. Kennedy hoots briskly, transmitting my hand signals, holding the sentries in place. *We're safe. We have the pups. Stay and watch.*

My brain is scrambling to catch up to what's just happened. It's not Friday night yet. I let myself take half a breath of sadness that the asshole dominants are going to smear the magic of this day, and then I decide to use it instead.

I look over at the shark squad. They all have pups in their arms, and some of them are shaking, but every last one of them has fierce eyes. "Stay tight together. The pups are safe. Those seven guys will never get past Rio and Ebony and Kel, and if they do, they're going to discover just how badass Reilly's bear can be."

He looks at me, quivering, but ready to do any damn thing I ask of him. I hate that it's this, but he's not going to let me sideline him. "Kennedy, I need you and Reilly to take the rear. Four o'clock and eight o'clock. I'll take the front with the pups tucked in between us. We're going to keep walking calmly back to the den."

Myrna nods and starts herding submissives into a triangle. No one argues—and Reilly takes four o'clock with a steadiness that earns him a proud nod from Kennedy. My wolf doesn't like leaving them out back, but the threat is in front of us and I can feel Rio's prowling menace in the woods behind them. Which means the chances of anyone getting as far as Kennedy and Reilly are minuscule, but that doesn't dim what I've asked of them.

My eyes land on the one person who isn't in position. Lissa. Her wolf should be huddled with the others, but she isn't, and she's vibrating with a need at least as fierce as mine. One she can't possibly act on with a small white wolf in her arms.

Myrna deals with that, too. She walks over and calmly collects Robbie. "I'll take him." She holds up a hand as Lissa tries to protest. "He's safe with me and you know it. You go stand for our pack."

Six words that give a name to the warrior light in Lissa's eyes and the energy storming inside her wolf. She looks at Myrna for a long, sharp moment, and then she nods and lets go of her son. "Thank you."

Myrna's grin belongs on a Valkyrie. "Give 'em hell, sweetheart."

Lissa's eyes shift. To the front. To me.

I watch as they cloud over, doubt finally catching up

with her instincts. Which doesn't get to fucking happen. I hold out my hand. There are some choices where she needs time. This isn't one of them.

She's so very clearly already made it.

I just need to hold her cape.

LISSA

The dominants are standing in a line when we emerge from the trees. Standing in a line *in our den.*

The growls from behind me are fierce. All the pups are wide awake, and even Kelsey's squeaky growl joins the chorus.

Hayden grins beside me. "I feel kind of useless."

I feel like he's practically holding me up, but I won't be that person. Not today. I robbed the bank and I did it so we could take our pack back and I won't be a wimp now. Even my wolf is clear on that. She's not trembling at all. Her alpha casts a big shadow and he'll do his job so that she can do hers. I squeeze his hand. His job is to be the teeth and claws, because the seven men facing us with their arms crossed don't have enough sense to value him for anything else. Except maybe Kenny, and today isn't about him.

It isn't really about the other six guys either. But it's going to start there.

Hayden quietly drops my hand. I'm not sure how I feel about that, which just makes my wolf snort. She knows what he's up to. Alpha business. Silly dominant games, even if they look good on him.

The wolves behind us spread out, which surprises me, but it shouldn't. They're standing in that big, safe shadow too, and they want to see.

Hayden stands a little straighter. A little taller. Proud of his pack.

Baird swaggers forward a couple of steps, Evan and Jake flanking him. I guess he's stepped into Eamon's shoes. I'm surprised it wasn't Colin, but he's always gotten more respect for his pool playing than his quiet thoughtfulness. He's down at the end of the line, but his eyes are angry, too.

Angry and embarrassed.

My wolf knows what that means. They intend to make someone pay.

Kennedy moves in silently, flanking Hayden on the left. Reilly moves in on the right, walking with steady, quiet confidence just like hers. I have no idea where Ebony and Kel are, but there's no way Kennedy left her post without permission, and no way Reilly is this close to unfriendly teeth and claws without hell ready to rain down on anyone who so much as breathes on him wrong.

More than one wolf is playing dominance games tonight.

I wonder if the men facing us have any idea how badly they're about to lose.

My wolf tips her chin up. Good pack. Strong alpha.

Faint amusement glimmers in Hayden's eyes. He

stands quietly, eyeing the seven who have come to adjust the world to their liking.

Baird eyes Kennedy and Reilly in the places of honor flanking their alpha, and snorts. "Are they the best you can do? I thought you had a couple of hotshot betas."

Hayden smiles. "Don't need them."

Reilly glows at my shoulder. Kennedy is entirely quiet on Hayden's other side, doing her best impression of nonchalant teenage girl.

Nobody's paying me any attention at all.

My wolf is fine with that. Her turn will come.

Baird dismisses Kennedy with a glance and fixes his gaze on Reilly. "Move, kid. The real men have come home."

Hayden grins at Reilly. "They must have really short memories. I didn't hear anything in there about doing chores, did you?"

Reilly shakes his head solemnly.

I desperately want to tuck Reilly in behind me where he can be safe, and Danielle must be an absolute mess, but oh, he's making me proud. His back is straight and his chin is up and his feet are set in the fighting stance Kennedy's been working so hard to teach him. A bear cub standing for his pack.

Hayden's eyes move back to Baird. "The requirements to rejoin the den are simple. You haven't met them. Get lost."

Baird snorts. "You took all our money, so now you get to feed us. Suck it up, Alpha."

My wolf jolts at the big, rumbling growl to my right.

"Don't talk to him that way." Reilly's voice is reasonably calm, but his eyes are fierce. "That money belongs to the pack, and if you want to be part of the pack, you have to be kind and helpful and do what's right for everyone."

"Riles has really big words, because he's a very smart bear." Kennedy cocks a hip, somehow communicating her utter disdain of seven guys in a single, easy movement. "What he means is you can't be assholes."

I dare a glance at Hayden. On the surface, he looks like a guy who just happens to be standing in the middle of a clearing while a ten-year-old and a teenager take care of business.

Apparently Baird sees that guy and not the wolf a hairsbreadth away from making him bleed. He shakes his head and shoots Reilly a look of utter contempt. "Kind and helpful? Is that what this is now? A pack for wimps and sissies?"

HAYDEN

I grab at the scruff of my wolf's neck. Again. He has no idea why I won't just let him beat up this asshole. It won't take him five seconds. Even Reilly has a better ready stance than this jerk.

I remind him that there are a lot of people in this pack who need to rebalance some ugly history, and one of them is a ten-year-old bear. Who doesn't need any more help than he's already got. Hopefully the trash-talking baby alpha who's designated herself as his sidekick realizes we aren't actually trying to goad the assholes into a fight.

My wolf snorts. That might be *my* plan.

Kennedy smirks at the guys who still haven't figured out just how crispy they are. "Seriously? You're calling a bear a sissy? You have rocks for brains, dude."

Reilly grins. "I think that might be an insult to rocks."

Baird glares, dominance pouring out of him. "You used to be a smart kid. One who knew there wouldn't always be people around to protect you."

My wolf claws for my skin. Line crossed. Bully. Bad wolf. Needs a lesson.

Kennedy takes half a step forward, hand flashing at the small of her back. A baby alpha, asking for permission.

My wolf growls. This is his fight.

Warm fingers squeeze mine.

My wolf stops in his tracks, listening to green-eyed wisdom.

Then he rumbles a quiet signal back at Kennedy.

Permission granted.

She faces the line of idiots, hands on her hips. "Baird, you're a jerk, and you're threatening my friend. That doesn't work here anymore. I challenge you. Dominance fight, Whistler Protocol rules."

I'm not sure the wolf she's facing knows what those are.

Kel steps silently out of the woods. Way too many of the seven guys look surprised to see him. "In case you need a refresher, Whistler Protocol rules are simple. The shifter who got challenged picks human or furry. The fight must be non-lethal, with no permanent damage, broken bones, or deep scarring. Keep it clean and win on skill."

Baird looks insulted. "You want me to fight a girl?"

"Friendly piece of advice?" Kel's grin is anything but friendly. "Develop some respect for girls. Fast."

Kennedy snorts. "Rocks for brains, remember?" She eyes Baird. "Only wimps and sissies walk away from challenges."

I manage not to wince. Her intentions are good.

Reilly rolls his eyes at her back. Lissa stifles a giggle.

My wolf relaxes. His pack knows dumb dominant posturing when they see it. The guys facing us are mostly clueless, silently egging Baird into a fight he's apparently not smart enough to know he doesn't want to have. Kenny is completely unreadable, even to my wolf. And Evan looks a little uneasy, which is interesting.

I catch Kel's eye. He doesn't look worried at all, which matches what my wolf thinks. He knows what Kennedy is capable of, and baby alphas need open ground to run. Ground that protects pups and friends is the very best kind to give them.

Kennedy shoots me a look. "Maybe I need to use smaller words, Alpha. I don't think he understands."

Troublemaker. "Try speaking wolf." I add a hand sign. Permission granted.

Dominance lances out of her, straight at the guy with scorn in his eyes.

Baird jolts to attention.

My wolf grins. That's not even a fraction of what she's got.

"Human or furry. Pick." Kennedy's words are quiet and deadly.

Baird snorts, but he's having to work harder at sounding disdainful. "I don't hit girls."

She smirks at him. "Don't worry, you'll never get close enough to land anything." Another lance of dominance, taunting his wolf. "Fortunately for me, I'm happy to hit assholes."

My wolf salutes her technique as he checks in behind him, listening for signs of trauma. Of fear. Of humans who aren't ready for what their wolves know needs to happen.

What he hears instead is a single, resonant, silent howl. The dominants waited too long. Their pack is ready to deal with them.

He might have to hold a lot of capes.

LISSA

I spent the last six years running from this, and now my crazy wolf wants to dash in there and nip Baird's heels and make this fight happen. Because it needs to happen. Teeth and claws, doing what they need to do. What they're meant to do. What my son, growling fiercely in Myrna's tight hold, *wants* them to do. What Kennedy has been hungering to do for weeks, and even I know this is the best kind of cause she could have chosen. Defender of a friend.

My turn will come after.

When Kennedy moves, it's a blur. She doesn't move first, but Baird's attack is halfhearted, a human man who outweighs her by a hundred pounds and thinks this is a joke.

Which means he doesn't stop the fist that lands in his gut, or the high kick that flies in over his wild, enraged swing and rattles his ribs, or the low kick that takes out his knees as he tries to suck in air. He lands on the ground with a bone-rattling thud.

Kennedy drops into a low fighting stance near his head. "Go ahead, hotshot. Hit a girl. I dare you."

He tries to get up. She snorts and takes his legs out again with the same low sweep that took down her alpha. Then she plants a foot in the middle of his back.

He tries to grab for her standing leg and she uses it to stomp on his fingers. The high-pitched sound he makes has Reilly's bear wincing.

"Oh, stop whining." Kennedy steps back, her eyes never leaving her quarry. "They're not broken because I actually follow the rules. When you remember how, maybe our alpha will let you come back. Now do what he said and get lost."

Baird rolls away, making noises that sound suspiciously like a whimper.

Kennedy shakes her head. "And maybe spend some time practicing your fighting skills. You're a disgrace."

Her gaze shifts, scanning the other six guys watching with varying levels of shock and dismay. "Anyone else want to fight a girl? Because I swear, I'll be happy to stomp on all of you."

Kel chuckles. "That's greedy, Kennedy. You could at least share a couple."

Dazed eyes turn his way.

It's Colin who finally speaks. "Did you teach her that shit?"

Kel snorts. "No. But I'd be happy to replicate it if you want to pick on someone your own size."

Kennedy pouts. "Betas, ruining my fun since forever."

Kel's laugh rings out honest and true, and every wolf behind me snickers along with him.

Colin's eyes turn slowly in our direction, and the menace in them has my wolf sitting up very straight. He's not a man who makes hasty decisions—and those aren't the eyes of a wolf who intends to crawl home. "You took all our money. This pack is nothing without its dominants. You might want to rethink that."

I let his words land, and I let the ripples of fear in my wolf happen.

And then I step forward, because it's my turn now. Fear can cause all the ripples it wants, but it doesn't get to own us, not ever again. I meet Colin's eyes, even though they're mad, and let his wolf see mine. "This pack is *ours*. The money, the decisions, the future, the power. The seven of you, you're remnants. Leftovers."

I can see the fury in his eyes—and the astonishment in his wolf.

I'm not done. "You're wrong. You don't matter unless we let you matter. We can be a good, strong, vibrant pack without you. Some of us will hurt that you're not here, but we'll hurt more if you're here without understanding what it means to be part of the kind of pack we intend to be. Reilly and Kennedy, they both know. If you ever want to be part of us again, pay attention to what they showed you today. Learn something."

My wolf channels all the fierceness, all the courage, all the need to throw punches that she can feel at her back. "And until then? *Get. Lost.*"

15

HAYDEN

My wolf lounges by the fire, drinking in the late-night antics of his pack. We should all be exhausted, but I know why every single one of them is still awake. They stood for their pack today, and they did it with big, bold words and fierce, united silence and low leg sweeps and the quiet certainty of a young bear who doesn't believe kindness is weak.

I look around for Reilly, who can still barely contain himself. He's been taking pictures with the pack phone and collecting eyewitness accounts and generally stoking the fires of our rapidly growing pack legend. The next edition of GhostPack News is going to be epic.

I spy him crouched down at the end of the big sitting log, getting an interesting angle on his shot of the women leaning against it. The shark squad, holding pups who aren't the least bit sleepy and regaling them with tales of this day. There are a lot of them, and I love that in every single one I've heard so far, I'm only mentioned in passing.

Kel drops to the ground beside me, one very content wolf. "Good thing you don't have an ego, Alpha."

I grin. "A bear came to my defense. I don't sound too feeble in that version."

He laughs. "A bear and a *girl*."

My pack is having a whole lot of trouble deciding which part of that they like best. A meek reporter and a baby alpha who absolutely refuses to take credit for anything besides making Baird whimper aren't helping them choose. "They were just the first blows. Lissa closed the deal." No amount of meekness on her part is getting her off that hook. Her words have been repeated over and over, tattooing themselves on our pack psyche.

Kel smiles as Reilly finally takes a picture. "She spoke for all of them. For all of us. Kennedy isn't the only one who's got a damn fine leg sweep."

Exactly. Tonight, words and fighting kicks both delivered powerful messages—the unique kind of strength that happens when a pack's dominants and submissives are on the same team. "I don't think those guys learned from any of it."

Kel shrugs. "It doesn't matter. Tonight wasn't about them."

He probably figured that out way faster than I did. "Those dominants lived at the center of this pack for way too long, and we let their shadows keep living there."

Baird might not have paid attention to Lissa's speech, but my wolf did.

Kel chuckles. "I'm pretty sure that's done."

No shit. I definitely wouldn't want to be the dumb alpha who didn't get that message. My pack isn't ever going to be meek and biddable again. "They were all growling. Every last one of them. Even Kelsey." I cast him a sharp look as my brain finally catches up with my wolf's sloshed happiness. "Did Rio have something to do with that?"

Kel snorts. "Do I seriously need to answer that for you?"

There's an odd look in his eyes. I cock my head. "Maybe, yeah."

He shakes his head slowly. "You really don't know."

My wolf sits up, vaguely alarmed.

Kel rolls his eyes. "The submissives growled. Reilly stepped into shoes two sizes too big for him and did them proud. Kennedy asked for permission before she rocked and rolled. Lissa's wolf, who nearly bled out the last time she faced down a dominant, could hardly hold herself back from taking a chomp out of Baird's tail."

I'm so lost. "I know all that."

He smacks the side of my head. "They were all standing beside you, dumbass. You held the center for what happened."

I stare at him. "I just stood there." Literally. My wolf didn't get to bite anyone, even though he really wanted to.

He grins. "Yup. And Ebony and I just hung out in the woods, drinking coffee and shooting the shit."

No damn way they were drinking coffee, but I'm starting to see his point. "They felt safe."

"They did. They felt safe and they felt valued, and because of that, they kicked some serious butt." Kel exhales slowly, and something that looks terrifyingly like gratitude lands in his eyes. "They stood for who they want to be in this world. And now they feel whole."

RIO

Kelsey snuggles deeper into my lap. The three smallest pups are all getting sleepy, but she's not. She's too sensitive to her pack to fall asleep while they're still this buzzed on joy. A situation my sentinel understands. Lissa's words rang a bell that won't ever un-ring, and every single shifter in this pack was lifting her up while she did it.

I know what it is to feel a pack rise from the ashes. I watched Whistler Pack do it after Hayden's father died. But today is one of the brightest acts of intentional, chosen healing I've ever been a part of, and I didn't do a damned thing.

My wolf thinks that's funny.

My human feels a little gutted.

Which is why Kelsey is curled up in my lap, a small red wolf handing out her special brand of medicine. She was in Eliza's lap earlier, soothing the hurts of a mama who had to decide that her son doesn't matter. It's not true, of course. There are seven wolf-sized holes in this pack where those men might fit some day. But Eliza joined in on the promise that this pack will be remarkable even if those seven holes never get filled.

Which means I have some work to do, because Damien needs to get his butt back here and remember his mama raised him right. He isn't heavy enough to tip the balance in this pack with his return anymore. Lissa dropped a big-ass submissive mountain on the scales today, and that means I have a lot more room to work.

I'm not in a hurry, though. Right here and right now is too damn good.

I stroke the soft fur of the pup in my lap. "Got it, cutie. Thanks for helping me screw my head on straight."

She turns her gleaming brown eyes up and looks deep into mine. Then she rights herself and hops out of my lap, licking my knee as she goes. Off to find someone else with wobbles that need a bit of steadying.

I shake my head. I know better than to underestimate any wolf, but I swear there's a wise and many-times-reincarnated elder inside that four-year-old body. I track her as she wanders around the fire, brushing against legs as she travels. She pauses in front of Shelley and asks to be lifted up. The older woman smiles and makes room on her lap beside Mellie, who's sound asleep.

I watch, curious whether it's Shelley or Mellie who's called to Kelsey's radar. Maybe both. There was a lot of dominant posturing tonight, and it didn't play out in the straightforward ways that would make sense to a toddler wolf. But it's Shelley who Kelsey butts gently with her furry head. The other bank robber. The quiet one who didn't speak, but who signed her name to the piece of paper that set Lissa's declaration in motion.

My sentinel reaches for the earth, but he doesn't sense any tremors coming from Shelley, just gladness. And hints of a woman who still doesn't think she deserves to be happy, but that's been receding nicely. Helped along by an attentive pup, no doubt.

I grin. I need to work on convincing Kelsey to leave me a few things to do. My wolf likes to feel useful.

LISSA

I shake my head as Robbie lands face-first in the dirt for the second time in two minutes. "He needs to sleep."

Ebony chuckles. "He's a dominant pup who got hit by all kinds of bossy juice tonight. He'll be awake for hours yet."

I grimace. "Mellie's asleep."

"She's not as tuned to Kennedy as Robbie is. I'm guessing it's a baby-alpha thing. They have a special kind of radar. It was everything Myrna could do to hold him while Kennedy taught Baird a few manners."

I don't think that lesson landed. I'm worried this one might not, either. "I'm not sure it's a good idea to teach

Robbie to fight. He hasn't got nearly as much control of his wolf as she does."

Ebony smiles. "That's why she's doing this in human form. She's helping him build that balance so he can be a dominant who uses his head as well as his teeth and claws."

Kennedy has dusted my son off and set him back in the careful fighting stance she's been teaching him, even though he clearly wants to learn the fancy leg kicks she used to take down the big, bad wolf instead. "She's really good with him. Slow and patient."

"You go at the speed of your student or you aren't a good teacher. He's slow on the words, but watch how fast he's picking up the moves."

I try to adjust my eyes so they aren't looking through the lenses of a worried mama. On the third try, Robbie actually manages to dodge the slow-motion kick Kennedy throws his way. She ruffles his hair and drops him back into his stance again.

He shifts into his fur and bounds at her, licking her cheeks when she lifts him up.

Ebony chuckles. "Okay, maybe he's got a ways to go yet."

He does—but I need to trust the words I said today. This pack is going to be amazing. I need to believe that's true of my son, too.

My white ball of fur snuggles against Kennedy's chest as she drops gracefully to the ground and nestles in to his special brand of cuddles. The contentment that hits her wolf is a palpable thing.

Ebony elbows me gently. "See? He gives as much as he takes."

I exhale. They're building the bonds of packmates. The exact balance doesn't matter. I know that. I need to do a better job of remembering it. "Kennedy's wolf is still restless. She didn't get to do much fighting today." I look over at the dominant wolf beside me. "None of you did." And they were all riled enough to do plenty.

She laughs quietly. "You've clearly never taught anyone to fight."

I snort. Bailey's made me learn a few things over the years, but my first and last instincts in a battle are to run.

Ebony nods her chin at the two who are still cuddling. "Someday Robbie will land a kick that matters, and every single shifter who has ever helped him learn will feel like they shared his foot."

It takes me a minute to understand.

She smiles. "Kennedy spoke for all of us tonight, and she did it with style and grace and guts and control. She made every smart dominant watching her fiercely proud." She leans into me. "And then she did exactly what teeth and claws are supposed to do and stood quietly while you delivered the message that mattered most."

I wince. I've spent all night trying to avoid becoming the heroine of this particular ballad and failing miserably. "It all mattered."

She shrugs. "Kennedy did the easy part and she knows it. Reilly did some harder stuff. You batted clean-up." She pauses, and I can feel something murky in her wolf. "Teeth and claws are only worth so much."

So many times in the past six years, hers have been everything. But she takes so very hard all the times they weren't enough. I lean into her shoulder.

"We can keep people from needlessly dying." She stares off into the trees. I don't miss the hitch in her breath. "But today, the heart of this pack did something way more important. You gave us marching orders for living."

KENNY

There are times I really can't stand the guys I'm shacked up with, even though I've earned that fate a thousand times over. So I'm off in the woods sulking. It's either that or listen to increasingly harebrained schemes for how a bunch of worthless men are going to convince themselves the universe gives a shit about their existence.

Lissa's words landed like a ton of bricks, whether they want to admit it or not. She called our bluff, the one Samuel spent six years erecting and we can't enforce.

Thank fuck.

My nose catches a hint of wolf upwind. I wait. They like sneaking up on me. They don't even make much effort to hide it anymore. This isn't one of the usual culprits, though. I wait until my human nose can figure it out. Shelley.

My eyebrows go up. She should be doing a victory dance around the den fire. There's no way they pulled this off without her. Banks don't just hand over money because people ask for it nicely. I'm glad she got brave enough to use the power Samuel stupidly left in her hands. He always thought she was his entirely biddable minion. He never understood what small acts of resistance cost a submissive wolf.

She walks out of the trees, pulling on a flannel shirt and clutching a paper bag with teeth marks that smells like something I won't ever deserve again. She holds it out to me. "Oatmeal spice. The pups ate all the ones with chocolate chips, so you get raisins."

Once upon a time, back when it was safe to have desires, those were my favorites. "Whatever you think I did to deserve those, you're wrong."

"You warned us."

Not really. I didn't have time to get close enough to do that. Someone must have ventured further from the pups than I expected. I was getting ready to trip over a twig near one of the sentries when I heard the alerts sounding. "You wouldn't have missed seven lugheads wandering into the den."

She smirks. "Nope, we wouldn't have. Take the damn cookies. My wolf doesn't like them."

I take the bag. I probably won't eat them, which seems like an appropriate form of torture for a guy who's done exactly nothing to help his pack. "You can take back a message for me." That way I don't have to wait for one of Kennedy's annoying visits. "Tell your betas they might want to route the food heading into the woods a different way. Jake stumbled across a trail yesterday and he's not entirely stupid."

She eyes me, and I get the distinct feeling I'm really close to having a paper bag yanked out of my hand.

I hold up my palms. "I don't ask, I don't tell, I don't talk. I don't know who's out there, but the guys are going to start spending more time prowling around now that you've cut off their beer supply and easy food, and even they notice shit when they trip over it. So get careful. And warn your sentries. Some of them aren't staying all that well hidden lately."

Menace, from woman and wolf both.

I sigh. "Give me some credit, woman. I know damn well that if I messed with any of them, the girl who dumped Baird on his ass today would pay me a visit." Assuming she could get to me before her alpha and her betas. They might have all stood around tonight pretending to do nothing, but there's a reason Shelley's wolf is capable of growling at me, and that isn't the kind of shit fourteen-year-olds know how to fix.

We gutted the submissives of this pack. They're sure as hell not gutted anymore.

Shelley stares at me awhile in the moonlight. Then she nods. "I have to go back. Eat your damn cookies."

I try not to listen to her, but my wolf whispers a traitorous message as she leaves. One that says maybe I could earn my way back to deserving cookies someday.

I shake my head and crumple the bag in my hands.

He doesn't know the half of what I've done.

HAYDEN

The moon is near full and the tug on my wolf is immense. We'll have a pack run again in a day or two, so we can sing it our new songs.

Tonight is for something more personal.

My green-eyed wolf is on top of the next ridge, the outlines of her clear in the moonlight. Her pup finally sleeps, and she disappeared shortly after his eyes closed. A wolf needing to be out of her pack's limelight for a bit, or at least that's what Ebony thought.

My wolf thinks differently. He remembers watching the stars the night I became alpha. When something really big happens, sometimes it takes the whole night sky to put it in proper perspective. I run up the rocks, scrabbling some in the dark. I don't know the way all that well, and the moon is blinding my wolf.

That and Lissa climbs like a damn mountain goat. Which is probably why Ebony grinned when she told me where to find my green-eyed packmate. I know her assigned run buddies don't follow her up here. Now I know why. I veer left, the sharp lines of Banner Rock below me, chittering pebbles mocking me as I run.

Lissa's wolf looks at me as I crest the climb, her dark fur glistening in the moonlight. Watchful. Waiting.

My wolf trots over slowly, panting. Trying once again, in this tornado of a day, to catch his breath.

Her eyes gleam. Silly alpha.

I pull up on my haunches beside her and inhale the scent of her warm strength. Then I drop down to the earth, letting it cool my belly and sending her the clearest signals I can. I'm not here as her alpha.

An odd tension beside me, and it's not coming from her wolf.

I lean my weight against her legs as carefully as I can. I'm not here as that guy either. I'm just here in case she wants someone to witness who she's becoming up here on this ridge.

A long pause, and then her chin lands quietly on the back of my neck.

I hold very still, and together, we watch the stars.

16

LISSA

I smile at the face on my laptop screen. She isn't who I messaged through ShifterNet, and I definitely didn't expect a video chat window popping up in response.

Jules grins at me. "Hey, Lissa. Planning on having my brother's babies yet?"

My cheeks do things that should be illegal in all ten provinces. There were definitely a couple of moments under the stars last night when my wolf thought that was a very good idea.

She laughs. "Sorry, I've been hanging out with the teenagers. They're a bad influence. You might want to work up a different answer for when my mom asks you that question, though."

I should have stuck to texting. "Hayden must have inherited his patience from his dad."

Jules laughs, even as her eyes get overbright.

My human wants to yank the careless words back, but my wolf knows they landed right where they belong. The Scotts want to talk about James, need to talk about him.

Jules smiles. "I remember one day I decided I was going to jump over the gate out of the nursery, just like the big kids did. I threw myself at it at least a hundred times. My father picked me up and told me he loved me and set me on my feet so I could try again for the better part of two hours."

I shake my head ruefully. "I'm not sure I'm equipped to handle a dominant pup."

She grins. "We can't be handled. We can only be loved and righted and allowed our bruises."

"Robbie's acquiring a really big collection." We all are. Yesterday got a little wild, and Kennedy's idea of a gentle fighting lesson last night added a few new layers to the evidence my son wears of his wondrous new life. "I have Danielle's tweaks to the table design, by the way. She liked your idea of splitting it in two."

"Less likelihood of a bear breaking it that way." Jules rolls her eyes at the trials and tribulations caused by her most demanding clients. "Tell her all my fall and winter orders want one. And all the orders from last year are yelling at me for not being psychic."

I imagine yelling at Jules Scott is about as effective as trying to move an anvil with a feather. "Are you still sending some people to learn the process when she and Eliza do ours?" That wasn't the CEO of HomeWild's first choice, but Hayden put his foot down when she tried to bribe Danielle into spending half the winter traveling to various shifter dens to make concrete tables and countertops.

"Yup." Jules grins. "One of them might be a bear. Consider yourself warned. I think my mom's ability to sit on him will run out by fall."

Ronan might be huge and disturbingly generous, but he's been nothing but sweet and kind to my favorite bear and to a number of very submissive crafters who have started casually dropping his name in conversation. "He's welcome here."

Laughter as Adrianna's head comes into view. "Say that any louder and he'll be there in time for breakfast."

Jules turns the monitor screen toward her mom. "She actually called to talk to you, and I have a meeting. I'll let you two wheel and deal while I go contemplate paint chips for the new spring line and why cats have such a strange fondness for bizarre shades of green."

Adrianna chuckles. "They do it just to mess with you, dear."

Hayden's sister flashes a grin. "I know."

I shake my head as Jules vanishes. Dealing with the Scott family is never boring. The one still visible on the screen is studying me carefully, like she knows all of what I've been up to for the last twenty-four hours. Which is entirely possible. Jules might not be psychic, but I would have no trouble believing it of her mother.

Adrianna picks up a cup of tea and smiles at me. "How's Robbie? I hear he had quite the day yesterday."

I have to laugh. "The newspaper isn't even out yet."

Myrna and Reilly are furiously polishing it. They don't let their standards slide even for a story this big—or maybe especially when the story is this big.

Adrianna sips her tea, merriment in her eyes. "There are currently several dozen shifters lazing about in the Whistler Pack dining room, eating their breakfast extremely slowly in the hopes it's coming out soon. Ronan heard from Reilly that it's worth waiting for."

I want, so very much, to hide it all under a bushel, but I can't. It matters too much. "The submissives spoke yesterday. It was a pretty big deal." I shrug, because I don't really know how to explain the rest. Then I remember that I'm talking to the world expert on shifter pack dynamics. I don't have to explain. She'll work it all out from a few of my favorite details. "It started with a water fight. Miriam and Eliza took Hayden out with an underwater attack."

Delight blooms in her eyes. "They didn't."

I grin. "They really did."

A chuckle, laced with pleased maternal glee. "Good for them. Who was brave enough to send two submissives after their alpha?"

I stare at her. Of all the questions she could have asked, I can't believe she picked that one.

She sets down her tea, her eyes never leaving mine. "Really."

It's way past time to change the subject. I bolt toward the only thing I can think of that might distract those eyes. "I was hoping to ask you for a favor."

She mostly keeps a straight face, but no way have I won this war. "Of course."

Next time I'll just let her pester me for grandpuppies. "Kennedy is reading a lot of your blog posts."

Adrianna's eyes change. "I'm honored."

"She has some good role models in her life, including Ebony." Who is the only dominant female I can name. "But I think she's seeking other ways to help her pack. More subtle ones that are less about teeth and claws."

"She's a very impressive young woman," says Adrianna quietly. "One who has fearsome teeth and claws. It's to her credit that she seeks to look beyond them. Not all baby alphas are so wise."

I look at the screen and at the wolf who probably understands better than anyone what it is to live inside Kennedy's skin. "I was hoping you might be willing to chat with her occasionally. Very informally. She was horrified about taking up any of your time."

Adrianna laughs. "She should see what exalted things fill up my time. I just finished arbitrating a dispute over the last jar of huckleberry jam."

Jam is serious pack business. "Who won?"

She snorts. "Neither of them. They're both headed to the woods with berry-picking buckets. I gave the jam to a young hawk who delivered some paperwork I needed this morning."

There are very good reasons nobody messes with the Whistler Pack alpha. "We'll have another batch of jam in a week or so. A big one, this time." The berries on the east slope of Ghost Mountain are always the slowest to ripen, but Myrna swears they're the ones that make the best jam.

Adrianna shakes her head wryly. "You're spoiling the heck out of my resident bear. And several dozen of his closest friends."

I laugh. "It's not my fault he's somehow convinced your pack to take jam as a form of payment. It wreaks havoc with my spreadsheets."

She grins. "We all have our burdens to bear."

It's really hard to complain about any of mine. "I'll let Myrna know she's causing jam wars."

"You do that." Adrianna's eyes gleam. "I'll send Kennedy a chat request."

That will probably make our teenage baby alpha's eyes fall out of her head. "You might want to wait a couple of days. When Reilly publishes his story, she's going to be a minor celebrity for a while."

A raised eyebrow.

Wolves are such curious creatures, even when they could likely find out anything they want to know by snapping their fingers. "When we got back to the den last night, the dominants Hayden threw out of the den were waiting. They were annoyed that they no longer have access to pack funds. One of them made a not-so-veiled threat in Reilly's direction. Kennedy challenged him. Whistler Protocol rules."

A long, slow nod. "I do like that young woman. I assume she made him eat dust."

My wolf grins.

Adrianna chuckles. "Good. In that case, perhaps I'll

be able to dissuade Ronan from paying the idiots in question a visit."

I wince. Ronan's a very big guy, and he really likes Reilly. "Tell him to read the whole article. Reilly stood up for himself just fine."

Adrianna's eyes soften. "Good for him. And good for all of you for making the right kind of space for a sweet, self-conscious bear to find his self-confidence."

That isn't on me. "Hayden and Kel and Rio have been really good for him." Men who think his big brain and soft heart and careful ethics have worth. "Kel especially, I think."

"He is rather good at walking softly and carrying a big stick. And he knows what it is to have a submissive heart that needs to stand for pack."

My wolf preens, like those words got spoken just for her.

Adrianna's eyes sharpen.

Oh, hell. "I should probably go. Thank you for making time for Kennedy."

The smartest alpha on the planet smirks at me. "I might have to go sit in the dining room and be impatient with the rest of my wolves so I can read the part of Reilly's story that will explain why you're so bothered."

I want desperately to duck my head inside my t-shirt like a turtle. "Not everything you read on the internet is true."

Her laugh rings brightly from my laptop's speakers. "You could just tell me, you know."

Something rebellious rises up in my wolf. She's proud

of her pack and she's proud of herself and this is a story worth telling. "There's a special place in our territory, not too far from the den. It's got a swimming hole with a small waterfall that only gets sun for a few days in the middle of the summer. We traipsed out there with loads of food and watermelon and Myrna's daddy's cast-iron frying pan and we had one of those magical days we won't forget for a long time."

Adrianna sighs quietly, a sound full of heartfelt pleasure.

It yanks the next line out of me. "Reilly's story probably won't tell you this, but Hayden's wolf was so happy. He just glowed, all day long."

Her eyes close briefly. When she opens them back up, they're bright with unshed tears.

I rush to say the rest before I choke on it. "When we got back, the dominants were here. Reilly and Kennedy did most of the work of showing them how things are going to be from now on, and then we threw them out, but I said a few words. Reilly's story will probably say way too much about that part."

A soft, slow smile. "You spoke for your pack."

My wolf and the truth I saw in starlight won't let me hide. "I did."

Adrianna picks up her tea. "You remind me so very much of my James. He would have liked you very much."

I gulp. "I'm just trying to take some small steps. Like you suggested."

She grins. "Oh, no. You don't get to blame this on me."

I sigh. "I'm a really ordinary wolf."

She takes a sip of her tea and smiles. A wolf who doesn't believe me at all.

HAYDEN

My pack needs more laptops and sat phones and other miscellaneous devices capable of talking to the internet, because the ones currently capable of doing that are all being shared by half a dozen wolves each, and they're all trying to speak at the same time.

I look over at Myrna and shake my head. "You've created bedlam."

She snickers. "I report on bedlam, mister. You might not be entirely responsible for this mess, but you had your tail in plenty of it."

I hold up my hands in the universal sign of wolf innocence.

She cackles. "When was the last time you declared a boys-against-girls water fight?"

I wince. "It was a spur-of-the-moment thing."

She snorts. "Liar. You figured Reilly would stick with Lissa and we'd clobber you easily."

Something like that. "There was steak to be eaten. Really good steak."

Her lips quirk. "Entire continents have been conquered with my daddy's secret marinade."

My wolf votes for using it to entice some of the lost

wolves in the woods to come home, but he's smart enough not to say that. Myrna might hit him with her frying pan.

Reilly laughs at Rio's laptop screen and turns fifteen shades of pink. Ronan, no doubt. Kennedy hangs over his shoulder, doing an excellent job of adding enough color commentary to take a story that started out somewhat resembling the truth and turn it into something sizable enough to regale a polar bear. It's not her part she's inflating, but Kel's discreet hand signals on the other side of Reilly's head are adding those details just fine.

I snort. Ronan does not need to be coached in the fine art of sniffing out all of the heroes in a story. "Reilly might actually get a big head from this." He's got exactly zero tendencies in that direction, but a certain polar bear has mad skills.

Myrna smiles fondly. "If he does, he deserves it. You don't know just how much some of those dominants harassed him. They respected his bear, but they had nothing but disdain for his sweet soul. For him to speak up on the side of kindness yesterday did my heart good, I can tell you."

She's telling everyone. Quietly, and without dimming Reilly's tale at all, but she made sure a few key details slipped into this edition's lead story. Details that enshrined kindness as part of our pack legend.

"I saw the photo you took of Danielle." A slightly blurry shot of her sitting by the fire, looking at her bear cub with her eyes full of mama pride. "One day he'll look at that and know why he grew up into a good man."

Myrna snorts. "He'll grow up a good man because he

lives in a pack full of them. Even if you all have terrible language and don't eat your vegetables."

"Kel eats a few." He eats all of them, actually, but for reasons I'm not entirely clear on, he hasn't let the rest of his new pack know that yet. I have no idea what long game involves a false dislike of broccoli, but I know better than to question a man with strategic skills capable of bringing large countries to their knees.

Myrna rolls her eyes. "Tomato sauce is not a vegetable."

I grin. "It is when you add puréed zucchini."

She pins me with a look. "You're not supposed to know about that."

Something Ebony says into the sat phone she's commandeered causes the entire shark squad to squeak. I don't ask what, but I can hear the cheering on the other end of the phone's video call from here. "You can't hide zucchini from me." I wrap an arm around wiry shoulders. "That's not a dare, by the way."

Myrna chortles and catches Braden as he tries to make a run for it. "No way, little man. Find a t-shirt and go stack your breakfast plate over with the others."

I shrug as he turns to me in mute appeal. "Those are the rules. If you stack all the plates you can find, you can come help me wash them." Which will take at least twice as long as normal, because Braden's wolf thinks dish soap is some kind of deadly threat that must be demolished, but I'm a smart alpha. If I don't want to be washing dishes for the rest of my natural life, I need to make sure all the most likely troublemakers are well trained in the appropriate application of soap bubbles and scrubbies.

"I'll take care of that." Myrna pats my shoulder. "You have someone else who needs you."

It doesn't take long to spy the wolf she means. Robbie is skirting the edges of the bedlam in his pack, a confused pup who can't figure out how to be a part of what he senses. It's all too fast and too loud and dealing with a medium that makes no sense to his human or his wolf.

More than any pup I've ever met, Robbie lives in the tangible here and now.

I drum my fingers on the ground, sending a message to his wolf. "Hey, Robbie. Come sit with me awhile."

He turns slowly, puzzled.

He swung on the rope for almost an hour yesterday and never lost focus. He's a pup who needs a purpose to get his feet back to solid ground. I cast around in my head for one deserving of his attention. It needs to be real and it needs to serve his pack. All pups see through fake tasks, but baby alphas have more sensitive antennae than most.

It doesn't take me long to pick exactly the right job for a couple of guys who don't want to be minions of chaos. I smile at him as he plops down in my lap. "I need to go make some deliveries. Want to come?"

His head tilts quizzically.

He uses so few words, but he never seems to need them. "Myrna saved some of that chocolate cake from yesterday for the sentries." I add a quiet owl hoot, which is how all the pups identify our tree-dwelling perimeter guards.

He nods solemnly.

"All the wolves who would usually go deliver it are busy talking."

He makes a face and puts his fingers in his ears.

I chuckle and ruffle his hair. "Exactly. So I figured I'd do it, but I don't know who all the sentries are, and some of them think my wolf is scary. I need someone to come with me who won't scare their wolves and who's good at climbing trees."

His eyes get big. He's been working hard on his tree climbing, but he's mostly had Kennedy climbing up right behind him.

I'll let him hit the ground shortly after I chop off one of my limbs, but he's a dominant and a baby alpha. He needs to feel risk and danger in his life so he learns how to respect it. "Think we can do that together?"

He pauses longer than any of the other pups would.

I wait. Rio says his wolf processes deeply. It just looks slow.

When he nods, my wolf beams. "Great." I hold up loosely fisted hands. "How many slices do we need to take?"

He contemplates my curled-up fingers. He reaches out slowly and straightens one. Then he glances at me.

I'm good with all the ways of doing pack math. I sit patiently.

He uncurls another finger, and then one on the other hand. Back to the first hand for a third finger. A long moment of contemplation and then a second finger on the second hand. My wolf is deeply curious about the two groups of sentries, but he knows better than to ask. Robbie might actually answer, and that would be breaking all kinds of promises I've made to wait for trust instead of demanding it.

I sit another minute, but Robbie doesn't move any more fingers. "That many pieces of cake?"

He nods solemnly.

That's one less than usual, but I don't question his math. We can always come back for more if needed, but I saw him roaming around with Ebony earlier this morning. He likely knows exactly who's out there. "How about I run to the kitchen for those, and you go collect the big bottle to refill their canteens."

He looks at me, and then he looks over at the cacophony and holds his hands in the shape of a phone.

Smart pup. We don't have enough phones to hand those out along with the cake, but that's not what Robbie is really saying. His wolf doesn't understand phones, but he has acutely sensitive radar for things that make his pack stronger, and wolves live for stories.

I slide a hand over one of Robbie's sensitive ears and cuddle the other one into my chest as I call out to our resident reporter. "Hey, Riles. Have you got printed news sheets yet?" We send a bundle of each edition out to the woods. Low-tech pack propaganda.

Reilly's head bobs up and down.

I hold up the same number of fingers as Robbie uncurled. "Can we have this many?"

I get a couple of interested looks, and then most of my

pack goes back to telling tall tales. Alpha antics aren't nearly as fun as rapt audiences.

Kennedy lopes over to us a minute later with a sheaf of paper in her hands. "You guys need help?"

"Nope." I uncover Robbie's ears and pat his shoulder. "I already have it. Tell Lissa we went to deliver cake and news and we'll be back before lunch."

Kennedy blinks. Then she studies Robbie, and I can practically hear her baby-alpha gears turning. She crouches down in front of him. "Cool. You get to practice being a bossy wolf with good manners."

Robbie nods solemnly. Then he tips his eyes down and curls over a little as he wiggles the part of his human that would have a tail. A nice approximation of a friendly submissive wolf. Excellent pack manners for bossy dominants, and not a lesson I knew he'd been getting.

Kennedy grins again and ruffles his hair. "That's perfect. I can see why Hayden picked you." She shoots me a look that says I'm maybe not a hopeless alpha. And one that says I'd better not miss when Robbie falls out of a tree. Then she heads back into the bedlam, a teenage wolf who's taken care of one kind of business and needs to get back to the others.

I shake my head. She'd be really scary if her pack loyalty wasn't the size of the Canadian Shield.

I set Robbie on his feet. Most packs this size don't have even one baby alpha, never mind two, and it will be an honor and a privilege to help both of them find their places in the world. "Let's collect our gear, little dude. I'll grab the water, since you have newspapers to deliver."

He holds the sheaf of paper like the precious offering it is, and walks big and tall at my side as we head to the kitchens. I look down at him, and a memory reaches out of the dim of my mind and stabs me right in the chest.

I remember that—the proud walk of a pup who feels as big as the sky.

I used to walk like that beside my dad.

17

LISSA

I collect up a couple of discarded t-shirts and one of Mellie's stray building blocks. Tidying a den that doesn't really need tidying, but my wolf is out of sorts.

She snorts.

Fine. My human is out of sorts, and my wolf got us into this mess with her need to be a hero. Reilly was doing a fine job speaking for pack yesterday and there were a dozen others who could have said what I said. But because the words came out of my mouth, the story can't ever be told without me smack in the middle of it.

I sigh. I know why I'm walking these unhelpful mental roads. My human has always been happier on the sidelines. My wolf likes the center. The bonds of pack are strongest there and they make her feel good. Which is great, but the eyes of my pack haven't left me all morning, and we're becoming the center of something even bigger, and that has me feeling all kinds of complicated things.

Our pack, our story—we're becoming a touchstone. A tale of healing and rebuilding and hope, the kind we would have read about and cuddled tight to our chests so many nights over the last six years. Which is a big reason I willingly spent the last couple of hours having really embarrassing conversations.

Telling our story in case it matters to someone else.

I'm still processing just how much it matters for us. The shark squad isn't talking much, but oh, their wolves are listening. Eliza and Miriam and Kelsey all got an earful from the shifters of Whistler Pack. Apparently taking Hayden down in a water fight is the stuff of instant hero status. Jules delighted in telling Kelsey that she was the last person to land a foot on Hayden's nose.

I sigh and drop my armload of random den detritus into a pile at the base of the tree that's turned into our mustering zone. Kelsey is handling her sudden fame far better than I am. She smiles, everyone melts, and then Kennedy or Myrna or Reilly or Ebony gracefully moves the attention to some other shifter.

Mostly me.

Maybe I need to borrow a page from Hayden's book and quietly disappear. It made my heart lurch when I realized Robbie was gone—and then lurch again when I realized who he left with. I know why Hayden took him away. This kind of noise and chaos is anathema to all the ways Robbie's brain knows how to work. The swimming hole was different. He knows how to be at the center of that kind of noise. The internet entirely confuses his wolf.

A hoot sounds in the trees, and a few seconds later, my human nose can smell my son's imminent arrival. I crouch down. Robbie surprises me, however. He doesn't arrive as a bouncy white pup. He comes out of the trees holding Hayden's hand and still wearing his shorts and t-shirt, both looking like they've had a lot of adventures since he put them on this morning.

Myrna pages Hayden from over by the fire. He pats Robbie's shoulder and sends him my way.

I stare a moment at my retreating alpha and the odd sense of reticence that seems to hang in the air around him. Then I shift gears, because I have a very excited son telling me stories about Hoot and falling out of a tree and climbing back up again and the cake only got a little squished and he had a bite but only one, because it wasn't for him, and they're all reading Reilly's stories and smiling a lot.

I gather him in my arms, because some of what he's saying is words and some is gestures and some is wriggling wolf in human form, but all together, it's more than Robbie generally says in a week.

He licks my chin and wriggles some more. A pup not yet ready to be contained.

I nuzzle into his hair and breathe in the smell of his happiness, letting it wash away the remnants of my cranky mood. Then I let him go, because holding him too tightly is something I'm trying to do less of these days. "How about a swim to wash off the tree dust?"

He looks confused, probably because he can't see his grimy face. Then he grins, because any reason to go swimming is a good one. His small hands reach for his t-shirt—and then he turns, his wolf at sudden attention.

A tired, dusty Ghost steps out of the trees on the other side of the river, meets my eyes, and nods.

I gulp. When I threw my pebbles, I didn't expect them to land all at once.

HAYDEN

My wolf jolts as a tall, scrawny man walks out of the forest. I have no idea who he is, but it's really clear from the reaction of my pack that the last twenty-four hours have just been prelude. I need to get my shit together, no matter how much I just got shaken by a stroll in the woods with a pup. A deep moment of truth has arrived, and he's looking at me with terror in his eyes.

A gasping cry arrows toward the stranger. "Ravi?"

My eyes don't move—they don't dare—but I know who's on her feet, shaking like a leaf. Cori. Jade's mom. One of the quietest, most nondescript wolves in this pack. Or she was until a second ago, when she started radiating agonized, furious, petrified love.

Holy hell.

I blink, and then I blink again, because she's one half of a mate bond so huge and so mauled my wolf can hardly see straight. Slowly and very carefully, I roll to my feet. I set my stance into the lines of an alpha who protects the pups and never, ever loses his cool, and look just over Ravi's shoulder. I don't speak. He's not ready for that yet. He needs to believe my wolf isn't going to tear him limb from limb, first.

Which makes my human vibrate with rage, but I absolutely cannot let that be any part of who I am right now. Ravi's wolf is a hairsbreadth away from bolting for the trees, and if he does that, he's going to tear himself in half and Cori right along with him.

The shaking stranger in my den averts his gaze, his eyes desperately seeking his mate. He sends her a look of terrible longing—and then his gaze lands on the small girl who's got her arms around Cori's legs.

The one whose eyes are the exact same shade of vivid green as his.

He sits down hard on the ground, every bone in his body gone, and stares at Jade.

My pack doesn't move. It doesn't breathe.

Ravi tries to swallow, but his throat gets stuck halfway.

My wolf inches forward. He needs to touch, to help Ravi breathe.

Ravi flinches, and his wolf yanks his eyes to the dirt at my feet. Cowering. Begging.

My human wants to puke, but this isn't about him.

"Ravi." A single, quiet word from a source I didn't even hear move. Ghost, a dozen feet behind him, her eyes fierce. "He's not like that, I promise you. Lissa sent me to fetch you and now you know why, and you know that she would never, ever put a pup in danger, so stop being stupid. You did good. You got here, which means Samuel doesn't have power over your wolf anymore. He can't make you leave. This is our new alpha. His name is Hayden and he thinks submissive wolves are really important in a pack, so he's going to be proud to have you." Her eyes burn into mine as she speaks to both of us. "You need to give him a chance."

Ravi's breath hitches. His head comes up, but he's not looking at me. Ghost's words broke the thrall of his wolf's fear, and his eyes head straight back to his mate and the pup he so obviously didn't know existed. The first words he tries to form are gibberish. He licks his lips and tries again. What comes out is a tortured, rattling whisper. "Why didn't you tell me?"

Jade whimpers.

Cori scoops her up in an instant, cuddling her tight and glaring at Ravi with daggers in her eyes. "Because you would have come for us. And then you would have been dead."

The sound that comes out of Ravi isn't one any living creature should ever make.

My wolf is beside himself. He doesn't know how to fix this. The teeth and claws causing the pain are inside Ravi's wolf and he can't fight them there.

He spies movement from Lissa. Hand signals. Ones he doesn't know, but the meaning is clear. *Move in. Be pack.* Surround the pain and let it be at the center. Rio's moving in right beside her, holding Robbie's hand, clasping Shelley's.

Warm fingers reach for mine. Layla on one side, Reilly on the other.

Ghost walks over and takes a seat between Kel and Myrna, a wall of submissive determination blocking Ravi's most obvious exit.

My wolf wants to clear them out of the way. The pain is so huge. We can't force him to stay.

My pack's answer is quiet and implacable and clear. *We can't let him go.*

"I'm Eamon's daughter."

It takes me far too long to realize Cori is speaking to me. Her eyes haven't left Ravi, but her words are meant for her alpha.

My wolf quivers as her words register, as their meaning lances his soul—as how she expects him to react makes him bleed.

He ignores the blood. It doesn't matter. So long, he has waited for this trust.

He puts his answer in his eyes. In his heartbeat. In his breath. He doesn't care who her father is. He only cares who *she* is. There is nothing she can say that will make her less a part of this pack or any less in her alpha's eyes. Only more.

She swallows hard. "Eamon and Samuel were cousins. We traveled together for a long time, beating up humans and taking their money and their pride. Then one day we came to this pack and everyone was friendly and they welcomed us and Ravi was nice to me. I fell so hard in love I could barely remember how to breathe, and somehow he fell in love with me back."

Another low, anguished sound from the man with tears running down his cheeks.

I can feel what once lived between them, the bright, shining, innocent strength of it. I don't want to hear what comes next.

Cori's chin wobbles. "I thought Samuel would just break things some and then we would leave, but he didn't. He killed the old alpha and then he had my father torture anyone who was still whole and strong and happy." Her breath rattles and her eyes fill. "He started with Ravi. With the beautiful man who dared to love me, and I was foolish enough to let him."

Ravi's whole body jerks.

The smile on Cori's face is the saddest thing I've ever seen. "I tried to leave with him. Eamon wouldn't let me go. So I told Ravi I didn't love him anymore, but he didn't believe me and he kept coming back until they made his wolf bleed so much he almost died. Then Samuel issued an alpha order and banished him."

My wolf writhes. I need that man alive again so I can shred him for his cruelty. Mate bonds have orders of magnitude, and this one is wild and deep. Forcing them apart would have been worse than sawing off a limb.

Cori's eyes fall to her lap. "Ebony took him away. I visited when I could." She lifts her head and her eyes dart to mine. "Ravi sent us money. As much as he could, to help feed the pups. He's a good man."

Her tears finally spill over, and it's not me she's talking to anymore. "I couldn't tell you about her, Ravi. I couldn't. But I tried to keep her safe and when she was a little bigger I was going to send her to live with you. I needed you to stay alive so you could love our girl and show her how to be free."

LISSA

I can't let go. That's all I can think about, all I know. I wasn't ready for this, but it doesn't matter. It has to be now and we have to be enough. I clutch Robbie's small hand and Rio's large one and let myself feel the soul-searing pain of two submissive wolves, one who couldn't leave and one who couldn't stay.

I don't know if holding tight will matter. I don't know if Ravi will let us love him. We've all spent three years lying to keep him safe.

His hands lift into the air, shaking wildly. He clamps them down on his knees again.

Cori strokes her daughter's soft brown hair. "Her name is Jade."

We all try to breathe for Ravi's wolf.

Cori whimpers a little and bites her lip. Locking down what lives inside her, just like she has her whole life. Hiding who she is and who she loves and how close she sometimes comes to not being able to do it anymore.

Fierce energy flows through Rio, his hand hot in mine.

Cori jolts, like lightning somehow found her on a sunny day. She opens her mouth and closes it again, a fish in very strange water. Then she looks down at her little girl. "Jade, this is your daddy. He's been living in the woods, but he sent the money for some of your favorite snacks and your cuddly boo and the book about balloons you like so much."

Jade's head tips to the side, a small, unblinking owl studying the man in front of her. The confusion of a pup who's grown up in a pack with no daddies.

Rio's fingers squeeze mine. A sentinel who has used his lightning—and now he can only do the same as all the rest of us.

Hope.

Cori tucks a stray lock of Jade's hair behind her ear. "His fur is soft and brown like yours, and your laugh sounds a lot like his, and he likes way too much maple syrup on his pancakes just like you do."

I close my eyes. There are all kinds of courage in the world, and hers has always gutted me. And yet, deep in her own hell, she still put herself between Robbie and Eamon more times than I can count. I take all of that gratitude and push it at the one wolf who might be able to back this away from the edge.

When I open my eyes again, Jade is tugging on Cori's hair.

Cori smiles and swipes at her tears. "Should we sit a little closer, love bug?"

Jade nods and glances at Ravi out of the corner of her eye. Curiosity, submissive-pup style.

I don't think he's breathed in three minutes.

With aching, majestic slowness, Cori inches her way toward Ravi's knees.

It's not the reunion of love and light I was stupidly, naively hoping might be possible. There's too much weight. Too much pain. Too much guilt and confusion and bludgeoned hope and seeping scar tissue. But still, Cori moves, inch by painstaking inch, closing the distance between their knees.

An eternity later, they sit, not quite touching.

Jade peeks out of her mother's arms.

Ravi is as still as a statue—and the color of a man right before he pukes up everything he's ever eaten.

A small girl's hand moves. Slowly. Cautiously. Reaching for the stranger. Testing the air between them. Hovering a long moment over the hand on his knee.

Her fingers land on his, light as a butterfly.

Lightning jolts the three of them again. The storm within, this time.

They don't even notice.

RIO

Sentinels are gamblers. We have to be. There are never any guarantees with hearts and souls and all the ways they manage to mangle themselves, and sentinels are the front lines of the battle to right the worst of that damage and help mangled shifters find their way home. But never in my entire life have I tossed the dice as fiercely as Lissa has this day—or fought as hard as she is on the grass beside me for them to land the way they need to.

My wolf isn't bothering to try to fix anything anymore. He's just throwing his weight behind hers as she gently blows on the embers of a small girl with curious, bright-green eyes. The one who has shattered a man into atoms and who just might give him the will to start putting them back together again.

I knew Cori was in hiding, and I knew she was in pain. I didn't come anywhere close to guessing why.

I give my head an internal shake. I wouldn't have thought it possible to miss a mate bond this strong in the pack I've taken as mine, but the earth didn't speak a word of it under my paws. Which could mean a lot of things, but I'm not going to expend any energy guessing. I'll be too busy listening and scrambling and trying to help Hayden hold his shit together—and paying deep attention to a pack that just maybe knows how to contain this and give it the time and space and love it needs to find its way home.

I wouldn't have thrown these dice. I wouldn't have dared.

Which is humbling as shit, because as the three people in front of me jumble into one awkward, shuddering, breathtaking whole, the earth under my ass is perfectly clear.

This absolutely needed to happen.

18

LISSA

I let out a very quiet sigh of relief as Cori's eyes finally close. Ravi conked out about three seconds after Jade finally gave in to her afternoon nap, a man so exhausted I'm amazed his ribs are still managing to breathe. Cori took longer.

I can only imagine what's churning inside her.

But once again, it's the simple routine of pack riding to our rescue. Shelley and Layla and Miriam and Eliza gathered up the smallest pups after lunch and herded them into a nap pile and started reading stories and stroking fur and building a gravitational well of sleep, just like they do every day.

Today, they quietly pulled in a couple of shattered adults, too.

Jade is nestled in her usual spot between Braden and Mellie, buffering the two dominant pups so that everyone sleeps, but her small, furry chin is resting on Ravi's hand. Cori has possession of his other one, her fingers wrapped around his wrist like he might try to run, even in sleep.

So much exhausted pain—and just maybe, the seeds of hope.

Or I'm seeing what I desperately need to see, because I'm the one who forgot that beating hearts and traumatized souls are really different from pebbles.

I look over at Rio. I've been doing that a lot these last two hours as we tried to move the pack gently through lunch, and give some privacy to two wolves drenched in tears while still wrapping them in pack.

He just smiles a little and keeps tapping some kind of rhythm into the earth with his hands.

"He's listening." Ghost sits down beside me and holds out a brownie. "Shelley says we need to eat these before the pups wake up."

I take half the brownie, but I can't take my eyes off Rio's fingers. "I thought he was talking. Some kind of secret sentinel code."

"Nope. Kel says he does that when he's human so he can hear the earth. When he's furry, he can just feel it through his paws." She nods at the two adults sleeping on the edges of the pup pile, waterfalls of tears still drying on their faces. "He's listening to their souls."

Something I should have done before I tried to turn my pack into a Hallmark movie. I stare at their ravaged faces and pray I didn't mess up really badly.

Ghost elbows me. "Kel said you need to stop that, by the way. He said you decided to be a bossy wolf and now you need to see it through and not get all wimpy because it's gotten hard."

My eyes widen. I have no trouble believing Kel said something like that, but I'm a little surprised he chose to use a messenger.

Ghost smiles faintly. "He's busy. He made me a deputy."

I'm not sure I want to know what's taking priority over giving me grief. "What's he doing?"

"Beating up on Ebony. She's feeling guilty because she couldn't stop Samuel and Eamon from trying to break Cori and Ravi, so Kel has to beat up on her so that she can start thinking clearly again. Kennedy wanted to do it, but she thinks maybe Kel needs to get beat up a little, too."

Pack, trying to take the unholy mess I made and turn it into something good.

Ghost's eyes shoot back over to Ravi as he makes a small, sad sound in his sleep. "Sorry it took us so long to get back. I found him pretty fast, but he had a hard time getting too close to the den."

I cringe inwardly for the hundredth time in two hours. I sent a teenager to do a job that needed a sentinel, a therapist, and a couple of knights with flaming swords. However, Kel's right. No matter how big a mess I made, I need to help clean it up. "Are you okay?"

She shrugs. "Yeah."

I study her. Cori isn't the only one good at holding her cards really close to her chest.

Ghost's eyes meet mine. "I know you're being really hard on yourself right now, but I think you're wrong."

I blink.

Her chin dips down, but the intensity in her words doesn't dim at all. "When I found Ravi, he was nice to me, but he felt invisible. Like his body was there, but the rest of him was barely breathing. Then I told him Samuel was dead and he could come home and his whole wolf lit up."

My hands curl into fists.

Ghost studies my clenched fingers. "I know he's hurting a lot and so is Cori, but I think all of him came back, even the parts that were barely breathing. So now the pack can help him get better and Ravi and Cori can be together and Jade can have a dad."

She has such faith. I need to have it, too. I wrap an arm around her shoulders. "You found him and you brought him home. Thank you."

"Thanks for sending me." She smiles at the ground. "It was a really good message to be able to deliver."

HAYDEN

Lissa's shoulders hunch over as Ghost walks off. I drop down into the spot the quiet teenager just vacated. "You need to listen to your own words."

She offers me a wry look.

Throwing my alpha weight at her might be overkill,

but I can't do shit to help Cori and Ravi, because both of them are terrified of everything I am and stand for, so she's damn well stuck with me. "One of our wolves came home today. That's everything. Don't you dare sit here feeling guilty for making it happen."

She curls her knees up tight to her chest. "They're both hurting so much. I thought it was the right thing to do, but there's so much pain."

I remember the day Kel came home with nothing but emptiness in his eyes. "Pain is a good thing. Trust me on that. It beats not feeling anything at all, and Ravi's wolf was really close to that edge." I don't even need my sentinel to tell me that.

She exhales slowly. "That's more or less what Ghost said."

The teenagers of my pack could rule the world. I'm damn glad they're mine. "She got him here." I have some experience herding broken wolves. There's no way that was an easy job.

Lissa sighs. "I can't believe I sent her off alone to find him. I only thought about her tracking skills. I totally overlooked the part where she was going to have to bring him back to the den that banished him."

My wolf is entirely done with his pack being stupid. They did something today that they wouldn't have been capable of doing yesterday, and they need to open their eyes and fucking look. I bump Lissa with my shoulder, hard enough to throw her off balance.

She throws out her limbs to catch herself and shoots me a dirty look.

I grin. She's so not scared of me anymore. "Stop beating yourself up."

She blinks at me.

There are things I don't remember about my dad—but I remember that on the days when the alpha of all alphas had doubts, he always had her back. I don't think Lissa fucked up at all, but even if she did, I will keep holding her damn cape until she puts it back on. "One of our wolves came home today. That's *all* that matters."

Her eyes fill with guilt and grief.

My wolf snarls. His pack isn't seeing what he sees and it's killing him. "Stop looking at Cori and Ravi for a minute and look at everyone else."

Her face crinkles in confusion.

"Eliza sang while she made lunch. Kenny crossed the inner perimeter at lunch to catch a glimpse of Ravi. Kelsey picked a handful of flowers and left them by her special tree." All of them reacting to the same elemental message. If one wolf can come home, maybe they all can.

She shakes her head slowly, but I can see my words landing. She knows what those flowers mean, even if I don't. "I keep throwing boulders instead of pebbles."

I run my hand slowly up and down her arm. Holding capes is mostly about listening.

She huffs out a sigh. "I was trying to take some small actions, except they haven't ended up so small and they're having a whole bunch of consequences I didn't expect."

I snort as a tardy dot finally connects. "I knew I shouldn't have left you alone with my mother."

A wry chuckle. "This isn't her fault."

She won't believe that. And she won't think my green-eyed wolf screwed up, either. "You know Adrianna Scott is the absolute mistress of boulder throwing, right?"

Lissa's lips twitch. "I bet she has better aim than I do."

I snuggle her in closer before my wolf strangles me. "If you believe that, ask her about the day a suicidal, tough-as-nails veteran walked into her office and tried to quit her pack."

Lissa sucks in a sharp breath. "Kel?"

I nod. That part, I've only heard in stories. All the parts after that, I lived through. "Rio and I showed up a few minutes later to work on my overdue math homework. She decided we were the solution to her Kel problem."

A pause as my green-eyed wolf thinks through all the implications of that choice. "It worked."

History is always easiest on the victors. "She didn't know that at the time. She assigned a ten-year-old to hang out with a guy who sharpened his knives fourteen hours a day. A dumbass ten-year-old who snuck into that guy's quarters and stole his t-shirts and held his favorite snacks hostage and changed his phone ringtone to a fart."

It delights my wolf that her first reaction is a reluctant snicker. He's still pretty proud of the ringtone stunt.

I rub my cheek against the top of her head. "When you start throwing bigger boulders than my mother, you can apologize and feel guilty and blame yourself. Until then, you keep right on tossing pebbles and asking your pack to catch them, because every time you do, you make us better."

She sighs. "I made a big mess."

I grin. "It kind of comes with the territory of asking your pack to be better."

LISSA

He's trying to make this easy on me. My wolf thinks he's cute. My human wants to kick him in the knees. She likes her guilt trip. It's a lot more comfortable than the alternative.

I sneak another look at Cori and Ravi and the pups snoring between them.

"He made it home, Lissa."

I squeeze my eyes shut as memory rushes in, of a conversation I had over soap bubbles and dirty dishes. The one that somehow took my cautious soul and turned her into a pebble tosser.

The story of the dad who didn't make it home.

I lay my hand against his heart. And I find my courage again, because whatever we need to do to help Ravi, he's alive and he's here and he's loved and this pack is full of people who won't let him forget it. My wolf straightens so that the man beside her knows she's done hiding her eyes under her paws.

Hayden huffs out a laugh. "Your wolf is a menace."

I roll my eyes. "She definitely has a mind of her own."

"Good." He squeezes my shoulders. "Tell me about Ravi."

I look at him, confused.

"I'm the immigrant, remember? You were his packmate. What was he good at? What used to make him happy?"

Such a simple, haunting, wise question. "He's sort of an older version of Kelsey. Gentle and patient, and he always seemed to know when someone needed a hug or a sympathetic ear."

"He's not that much older than you are."

I smile. "He always seemed a lot older. He was like a big brother to most of the pack juveniles. He didn't play favorites. He knew how to make everyone feel special. He spent four months teaching me how to play a song on his guitar so I could sing it for a friend's birthday."

Hayden's hand strokes my wolf. "So he's good with pups."

I lean into his touch. "Yes. The older ones especially. You know that age when your human wants to be your own person and your wolf just wants to be pack?" The special demons of shifter puberty.

Hayden chuckles. "Oh, yeah."

"Ravi gets that." My brain meanders out of the past into the present. "He'd be really good with Reilly. Or Kennedy." He was wonderful with Bailey and her oversized, fragile dominant ego.

A thoughtful silence. "He plays the guitar?"

"He used to." He had an old, banged-up one that hardly ever left his side. I don't know what happened to it, but I can guess. We always needed money to feed the pups. My inner bookkeeper starts squeezing budget lines. "There's a pawn shop in town where we can maybe get a used one."

Hayden nods slowly. Listening. He's so very good at that.

My wolf finds more to tell him. "When Ghost was Robbie's age, she would sit and listen to him for hours."

He hums happily. "Reasons for her to spend more time at the den. You're good at this bribery stuff."

He's good at steadying the very center of me. "Shelley used to sing with him sometimes, too. She'd blush a lot and go back to her baking after, but she can make really pretty harmonies."

His cheek nuzzles against mine. "Sounds like a plan."

Music is wonderful, but there's no way it can fix all of this. "It's not enough."

"Of course not." He kisses the top of my head. "But it's the piece I was missing, and my betas are too busy causing each other bruises to do all my work for me this time."

I stare at the alpha wolf suddenly riding in his eyes.

His fingers brush my cheek. "You did the hard part, beautiful. You got him here. Trust me to do my job and help him stay."

I lean into his touch, wordless.

He smiles, his hand strong as it cups my face. "I've got a really big catcher's mitt. You keep throwing all the boulders you want."

19

HAYDEN

It takes less time than I expect. Naps are over, the pups are finger painting on the huge rock by the river under Shelley's watchful eye, and Ravi is starting to think. I can see it in every line of his body, in the careful way he's trying to ease Cori away from the melded state they've been in for the last few hours, in the worried attentiveness building in the packmates who grew up with him.

Lissa's helping with the finger painting, but her eyes travel from Ravi to me, and I can see the question there. I let my wolf answer. He's got this. The bad alpha is gone, but his legacy lives, and sometimes teeth and claws are exactly the right answer.

She looks a little startled.

I snort. Wolves suck at metaphors. Fortunately, mine doesn't suck at the job he needs to do now. It's the last gift my dad gave me. The wolves who make it home don't scare me at all. They're a chance to make sure Jade never cries herself to sleep every night for a year like Jules did. My mother figured that out when I was ten years old, and she's been attaching me like a burr to reluctant prodigal shifters ever since. I might not have Rio's nose for precisely where to push on someone's pain, but I have persistence down to a fine art.

And when that doesn't work, there are always fart ringtones.

Ravi gets up to collect a mug of water, and when he sits back down, there's a foot of space between him and his mate.

I shoot Kel a look. He's casually leaning against a log —and neatly blocking the easiest route out of the den. Ebony's reading a book smack in the middle of the other one. I snort. My betas are looking a little worse for wear, but apparently they're back to doing most of my work for me.

I take another look at Ravi. If he wants to be a domino, I'll give him a push. "I'm glad Ghost found you. It sounds like you were a long way off."

He shrugs, holding up his mug of water like it can maybe protect him from intent alphas and other monsters under the bed. "I usually am. I'm a lone wolf. I landed a little work up north, was on my way back. She tracked me down as soon as I crossed the territory line."

Some of that is true. Some of it's the lie he's been using to keep his wolf together for the last six years. I hide a grimace and start applying alpha claws to the part of that story that needs to die. "Lone wolf, huh?"

Cori looks stricken.

He shrugs. "It suits me."

Lie.

Some lone wolves are born, and some are made, and some are the product of bleeding that has nowhere else to go. Bleeding he doesn't know how to stop, because the alternative is wearing the yoke of fidelity and allegiance to pack, and the last time he did that, his alpha put him in a blender and pushed all the buttons.

"I was thinking I'd stay for a bit. Then I'll go, find myself more work." He carefully doesn't look at his mate or his daughter. "Circle back in a while."

"That's bullshit." Rio looks up from whatever tinkering he's doing on his tablet and casts a pointed look at Cori and Jade. "Your wolf will rip you to shreds if you try to leave them."

Ravi shudders. "He'll shred me if I stay, too."

Truth.

Rio just waits, a big, black storm willing to wreak havoc if he needs to.

I don't think he will. I hold my breath, because the most potent storm of all is inching in the direction of the man she loves.

Cori's fingers reach for Ravi's.

He clutches her hand as his face collapses. "I want to come back. For my mate and my baby girl. But my wolf, he's going to have trouble. He's been a lone shifter for too long. He's got a big hate on for alpha wolves, and he doesn't think he needs a pack."

Truth.

I smile at Cori and let her see her alpha's pride. "That isn't a problem."

Ravi's eyes snap up to mine.

I shrug, keeping my body language easy and confident, knowing I'm speaking as much to his wolf as his human. "Whistler Pack deals with screwed-up shifters all the time, so we're going to borrow their system. You'll have two pack buddies. Their specific job is to help you integrate."

Ravi stares at me.

Cori stares harder, and the unspoken question in her eyes is the far more pointed one. I meet it head on. "You and Jade are his reasons for staying. His pack buddies will be doing something different. They'll be working on breaking down his reasons for leaving, and helping him remember the normal stuff about being part of a pack." I grin at her. "That usually involves harassing him a lot, which isn't your job."

That gets me a small smile—from her. Ravi is an entirely different story.

KEL

My turn.

Lissa did the part that only someone innocent of this particular kind of trauma would dare to do and Rio blew away the bullshit and Hayden has drawn the lines he needed to draw. Now Ravi needs to hear from someone who knows what it is to drink from the bottom of the pain bottle.

And if I don't miss my guess, so does the woman sitting beside him, trying to pretend she's not as flayed as he is.

I clear my throat, which is all it takes to have Ravi's eyes jerking my way. Hell is an especially horrible place for submissive wolves. "A friendly warning from a guy who's had a couple of those special pack buddies? They suck. You'll hate their guts and hate their persistence and want to crawl back into the dark and stay there because it's quiet. They're annoying, uncomfortable thorns who will never leave you alone."

His face creases in confusion.

I let him see my pain bottle. "Let them stick."

Ravi's eyes widen.

I nod my head at two guys who are looking way too full of themselves. "Hayden and Rio were mine when I got back from my final Special Forces tour twenty-two years ago. As you can see, I'm still having trouble getting rid of them."

The entire pack stares at me, at what I'm letting them see. I steady my wolf. Sometimes the most important thing we can offer to others is to let them look. I keep my eyes on Ravi. "Trust me, my wolf was at least as fucked up as yours. Still is, some days."

That isn't what he wants to hear. Neither does anyone else who's listening. I can feel Hayden's glare and Rio's sentinel crap trying to dig holes in my skull, but I ignore them both. I get to send this message my way.

"The difference between those days and this one? I trust pack to get me through it."

The alpha glare and sentinel skull-digger abruptly vanish.

I hide a smirk. You'd think those two would learn. Just because I was fucking up an hour ago doesn't mean I'm fucking up now. I aim a pointed glance at our boss wolf. "You didn't mention who his pack buddies would be." My beta brain has several suggestions, but Hayden hasn't asked for them, and he's not the kind of guy who's arrogant unless he's sure. Rio's an obvious choice, but the buddy system at Whistler Pack is living proof that weird and unpredictable work really well.

Hayden smiles, and I have exactly long enough to hear the pin pull out of the grenade. "I was thinking Reilly. And you."

Fucking hell. I try to glare at him, but I can't. My wolf is too damn pleased. Chosen by his alpha and all that crap, which shouldn't work on a hardened asshole like me, but it has, ever since he was ten years old and fucking with my phone.

I can't argue with his other choice either, even though I really want to. A dominant wolf won't work and Reilly and I are both big enough to sit on Ravi if he tries to leave. But that's a hell of a thing to load on a bear cub.

Hayden meets my gaze with that whole boss-alpha look he does far too well. Then his eyes slide sideways to a bear, sitting on a tuft of grass, shaking with the enormity of the job his alpha just laid on his shoulders.

My wolf is moving before my human manages to get

a word in edgewise. I plop down beside Reilly and nudge his bear with my shoulder, hard enough to get his attention. Then I nod my head at Ravi. "What do you think, should we make him do chores first, or take him for a run, or show him the bear-slide game?"

The panic in Reilly's eyes flees with the relief of knowing the right answer. "I can be a slide. Jade loves that."

I grin as pups covered in finger paints all start jumping up and down by the big rock. "You're going to be covered in green and orange handprints, dude."

He sighs philosophically as he swings to his feet. "Paint is better than maple syrup. That really sticks in my fur."

My wolf is on the move again. This time he lands where I can sling an arm around Ravi's frozen shoulders and surreptitiously squeeze Cori's hand while I'm at it. "The hard life of a bear who's the small pups' favorite toy."

Ravi manages to blink. "They slide down his bear?"

I grin. "Yup. Which means we're on catching duty, because they usually don't make it all the way to the bottom." It's an excellent drill for hand-eye coordination, and it also seems like a good way to pin a man down until his wolf gets through his first case of the shakes.

Sadly, it also makes it hard for me to go yell at the guy who gave me this job.

I shoot Hayden a glare as I herd Ravi over Reilly's way, but I don't expect it to make a difference. Twenty-two years ago his mom gave him a job and he's never let it go. He's still pinning my tail to the pack donkey every damn day.

LISSA

I have no idea how we won the water fight.

I stare as Rio, Hayden, and Kel work like a well-oiled machine, so smooth that it almost looks accidental, and neatly run Ravi off at the pass he was trying to leave over. His wolf is entirely disoriented now, stuck in the middle of five bouncing pups who are doing their best to sound like twenty.

The shark squad is gathering behind them, trying to make sure the pups don't pull out too much of Reilly's fur while they're at it.

Pack math does its job and Kelsey pushes Jade to the front of the line. The toddler with her daddy's green eyes giggles and takes hold of a couple of handfuls of Reilly's lush belly fur. My wolf cringes in sympathy, but he assures us it doesn't hurt. It just tickles sometimes, and those moments are a pup favorite. Reilly's whole bear jiggles when he laughs.

Which is why there are five other adults all within arms' reach of his belly. Bear sliding is not for the faint of heart.

Jade works her way over the top of Mount Reilly and points her nose straight down the other side. Ravi gulps and grabs the back of her shirt. "Maybe don't go down face first, sweetie?"

She offers him a cherubic smile. "My like this way."

Myrna pats her bottom. "No way, chickadee. Not unless Reilly's in the water, or you'll get grass up your nose, remember?"

Ravi looks relieved and overwhelmed and several things far more complicated, but he carefully holds Jade's hand as she switches around to come down feet first. Then he has to juggle fast, because Mellie waits for no slow sliders and hurls herself down hot on Jade's heels. Which ends in the predictable pile of two small toddlers sitting on top of one dazed adult wolf who hit the dirt on his way to catching them.

Kel grins down at Ravi. "Nice. I pick you for my baseball team."

Reilly growls.

Kelsey, sitting on the top of the slide with her arms around Braden, giggles. "I think Reilly wants you for his team, Ravi."

I grin. Our version of pack baseball barely remembers it has teams.

Jade bounces on her daddy's belly. "Again."

Mellie, happy to catch a case of exuberance, starts bouncing, too.

One lone wolf, held to pack through the sheer force of gravity.

Hayden and Ebony join me, carefully keeping their dominant selves distant from the playground. I shake my head ruefully. "I would have tried something silly like talking to him."

Hayden shrugs. "The time for that will come."

Probably. Ravi was a good talker once, a deep thinker who helped me find my way more often than I probably remember.

Ebony eyes her alpha. "That buddy system is pretty smart."

"It's genius," he says quietly. "And my mom pulled it out of pure thin air."

I take a moment to thank the universe for the staggering depths of Adrianna Scott's compassion. And for the son she passed it on to, because he might not take credit for the man he is, but his pack needs to not let him get away with that.

I brush my fingers against his.

Ebony's gaze flicks to my fingers and away again. "Kel's mad you assigned him."

I study the guy joking with Ravi about cannonball pups. "He's perfect for this. And he'll be great at helping Reilly figure out what to do."

Hayden chuckles. "Other way around. Reilly's going to be leading this gig by sunset."

We both stare at him.

He shoots our bear cub a fond look. "It's not skills or experience or a level head that make for a good buddy. It's persistence and faith. Pack buddies don't teach. Their job is to be contagious. That's why Kel is trying to be mad. He doesn't think he has enough faith for the job."

We're both still staring. Ebony finds her words first. "Faith?"

He smiles. "What does Reilly believe, right down to his bones?"

It's my wolf who finds the answer. "Pack matters. Kindness is a strength. Pups who have good dads are really lucky."

Ebony nods slowly. "You're a really smart alpha, Hayden Scott." Her eyes travel to me. "That's good. Someone needs to be able to keep up with Lissa."

My wolf blinks.

Ebony grins at me. "I didn't know you had this in you, honestly. But I'm really glad you do."

Hayden snorts and wraps an arm around my shoulders. "Head rabble rouser?"

I squirm. "That's Myrna's title."

Ebony looks up at the sky and pretends to think. "Criminal mastermind?"

Good grief. "I only robbed a bank once."

Hayden catches a streaking white wolf and tumbles him onto his back. "Mama to trouble?"

Robbie yips, perfectly happy to accept any title that comes with belly rubs.

Ebony laughs. "Ringleader of chaos?"

I shake my dazed, confused head and try not to be amused.

I'm just an ordinary wolf.

20

LISSA

I tuck the last of the dry dishes away in the cupboards near the sink and look around. I'm on dish duty alone tonight, which took some doing, but I wanted time to think. To prepare for the two conversations I need to have. I'm still not feeling ready, but there's only so long I can hide behind soap bubbles, at least if I want to keep feeling like a pack grown-up.

Which seems so much safer than the titles Ebony and Hayden were inventing. I'm just an ordinary wolf trying to help her pack—but what's inside of me right now doesn't feel ordinary at all.

I turn off our makeshift lights and raid the cookie jar on my way out of the kitchen. They're peanut butter, which makes my wolf start drooling.

I promise her one if she lets me do the talking.

She lies down, nose on her paws, and pouts. She loves peanut butter.

I smile. It was good and brave and right that she wanted to bring Jade's daddy home, and now she needs to let me take care of some of the details that wouldn't occur to a wolf, but that are sitting heavy on my human heart.

She puffs out a sigh. She's not a fan of talking, but she understands my need to do it, and she definitely thinks it beats hiding behind soap bubbles.

I walk through the dark and the sounds of pack having the most ordinary summer's evening we could manufacture on short notice. I hope it's helping. Ravi's wolf settled a lot after bear-slide duties, but the way Kel's been watching him, it probably won't last.

Somewhere in my soap-bubbles meditation, I got okay with that. We'll just keep inviting Ravi home until it sticks.

I look around as I get back to the bend in the river. Cori is sitting with Eliza, watching the antics of the pups, who are all up on a log that stretches out over the water, dropping twigs and leaves into a small current. It's an activity Reilly started as a science project, but it's turned into an excellent way to settle pups in the evening.

I smile as Robbie and Reilly set two twigs in the current right next to each other. He really is a contagious bear, and a wonderful friend to my son. He's also casting careful looks over at the far side of the river where two men sit in the shadows. A bear taking his new pack-buddy duties very seriously.

I angle toward the log, intending to leave the guys in

the shadows alone, but Kel motions me over. I wade through the shallows, enjoying the feel of the cool water on my bare feet. I have shoes somewhere, but I love the parts of the year when I don't need them.

Kel sniffs as I approach. "Did you bring enough for the sentries? I'm about to do a circuit, and they like me better when I come bearing gifts."

I grin. "Maybe. Ravi eats a lot of cookies."

Ravi snorts, which clearly astonishes him. Then he gathers himself inward again. "I'm fine without. Dinner tonight was wonderful."

It took way too long to convince him that spaghetti and meatballs are no longer a scarce pack resource. I sit down on the warm ground Kel just vacated and pull two cookies out of my sack. I hand the rest to my poker-faced beta. I can always go raid Shelley's cookie jar if we need more.

Ravi sits taut and still beside me, a man clearly torn.

I wave a cookie under his nose. His wolf is a total sucker for peanut butter. "Shelley dispenses happiness in cookie form, remember? She'll be really cranky if you don't eat some."

His eyes fill with something that doesn't need to run away. "Does she still make the ones with the candied walnuts that make you sneeze?"

Guh. I wrap my arms around his neck and cling like a monkey. "I've missed you so much." He rarely made it any closer than the far reaches of Bailey's turf, and with Robbie unable to shift, I rarely made it out that far.

He sighs into my ear. "Missed you too, runt."

I huff out a laugh as I let him go. "I got bigger."

He grins at me. "So I can see."

I take a bite of my cookie and glare at him until he does the same. He chews and swallows, and then his wolf wriggles like Robbie the first time he tasted strawberries. I laugh. "I should have sent some with Ghost."

He makes a wry face. "They might have made her job easier."

I lean against him companionably. "I'll keep that in mind in case you take off and we need to collect you up again."

Air whooshes out of him like I punched him in the gut. There's a long, slow pause as he eases his way back into breathing. "It matters. That you'd come find me."

There's the Ravi I remember. The one who knows how to cut to the very heart of what's important. I take another bite of my cookie. "We would. So if things ever get hard enough inside you that you need to leave, know that it's okay to go. You can run and your pack will come for you."

Silence, but I can feel his wolf struggling beside me, torn between a desperate urge to head for the hills and a violent need to stay. I don't know if I can help, but I need to try. Leaving will feed the wrong parts of his soul. I lay a hand on his arm. "Talk to me."

He swallows. "The worst part is looking at the little girl I didn't know I had and imagining what she lived through. Cori was here too, but she's so strong inside. Jade's just a baby. When I look at her, the guilt nearly drowns me."

I know that guilt—and the corrosive helplessness that lives underneath it. I rescue the cookie he's turning into dust and reach for the dark ooze that still tries to slime me far too often. "Has anyone told you how Samuel died?"

His whole body shudders beside me. "No."

"It was the day Robbie finally shifted for the first time." A memory that rakes claws over my soul, but pebble throwers don't get to stand on the water's edge and ignore the ripples of pain they've caused. "He was this adorable little white wolf, but it turned out he'd been hiding a big secret."

Ravi nods slowly. "He's really dominant. Cute as all get-out, but my wolf definitely noticed."

I close my eyes. "So did Samuel. He took one look at Robbie and dragged us both off to the woods." I won't have to tell Ravi why. "Hayden showed up just as Samuel charged."

A hushed, horrified curse.

I wrap my arms around my ribs, trying to hold steady. "We were going to die because I didn't leave the pack in time to keep Robbie safe." I pause and get out the part he really needs to hear. "And because I'm not a wolf who can use my teeth and claws to protect my child."

Pain blazes in Ravi's eyes.

I know that pain. It still haunts me in a way that I'm just beginning to understand won't ever truly go away. "I know what it is to have had a pup in danger. I know what it's like to feel every kind of helpless that I couldn't protect him, and to want to puke every time I look at him even though I love him so very much. I know how awful it is to sit for hours in the dark and question every choice I've ever made." I take a shaking breath. "I also know how hard it is to stop feeling all those things."

His fingers find my shaking, cold ones.

I hold on tight. "But if we keep thinking like that, Samuel wins."

He turns his head to stare at me.

"He wins if we keep believing like that, Ravi. Even if he's dead." I push the words out because I so need to say the ones that come after. "Our wolves have strength. So much strength. Just not that kind. We need to use the kind we have and make that matter. It's the only way to stop feeling so awful and so weak."

He studies me for so long I start to wonder if I'm accidentally speaking a foreign language. Then he smiles slowly, like every muscle on his face has to figure out what to do. "That's what you did. When you sent Ghost to find me."

I grimace. "That might be a bad example."

His head cocks, his wolf curious.

I sigh. His wolf might understand. My human is still really fretting. "You and Cori are good, smart, loyal people who deserve the right to make your own choices in your own time. I didn't let you do that."

His chuckle is as rusty as his smile. "Still thinking things to death, huh?"

I smile at the man who spent most of his life being my big brother. "Kind of, yeah."

He lifts his free hand and ruffles my hair, just like he used to do when I was small. "You did good, Liss. I know my wolf's having a really hard time, but he was having a hard time out there, too." He looks over at the log where a sleepy Jade is nestling in against Kennedy's side. Then he looks at Cori, and the sigh that comes out of him is laced with a thousand shades of remorse and pain and love.

I lean in a little more and hold up the crumbled remains of his cookie.

He huffs out a laugh—but he picks up a few of the crumbs and eats them.

BAILEY

She's an idiot. She might be my best friend, but sometimes Lissa literally cannot see past the end of her own nose. Especially when it's trying to stick itself into all the guilt in the universe.

I shouldn't be here. It's a dumbass idea because the new alpha isn't blind and neither are his betas and at least one of them has to be expecting me, but my wolf wouldn't let me stay away, and now I know why. It's always been my job to punch things that try to make Lissa less, even if it's her own overdeveloped sense of guilt.

I have a few things to say to the guy she's stuffing full of cookies, too.

Of course they're peanut butter. The universe can be vindictive that way.

I take another good sniff around. Then I shift and pull on the oversized t-shirt and leggings I had slung over my shoulders. I don't care about being naked, but the nights are starting to hold the first hints of coming fall, and getting cold too easily is one of the weaknesses I've never been able to overcome.

I step out of the shadows, easing in behind the two I've been spying on. "Hey, guys." I keep my voice low. We're downwind, but if either of them sound an alarm, the claws of hell will arrive in an instant.

Lissa whirls. "Bailey?"

I snort at her quietly hissed greeting. She sounds more astonished than if a cute prince suddenly showed up in her forest. Although that's pretty much what happened. Hayden Scott is as close as shifters get to royal progeny.

At least he's not a dick about it. "Stick your eyes back in your head. I heard Ravi came back." Word of his arrival landed in my camp like thunderous, awed dynamite. I look carefully over his shoulder. He's usually fine with my bossy self, but his wolf is pretty spooked. "Your little girl is a sweetheart. She's worth every step of the walk through hell this is going to be for you."

He exhales slowly.

I'm not a nice wolf. "Know that if you don't stay, I'll kick your ass every second you have to spend crossing through my turf to get out of here."

Lissa nearly growls. "Let him go if he needs to. We'll keep bringing him back."

Somebody's wolf is getting saucy. I like it. I also have to give unwilling credit to the pack immigrants who are holding space where she can be that kind of wolf. But she still doesn't get to tell me what to do. "Consider me the front lines of sending him back."

I meet Ravi's eyes for a moment. Long enough for him to see the burning intent inside me, because I never would have picked him for this job, but since Lissa did, I'll do everything I can to make it work. "You need to stay. For yourself and for Jade and for Cori, and for all the others out there who are even more fucked up and who dream of coming home."

He swallows hard. "I know."

He does. He roamed the edges of our territory along with all the other ghosts. His human isn't as far gone as some of them, but Samuel did a number on his animal. One I've never been able to make so much as a dent in, but I've never been able to offer what he needs most. I reach out a hand and squeeze his shoulder gently. "I know you think your wolf is weak, but that's a damned lie. They tried to break this pack, Ravi. It still lives because wolves like you refused to stop breathing."

The whimper that leaves him is almost violent.

I'm not quite done. "Now you get to do more than breathe. Don't fuck it up."

Lissa rolls her eyes at me, but there are tears in them. Good. I hope her wolf was listening, too. Idiot submissives. They're the best of us, always, and the ones we fucking assault when we can't handle just how much more important they are.

I throw an arm around her shoulders and hug her fiercely. Time to get out of here before I have to fight my way out.

Her hand grabs mine and refuses to let go. "Stay a minute." Her eyes flick pointedly in Ravi's direction. "I'll be right back."

I stare as she bounces up and runs off. "The heck is she going?"

Ravi chuckles. "No idea, but apparently you're my designated babysitter."

My wolf growls. "Do you need one?" I have to clear out. There's no way the next perimeter check isn't going to find my scent trail, and the pack betas are even more paranoid than I am.

Ravi shrugs a little, but his eyes are worried.

For good reason. His wolf is barely managing to sit still.

Dammit. I'm going to kill him, and then I'm going to kill Liss, even if she comes back with peanut butter cookies. I slink a little deeper into the shadows and try to smell like forest.

I have a really bad feeling about this.

21

LISSA

I don't run. Quite. I don't want to set anyone off, but I don't have much time. I might have pinned Bailey down temporarily, but it won't take her long to figure out how to drop a rock on Ravi's tail so she can bug out.

I stick to the trees. The wolves I'm trying to find all prowl at this time of night.

"Who the hell is she?" Kel slides out of the shadows like he was born from them, his eyes fierce. "Ghost told me to let her through, but she's way too close to the pups. And to a wolf you're supposed to be sitting on."

I hold up my hands in the universal sign of submissive wolves trying to calm flaming hotheads. "She's a friend." Which won't be nearly good enough for him. "My best friend. I vouch for her unequivocally." Well, except for the part where she'll keep sitting on Ravi. That I can't be totally sure of, although she'll probably help us round him up again if he bolts. "Don't spook her, please. There's something I need to go do."

His eyebrows go up. "She's dominant and she breached my perimeter."

Old loyalties crash against new ones. I steady my wolf. They're the same loyalty, even if it's complicated. "She's got reasons for sneaking in. I'm surprised you saw her."

He scrutinizes me with a look I can't interpret. "I saw her cross while I was chatting with Ghost. She's good. I wouldn't have seen her if I hadn't been up that particular tree. I assume she's the reason we have a contingent of sentries with better woodcraft than most Special Forces teams?"

He's dead serious, but I have to smile. "One day, I hope she gets to hear you say that."

He huffs out a sigh. "Go. Do whatever you need to do. I'll keep eyes on her."

Kel and Bailey are two peas from a suspicious pod. Ones who lay down their lives, over and over again, for those they choose to protect. "You can trust her. She doesn't take orders and she doesn't play by the rules and she can be a very pushy wolf, but she would set herself on fire before she caused harm to this pack."

His eyes are on the shadows where she's lurking. "You, I trust. Her, I'll watch. Go. Hayden's in the trees around the other side of the log."

I shake my head. "Do they give betas an extra dose of psychic powers, or something?"

His grunt sounds amused. "There's no greater gift

you can give him than bringing his wolves home. Next time, warn me so I don't rip anyone's throat out."

I wince. "She's not here to stay."

He smiles faintly. "Yet. Hayden can be a really persistent asshole."

I have to laugh. That's pretty much what it's going to take.

Kel sighs. "Tell her to keep her eyes open when she leaves. Shelley and Rio are out for a run, which is the only reason the big, black wolf of death hasn't already crawled up her ass."

I wince again. Teeth and claws can be really touchy, even if they're all on my side. Which means I need to hurry. I fade into the shadows Kel emerged from.

This time, I run.

HAYDEN

I hear her coming, which isn't a huge surprise. The look in Lissa's eyes when she charges out of the trees is, though. She grabs my hand. "I need you to come with me, and I need you to not rip out her throat."

That's not a line I hear often, especially as I'm getting dragged through the woods. I don't resist, though. I'm not sure I could. My wolf is enchanted. The determination emanating from Lissa is some kind of wildly enticing drug.

I shake my head. He's the strangest kind of romantic. "Care to fill me in a little so I can avoid being stupid?"

She yanks us hard left so I don't run into a tree. "Just hurry and don't pick a fight."

I whack my wolf upside the head and tell him to pay attention. Clearly someone is in our woods, and my human nose can't smell anything. "Did you signal the sentries? Or Kel?" Because I'm not nearly the scariest guy in this forest.

"Kel's watching her. She's watching Ravi."

That leveled up fast. I duck under another tree branch that's at just the right height to brain befuddled alphas. "Is it one of the sentries I haven't met yet?" Even as I ask, I know that isn't right. None of them would pick a fight with their chocolate courier.

Or have Lissa this worried.

My wolf whines. I grab her arm. "Shit. A pup?"

She rolls her eyes and keeps dragging me. "Do you really think Kel would just sit there watching if a pup had wandered in?"

Good point, but my wolf isn't listening anymore. He's trying to take over my skin, because the nose I'm giving him to work with is utter crap, but he can smell faint edges of something and it's making him crazy.

Then the wind gusts a little and I get a bigger whiff.

My eyes widen. I know that smell. The sentries carry it sometimes. So do the pups when they come back from the woods. My feet start moving a whole lot faster. A dominant invader Kel hasn't ripped to shreds, and Lissa clearly trusts with her life. There's only one wolf I can think of who fits that description.

The leader of the shadow pack is here.

BAILEY

I smell him coming. Which is completely unnecessary, because my wolf's fur stands on end long before I get a whiff of him.

I grab her in the kind of choke hold that only comes from very painful practice. Just because every dominant male in this territory has been an asshole for the last six years doesn't mean she gets to shred this guy at first sight.

The rumble of her growl shakes me where I sit. She hasn't gotten to shred nearly enough of them. There were always too many innocents to protect.

I gentle my hold as much as I can. In her own way, she's as banged up as Ravi's wolf. Unfortunately for her, she's a lot more deadly, which means she can't sit here and eat cookies and shake. She needs to be in control and she needs to be smart.

Lissa splashes through the shallows, followed by a guy who's somehow managing to give off a pretty good alpha vibe even though he's being dragged along by a woman half his size. Which I have to give him points for. Dominant wolves don't give that kind of permission easily, and I don't feel any resistance from his wolf.

Mine's ready to pounce on him just for the sin of touching Lissa's heart. There's no way he's worthy.

Ravi's fingers brush my arm, which is an act of courage so stark it shocks my wolf into stillness. "He's a good guy. Really good. Don't mess up what he's doing here."

Shit. I rein in my human along with my wolf.

Alpha guy watches me, amused. He's figured out the math too. There's only so much posturing and aggression either of us will let out near pups and traumatized submissive wolves, which means we have to be nice. Something I'm pretty sure he has way more practice at than I do.

He strolls over and sits on the ground beside Ravi.

I'm not fooled. He could be all over me in less than a second, and he's clearly considering it.

Lissa sits down where she can keep an eye on both of us. Smart wolf.

Alpha guy tips his head, giving me permission to exist. For now. "I'm Hayden Scott."

I'm the idiot wolf who got trapped by her best friend. "The new alpha. I know."

Lissa growls.

Fuck. There's nice, and then there's overly trusting and stupid. But there's no way I'm getting out of here without giving him at least a little. "I'm Bailey Dunn. I hang out in the woods."

He studies me for a while. "You're the one who sent us the sentries."

My wolf scowls. She doesn't understand his game,

asking questions when he already knows the answers. "Yes."

He smiles, and it lights up his eyes. "Thank you. They've kept the pups safe during a stretch when we've been pretty short of teeth and claws."

An alpha who offers thanks to an asshole wolf who strolled across his perimeter without asking. An alpha who admits weakness. I blink. This man is a very potent puppy.

Lissa hides a grin. Mostly.

I manage not to bite her head off, but I want to. She's put me at a huge disadvantage, one I never would have chosen for myself. I'm not a wolf who's good at mind games. I'm good at fighting and surviving and keeping scarred wolves breathing, and I have no fucking clue what to do right now. "You're the guy who's been sending food out to us." Not an admission of weakness. Quite.

"Lissa and Shelley and Ebony take care of that." He shrugs, like it hardly matters. Like they hardly matter.

My wolf nearly rips his heart out. Then Lissa's glare lands.

Shit. He's not an asshole. I don't know what he is yet, but I need to behave until I do. "It's appreciated."

Wry amusement hits his eyes, but it's somehow not at my expense. "Do you need more?"

I don't want to answer that. Any answer tells him far too much, but those eyes are doing a number on my need to rip things to shreds, and I don't have anything besides words I can use as a shield. Not if I want Ravi's wolf to stop bleeding anytime soon and my best friend to keep speaking to me. I scowl and give him a reply I can live with. "No."

Lissa glares at me again.

Hayden just waits.

My wolf wants to shred things. Any things. Tree leaves. Annoying rocks. Stray assholes. Anything to get rid of this bottled, twisted feeling inside her, but that would be wrong because this guy isn't an asshole and Lissa trusts him and I can't afford to be broken right now. He's offering something I need far too badly. "The wolves who hang out with me, we're good. There are others we could feed, though. If you sent smaller packages."

Yellow-gold ferocity rises in Hayden's eyes.

My wolf claws against my skin. Don't tell him about the ghosts. They're so fragile. So very close to gone. Always, we must protect them. Hide them. Fight for their right to keep breathing—or to die on their own terms.

His eyes never leave mine. Magnificent, gentle eyes, full of implacable demand.

My wolf lunges inside my ribs.

He meets her challenge, fierce and swift.

I suck in a breath. I'm not ready for this.

Lissa reaches for his hand, a single, soft touch that changes everything inside him. I stare as his wolf catches himself in mid-air and wrenches back to the ground.

"B." Lissa's eyes are glued to mine and the raging battle that lives there. Asking the rage to stand down and the trust to stand up and my damn heart to keep beating in the name of goodness and softness and light, even when it hurts so much I can hardly stand it.

A fight she's taken on for six years.

The only reason I'm not a ghost in my own woods.

My rage finds its exit valve. Lissa trusts this man. She brought him one ghost, and Ravi might be a quivering mess beside me, but he's here and he's got a chance and maybe, just maybe, I need to not rip into the guy who just asked how he can help.

Hayden's wolf eases a little. Slowly, letting mine adjust. Holding the careful balance between us so that two aggressive, dominant tempers can get themselves back under control without either of us needing to start a fight the next time we meet.

It's far harder than it should be.

My wolf is way too scared about what might happen if we don't fight.

Which is the kick I need to finally get my human arms back around her neck. I don't take my eyes off Hayden Scott. I can't, no matter how gracious he is, because he's the first wolf I've ever met who could pound mine into sand, and that has every instinct I have priming for battle.

A hand strokes my back. Ravi. Idiot wolf. I could take a huge bite out of him right now and barely notice.

Lissa's eyes are full of love and certainty that I would never do that.

I huff out a breath that admits far more than I want it to and dip my chin at Hayden. Not in submission—my wolf would never tolerate that. In apology. In embarrassment. I never should have let that happen. I don't lose control. Ever. There's too much at stake.

His hand reaches out, slowly and calmly, and settles on my shoulder. "What should we send?"

I know he's spoken words—I just don't know what they are. All I can feel is the message in his touch. The warmth in his fingers touching the armor I've worn for six years and acting like it doesn't exist. Like it doesn't matter. Like he can hold its weight for as long as I need so that I can take a breath.

My wolf trembles. She has no idea how to do that.

He lets the weight settle again on my shoulders. Gently. With a message of gratitude for carrying it.

My wolf lurches.

He knows. He gets it. He sees me.

He's *proud* of me.

"Human food." Ravi's fingers scrunch up the knees of his ratty jeans. "We should send human food. To help their wolves remember."

I stare like someone who's just landed fresh from an alien abduction.

Lissa's hand finds mine as she smiles at him. "You know what some of their favorites are. Maybe you can help Shelley put some packages together."

Hayden's voice adds to the conversation. Honoring Ravi. Including his wolf. Smiling at Lissa, clearly adoring her. Supporting a simple conversation about food and deftly not asking about the wolves he can obviously feel.

I cling to Lissa's fingers.

I had no idea.

He *knows*. About all of us. I can feel his awareness, his intent, his certainty, streaming through the hand that still rests on my shoulder. We're all his wolves. The broken ones, the ghosts, the ones so full of rage they can barely see straight.

All of us.

My heart tries to lurch. It can't give him what he wants. There's too much left to do.

His touch eases. He'll wait.

I hear a shaky breath. It takes far too long to realize it's mine.

Holy fuck.

LISSA

I have no idea what he's done, no idea at all—but for the first time in six years, Bailey's wolf isn't fighting.

She's listening.

I drink in the miraculous sound of Bailey's heart, beating naked and uncovered. Then I sit up straight, because even before Samuel turned these forests into the pits of hell, she's never been able to handle being that kind of vulnerable without consequences.

And all of Bailey's consequences come with fists.

I know we just did something huge and sacred and important, and if we can work with her to reach the ghosts, maybe the terrible weight on her shoulders will finally ease just a little and she'll be able to breathe. I want, so very fiercely, to be able to give her that, and I want the man sitting so steadfast and calm at my side to have his wolves come home.

But first I need to make sure nobody gets punched in the nose.

I run my hand along Hayden's forearm, because Bailey's wolf is way beyond words, and his might be, too. We need to get this back to safe ground, and for her that means a way to bug out while looking like the tough warrior she's always needed to be.

His fingers find mine and squeeze.

My wolf relaxes—and then she jerks, because he's not easing off at all. He's pulling me in somehow, into whatever magic soup he's pouring down Bailey's throat.

She stares at him. At me. At him.

She growls.

His wolf rises—at my back.

Bailey's eyes widen.

My wolf flails.

I hear the laughter of his wolf. The certainty. The trust.

I shake my head, but that's a human answer. My wolf is already straightening, her eyes blazing with pride. Her alpha has asked her to speak for pack. She gathers everything—strength and patience, fear and trembling, resilience and hope—and holds it out. Offering the bonds of pack.

Bailey trembles, a wolf utterly undone.

Her fingers slide out of mine, shocked, numb.

Her eyes stare, blank and fierce, as she takes one slow

step backward, then another, never taking her eyes off the monstrous threat sitting cross-legged beside me.

The shadows close in around her.

Hayden holds absolutely steady beside me as she vanishes.

Ravi whimpers, his wolf thoroughly confused.

Mine isn't. She knows exactly what just happened, no matter what it looks like and no matter what the woman currently fleeing through the woods is trying to tell herself.

Bailey Dunn just took her first step home.

22

LISSA

I don't have to find Cori. She finds me, right after the pups leave for a romp in the woods, with Reilly in the lead and Rio and the betas herding stragglers at the back and Ravi in the middle with Jade wrapped around his neck like a monkey.

Something about giving all the moms a break.

I shoot Cori a wry look as she sits beside me and sets down a pile of the pillows she's working on trimming. "Is your wolf okay with this?" Motherhood is a strange journey of way too much and never enough, and Jade is rarely out of her sight.

She makes a face. "Maybe. I'm not sure. Eliza went with them."

Sister wolves. That will help. I reach for pins and one of the pillows. I can't sew to save my life, but I can put pins in approximately the right places. The trim she's adding is red and shiny and feels a lot like wolf fur. My hand pets it instinctively, which is probably the point. "I should have asked you before I sent Ghost after Ravi. I'm sorry I didn't."

She shoots me a surprised look. "You're kidding, right?"

I sigh. I'm really not. "You've spent so much of your life not having choices, and I took a really big one away from you."

Her head tilts as she threads a needle. Thinking. "Maybe. But I wasn't making it. I've spent so long hiding. I think I maybe needed someone who could see what I needed. And Jade, too."

I squirm. Sometimes walking the line between human needs and wolf ones is really tricky. Wolves wouldn't need to have this conversation. The part of me that believes in consent and freedom and self-determination really does. "I still should have asked."

Her smile is slow and sad. "I don't know if I would have given you the right answer."

I pin silently, honoring her courage and her pain the only way I know how. I spent the last six years in hell. She's basically spent her whole life there, and somehow she's still the kind of person who wants to sew shiny red fur onto pillows because it will make other people happy.

She exhales softly. "I'm glad he's here."

I close my eyes. I wasn't seeking absolution, but she's granting it anyhow. "I wanted him here for me, too. He's a really good guy. He makes our pack stronger."

She makes a face. "It might take him a while to believe that."

That's true of every single one of us. "It's hard. Realizing how much we matter."

Her eyes dart to mine, surprised. "You've always mattered. We would have all gone crazy without you here. Or starved. Myrna swears you have a spell for turning earthworms into grocery money."

That would have made things so much easier. "We would have been wearing earthworm skins if it weren't for you and your sewing needle."

Her nose wrinkles as she pretends to scoot away. "Eew. That's disgusting."

I contemplate a pillow covered in lime-green googly eyes and snort. "Who knows where these eyes came from?"

The giggles squirt out of Cori so fast she can't catch them.

I close my eyes, trying to hold back the sudden tears, because I don't think I've heard that sound from her, ever. It does something to the guilt inside me that a waterfall of words couldn't. Even with everything that's ravaging her and her mate—she can laugh like that. She can let us see the person she is underneath the solemn, laced-up caution she's always worn like a cloak, and she can dare to let a small moment of happiness really touch her.

My wolf has a shorter version.

That giggle means we did a good thing.

Which means I need to get over myself. Preferably

before I have to figure out how to attach googly eyes to a pillow.

Cori's knee nudges against mine. A very tentative touch from her wolf, which isn't something I'm used to either. "Was Bailey really here last night?"

I roll my eyes. "I can't believe she thought she could sneak in here without everyone noticing."

Cori strokes the bright green velvet of the pillow she's working on and smiles. "She came for Ravi."

She did—but as I lay in the dark last night staring up at the stars, I decided maybe she came most of all for herself. Not that she'll admit that anytime before the next ice age, especially after the whammy Hayden put on her wolf. I pin red fur trim to wide-wale corduroy, which is an oddly appealing mix. "Everyone's focusing on Ravi. How are you?"

She blinks. "You're usually more subtle than that."

I laugh. "I volunteered to help you with sewing this morning. I figure subtle is kind of a lost cause." I like sewing about as much as Robbie likes broccoli.

Cori grins down at her pillow. "Maybe. Ravi said you'd dig it out of me, so I might as well just talk to you."

It unclenches some of the tight places inside my gut to know they're having that kind of conversation. "I learned from the best. Ravi was usually the one who would come find me and dig out whatever was bothering me."

A small sigh, one full of wistful memory. "When we first came here, he sat down and tried to talk to me. I never talked to anyone ever, so I tried to ignore him. It took him less than ten minutes to have me spilling all my secrets."

Sweetness and sadness reach up and try to choke me.

Her knee nudges mine again. "I felt a little bit of that guy last night. After Bailey left."

I push sadness to the side and reach for the sweetness. "That's good."

"It's hard. I don't know what to say and I don't know how to help him, or me, either." Cori's eyes squeeze shut as the words pour out. "I just want to grab him close and never let go, and then I wake up the next morning and I'm all tense and stressed and I just want my space."

My hands reach for her back. Her hair. Stroking. Soothing. Trying to figure out what to say when I have no idea, when I have far too much of that same push and pull still living inside me. I try to think of what I read online about trauma and stages of grief, but it all feels far too complicated.

Then I realize our wolves, their cheeks nuzzled together, have a far simpler answer. "I'll pass on some really smart advice someone recently gave to me. Listen to your wolf."

The stiffness in her spine eases a little.

I try to let some of my own go, too. "They have good instincts and sometimes they can see answers when our humans can't."

She leans into my hug. "It's hard to hear her sometimes."

My wolf snorts.

I ignore her. She needs to take some days off in between throwing boulders around.

She doesn't say anything. She just pulls up the memory of Cori's eyes when Ravi walked out of the woods.

I sigh. In my next life, I want a nice, well-mannered, patient wolf.

She swishes her tail impatiently.

I tug on the ends of Cori's hair, calling gently on her wolf. "What was your first reaction when Ravi showed up? Before all the worry and hard thoughts landed?"

Her smile is achingly vulnerable and real. "I was so happy, Liss. My heart nearly split in two."

I blink hard and hug her fiercely. "Hold on to that. Give your human time if she needs it, but let what your wolf knows hold you steady."

She huffs out a slow breath. "When did you get so wise?"

My wolf snorts again.

Troublemaker. "I feel like I'm flailing most days. I think that's kind of how this life thing works."

Cori studies me for a long time. "What was your first reaction to Hayden?"

I make a face. "What happened to shy Cori who never sticks her nose in other people's business?"

She shrugs a little, but there's mischief in her eyes—and another peek at the woman she might become if hope and love stick around.

I don't want to go back to that day, but she deserves at least that much from me. I take a deep breath and let myself remember the crazed adrenaline and abject fear and the horrible, echoing emptiness where my wolf used to be. The surreal, jittery, teeth-chattering moment when my eyes first struggled to focus on the man who just saved us—the one lying on the ground, naked and pale, while his friend tried to stop the bleeding.

But that's what my human remembers.

My wolf has a different memory entirely. Wounds and blood and fear are part of life, and he was so much more than that.

Warm.

Strong.

Sexy.

Safe.

I sigh quietly. "My wolf passed out for most of the fight. When I opened my eyes again, Hayden was lying on the ground. Kel was doing field first aid on his leg and shoulder and asked me to help. To touch Hayden. To keep him warm."

Cori's eyes are wide and solemn.

"I should have been terrified. I was. But not of him." I swallow. She'll know exactly how much the next words mean. "I felt safe."

She sighs, as quietly as a falling leaf, and smiles down at her hands. "That's how Ravi made me feel when I first met him. Maybe that's what I can give back to him now. Maybe it's that simple."

There's nothing simple about feeling safe and nothing simple about giving it, either. But she's not really looking for simple. She's looking for a way to sit quietly with her heart as she walks alongside a man who's trying to make his way home.

A journey we're all on. I offer an apology to my wolf. I didn't want to remember. I didn't want to see.

She nuzzles inside me. Contentment. Forgiveness.

She deserves more than that, but first we have another pebble to toss. One my human came up with so that she doesn't get totally left in the dust.

My wolf smirks. Her paws are fast.

Definitely a troublemaker. I pat the laptop I brought with me and channel my inner bank robber. "Want to shop for a guitar?"

Cori tilts her head like a perplexed owl.

I open the screen. "I found a shop near Whistler that sells second-hand instruments. They have a lot of their inventory online."

She squints at me, still confused.

My wolf grins. She likes this plan. "They have guitars. Ones we can afford. And we know lots of hawks who will deliver for jam."

Wild, soft hope hits Cori's eyes—and then she locks it down behind the caution that's been her shield the entire time I've known her. "He'd be really mad if we spent pack money on him."

I'm a far smarter bank robber than that. "We're not. We're spending it on pack. Wolves love music. You know that."

Cori blinks slowly, an owl suddenly dumped into bright sunshine.

I double down on wild, soft hope. Our instincts are so

much smarter than our doubts. "How much better will our campfires and lazy afternoons by the river be with some guitar playing?"

It takes a really long time—but the smile that finally takes over her face is breathtaking. "Yeah, that will work. That will totally work."

I elbow her. "Of course it will. What, you think I'm new to this bribery stuff? The other day I told Rio that we needed more candy because otherwise the pups won't eat any because they're trying to save it all for him."

She huffs out a tiny laugh. "He fell for that?"

Possibly only because Kelsey was listening with bright, laughter-choked delight, but I'm sticking with my story. "Absolutely."

Cori shakes her head, but there's merriment in her eyes.

I open up the webpage I bookmarked earlier. "There are some really ugly, beat-up ones in our price range that supposedly sound pretty good."

She grins at me and we lean our heads in together, peering at the laptop screen and scanning rows of guitars that mean almost nothing to us, but will mean everything to the guy we're shopping for.

A small hand reaches in and points at a hot-pink child's guitar. "I like that one."

I look down at Kelsey, who has somehow wiggled in between us, holding a clutch of posies.

She slides into Cori's lap and holds up the flowers. "I picked these for you. You can give them to Ravi. He likes flowers."

Cori's eyes glisten as she takes the small bouquet of wildflowers. "Thank you, sweetie. I thought you went for a romp with all the other pups."

Kelsey shakes her head, her eyes on the laptop screen. One pack psychic, entirely tuned in to the important stuff. "What do they do?"

It kicks me somewhere really hard. She's never seen a guitar. Never heard one. This child who loves music, who sings it from the most precious parts of her soul, has never sat on a river bank on a lazy night with Ravi's quiet fingerpicking wrapping around her heart.

I gulp down the sadness and the guilt and the grief. I'll save those for what can't be changed. This can, and we can do it in a couple of days. I smile at Cori and reach for the keyboard, already rearranging budget lines in my head.

One battered guitar and one hot-pink one, coming right up.

23

LISSA

I reach into the basket of clean laundry beside me and fold a small, berry-stained t-shirt, watching the pups play with their alpha. They came back from their romp chattering and full of energy, but most of them are mellowing out now, cuddling in to Hayden's side or licking his nose, or in the case of my son, chasing the yellow-gold tail that keeps helpfully thumping.

I wince as sharp teeth manage an interception. I know just how sharp they are.

"I'll deal with this." Rio sits down beside me and pats the clean clothes. "You go do something fun."

Clean laundry on a sunny day isn't exactly drudgery. And it was nicely reinforcing my ordinary-wolf status. "I'm good."

He grins and pulls the laundry basket out of my reach. "Now you're better. Go."

I shake my head. "We all have pack chores."

He rolls his eyes. "Yo, Kel. Make Lissa go do something fun."

Kel, walking by holding a bunch of really ancient wiring and something that might be a shower head, just snorts.

I contemplate making a grab for the basket, but Rio's wolf could squish mine flat without even trying hard. Which means I need to be smarter. Or sneakier. Or I could just let him fold laundry and find something else to do. My wolf looks over at the magnificent yellow-gold creature sprawled on the ground with pups climbing all over him. She has ideas.

I roll my eyes and watch as my son, tired of tail chasing, tries to nuzzle in next to Hayden's cheek.

A big nose gently pushes him in the direction of the other pups.

Robbie, about as easily deterred as a storm wind in winter, tries again.

The nose patiently returns him to the pup pile.

A fuzzy white pup stays where he's put this time. Quiet. Smelling the reticence my wolf has scented, too. She watches, wary, confused. One of the pups often gets a special cuddle. Why not hers?

Rio's hand brushes my shoulder, but his eyes are also watching.

I make myself take a breath, and another one, pushing away the stories trying to invade. None of them are true, no matter what the last six years want me to believe. Hayden has been nothing but kind and patient and accepting of Robbie, and I won't believe anything less is true now. Something else is going on.

Something that was happening the other day, too.

I look at Rio, a silent question in my eyes.

He tips his head down. A sentinel, holding secrets. Keeping them safe.

I stare at my son, and at the yellow-gold wolf lying quiet and somehow distant in the sun, and wonder just what I haven't seen.

Golden eyes meet mine, and I imagine I see guarded sadness there.

My wolf tugs at me.

I make it to my feet—and spy Ebony, looking straight at me with a question written all over her face and a box in her hands.

Reticence flees Hayden's wolf and attentive alpha lands instead.

I sigh. More ripples, coming home to roost.

Ones with really sucky timing.

HAYDEN

When Ebony walks over and hands me the simple wooden box, I don't expect it to flatten my wolf.

It does, with all the force of one of Kennedy's roundhouse kicks.

It's filled with food. Wild foraged, all of it. Which means it can only have come from one place.

I close my eyes. We sent our first delivery of small packages out to the shadow pack yesterday. Carefully prepared offerings of food that can't be easily found in the woods. This is so very obviously their reply. Delicacies, especially for those of us who have consumed a few too many hot dogs and marshmallows lately. And who've been holding back on raiding the berries close to the den so they get left for the pups.

My wolf knows the box isn't a trade or a pay-off or a gift. It's something far more basic and important than that. Pack providing for pack.

A bunch of faraway wolves, turning their paws toward home.

I look over at Lissa, but she's hanging back. She's maybe got reasons. She didn't miss what my wolf just tried to do with her son and neither did Robbie, and that's a conversation we need to have, but alphas don't always get to pick the order they deal with things, and this box is fiercely important. I don't get to fuck it up because my wolf is having wildly inappropriate yearnings.

I inhale deeply, collecting the scents of pine and nuts and berries and wolves I haven't yet earned the right to know. I don't ask if they can spare the food, even though it nearly kills me. The underground management in this pack doesn't deserve that kind of disrespect. Instead, I gather my focus and scrape my wolf up off the ground and tell him to get his shit together.

There's only one right way to respond to this, and it isn't with words.

The box is lined with pungent greens I don't recognize. One corner holds a rough wooden bowl filled with nuts. My eyes widen. "There are hazelnuts in our territory?"

"Some." Ebony smiles. "Ghost Mountain has lots of secrets."

It also clearly has lots of berries. The rest of the box is overflowing with them, at least four different kinds. I close my eyes as my mouth waters and my wolf swoons. It's not a tasty bunny snack, but he's been along for the ride when I've hunted berries in every nook and cranny of Whistler Pack's territory. He knows they're my kryptonite.

Something I need to let my pack feel today. I've had lots of good, pup-sized reasons to keep the full extent of my berry obsession hidden. This box vetoes all of them.

The ones who sent it deserve to know just how well they've aimed.

The first berry I try is a wild strawberry, an old friend that delights my tongue and makes me really sad there aren't acres more of them. The next is a huckleberry, and if there's a decent supply of those somewhere, Ronan has just become our very best friend. The third isn't a berry I know. It's round and plump and a deep, juicy purple that tastes like bottled summer. Something far too close to a whine sneaks out of my throat. "Please tell me the pups hate these."

Ebony's chuckle comes all the way from her toes. "Sorry. I can't lie to my alpha."

Damn. I swallow and stare forlornly at the few berries left in my hand.

The sound that comes out of my fierce, sturdy beta is almost a giggle. "We call them sun berries. They're some kind of mutant huckleberry that only grows in this area. I think the cats have some on their land, too."

If Ronan finds out about these, this pack will end up with two bears.

It's not a very big box. I can't be a greedy wolf. "We should make some pancakes." That way maybe I'll be able to behave. Another two minutes of this kind of torture and I'm going to eat the whole box. I wasn't all that steady when it arrived, and the sun berries are fiercely eroding what little maturity I have left.

Ebony snorts. "They were delivered with instructions." She winks down at the small girl who's magically appeared at her side. "Right, Kels?"

Kelsey nods, her eyes solemn. "They're for you."

I can't eat a whole box of berries while the pups watch. Except it's suddenly really obvious that's exactly what the shifters who sent it intended. Which means they're devious and evil and know me far too well for comfort.

I man up as much as I can and whimper at my beta instead of an innocent four-year-old. "I can't eat them all."

She snorts.

I hear a scuffle behind me. It doesn't surprise me that it's Reilly, or that he's holding up the pack sat phone. "Could you make that face again?" He shoots me a pleading look. "I tried to get a picture but it happened too fast and the people who picked the berries really want to see it."

It's not hard to replicate. I pick out two more sun berries as my reward, and then I try to hand the box back to Ebony.

She gives me a look that says if I fuck this up, I'm going to discover just how badly she can beat me up when she's really trying.

Dammit. I look around for Kel, or Rio, or anyone who understands why I need to be rescued. All I see is a sea of happy, expectant faces—and a green-eyed wolf with a bemused smile. One that somehow sees the hurts and wishes and longings of the small boy I sometimes still am, no matter how much growing up I've tried to do.

Reilly snaps another photo, dancing from one bare foot to the other, a reporter delighted by his latest scoop. I sigh and give in to the absolutely inevitable force that's just applied itself to my life. If I'm going to be front-page news, I might as well make it good. "When I was Mellie's age, I once went for a whole six months when I wouldn't eat anything but berries."

His eyes widen. "Really?"

I nod solemnly. "Ask my friend Ronan. He can tell you all my embarrassing berry stories. I ate so many wild strawberries once that my mom thought I might turn into one."

Reilly's eyes gleam. "Does Ronan know any more embarrassing stories?"

Oh, about a hundred editions' worth. And I'm sure he'll

be happy to share all of them, especially if he gets to talk to our resident bear while he's reminiscing. My wolf sighs. The things he does for his pack. "A few. Ask him about the time I gave a basket of blueberries to a girl I liked. She was allergic. They made her itch from her ears to her toes."

Ebony somehow manages not to bust up laughing, but it's a close thing. "I think gossip is Myrna's column. Reilly here does serious journalism."

Reilly clears his throat solemnly. "I could make an exception."

I shoot one last pitiful look at Ebony before I give in and cuddle the box to my chest. "I still want pancakes."

Her lips twitch, probably because her alpha sounds like a petulant toddler. "That can be arranged."

Good. So can bribing pups to eat some berries along with their pancakes. That way I won't feel like a total monster. Although given how quietly Braden is hanging out in Miriam's arms, I may have some issues on that front. I scowl. Now is a really bad time for the pack toddlers to develop self-control.

Except that's not really what this is. It's a very bossy, complicated wolf sending me a message, one only a dominant could have delivered. My wolves need to meet their alpha's needs. Which means I have to let those needs be visible.

Claws scratch at my insides. I sigh. My wolf has spent way too much time hanging out with hawks and bears. He likes to hoard his treasures. I look at Ebony. "Once it's empty, can I keep the box?"

Her eyes soften. "Yeah, you can."

I pick out a single sun berry and hold it on my palm. "Are you going to tell me who sent it?"

She snorts. "Do I need to?"

I glance over at my green-eyed wolf, who's still busy trying to look innocent and failing miserably. "No. How much did Lissa have to do with this?"

Ebony pitches her single-word answer so quietly I barely hear it. "Everything."

My wolf rolls over.

Done. He's entirely done. Entirely hers.

She just needs to say when.

LISSA

The pancakes are delicious. Watching Hayden's face as the pups keep bringing stray berries for his plate is even sweeter. We all knew he liked berries. We're discovering this morning just how big his love is, and just how hidden he kept it.

Foolish alpha. This territory has more berries than we could ever eat.

And Bailey will always sniff out a secret.

Kelsey arranges a handful of sun berries into a happy face on the top of Hayden's newly delivered pancake, hot off the griddle. Myrna's been making them in her daddy's frying pan for more than an hour, and she's flatly refusing to share her duties. Which means the rest of us are stuck watching and soaking in our alpha's embarrassed delight.

It's a hell of a warning shot.

Bailey might know which way she's heading now, but she isn't going to make it easy on him. Especially when she sees Reilly's pictures. Which will be very soon. Kennedy showed up right about the time the first pancake came off the griddle, and took off fifteen minutes later with a full belly and a handful of carefully printed photos in her pocket.

I know why Bailey sent Hayden the box, but for her it was a cautious act. A testing one. I don't think she actually expected to shoot an arrow right smack into the most vulnerable parts of him.

It won't be the only one. Bailey doesn't stop battles once she starts them. The skirmishes won't always point forward, because only the pups of this pack seem to know how to reach straight for the sunlight. But she sent the berries and Hayden is eating them with a relish that's amusing every last woman and pup in his pack, and as first skirmishes go, that's about as well as this one could have gone.

Now I just have to find a way to make sure Hayden understands he's in a war. My best friend isn't going to make it home any other way.

That can wait until the berries are gone, though. I snuggle the sticky pup beside me. Robbie's been happily eating pancakes drowning in maple syrup, but he hasn't touched a berry. Even Braden hasn't eaten more than a few. Some things matter even more than sun berries, and watching Hayden come first in this pack for once is apparently one of those things.

Which Bailey clearly knew and the submissive wolves of the den never figured out, and I'll kiss her for it the next time I see her.

Right after I yell. It won't make her be any nicer, but it might make me feel better, or a little less guilty, anyhow. My wolf isn't letting me forget the guarded sadness in his eyes right before the box arrived.

Rio sits down beside us holding a plate laden with gummy bears instead of berries, because he's a very smart sentinel. One who's apparently not letting Hayden wiggle off Bailey's hot seat all that easily, which is interesting. He offers Robbie a sausage and eyes me casually. "I hear she's a friend of yours."

I look down at Robbie's head, but he's busy dipping turkey sausage in his leftover syrup. "She is. That doesn't mean she's going to be gentle with him."

He snorts. "No kidding." He dips one of his sausages in Robbie's syrup. "Are you?"

I blink.

"When Kel came home, he used to sit and watch. Just like you do." Rio's words are casual, but the sudden intensity in his wolf is hard to miss. "He didn't ask questions, he didn't share—he just kept his eyes on everything and everyone."

That hasn't changed. "He still does."

Rio ruffles Robbie's hair as my son offers up a bite of sausage for his big friend. "He talks now, too."

There's a point here, and I'm afraid I'm missing it. "You think I need to talk to Hayden?"

He looks at me and says nothing.

I make a face and try harder.

Rio chuckles and ruffles my hair. "How did it feel earlier today when Cori sat with you and talked and laughed and told you things you already know?"

I side-eye him. "You were romping in the woods with the pups. How the heck do you know that?"

He grins. "Sentinel woo."

Troublesome wolf. I consider sticking my tongue out at him while Robbie's not looking, but then what he said about Cori somehow makes it through my ribs. I stare at green leaves that blur as something inside me rearranges and finds clarity. "Traumatized wolves watch. Healthy wolves talk. They give each other words."

"Not always." Rio casts a fond look down at Robbie. "Sometimes watching is a really important job. But talking can be, too."

I sit there a long moment, trying to figure out what I'm supposed to say to Hayden. My wolf snorts and nudges my brain in the direction it needs to go. "Or asking the right question and listening to the answer."

He offers Robbie his last sausage. "Or that."

Tricky sentinel. I steal two of his gummy bears, green ones that match my eyes, and chew on them as I contemplate all the people who've sent me messages today.

And all the things I want to do with them.

24

HAYDEN

Some days look sunny and innocent on the surface and have hurricane-force winds blowing underneath. This is one of those days. I look up at the hawk winging in from the southern peak she flew over just for kicks, and shake my head. Kendra's capable of stirring up a hurricane all by herself, and she sure as heck isn't going to ignore one already in progress. Not if it's my ass in the wind, anyhow.

Hawk alphas have some really funny ways of showing that they love you.

She's got awkward, easily recognizable packages in both claws, but that doesn't stop her from a landing that would do a fighter pilot proud. She lets her hawk preen for my suitably awed wolves before she shifts into a faded yellow shirt and raggedy denim shorts that don't make her look a feather less deadly.

She grins at the pups first, because hawks are suckers for babies with sharp teeth. Mellie waves her arms, already toddling over for a ride. Kendra squats down to meet her. "Not yet, cutie. I have a couple of deliveries to make first. Then we'll fly."

Mellie plops down on her butt, the pouting of a denied dominant pup warring with innate wolf curiosity. Nobody bothers to intervene. We've had enough hawks fly through in the past few weeks that my whole pack knows they handle bossy pups just fine. Kendra winks and holds up the smaller of the two packages she flew in with. "This is for a special girl who sings the prettiest songs of anyone I know."

Mellie turns, a bossy pup who knows her pack very well.

Kelsey stares at the hawk alpha's knees, her hands twisting in her lap.

Half a dozen submissive wolves stir, but I flash them one of Kel's hand signals. Kendra won't get this wrong. She might be one of the most dangerous women I know, but I've seen her with a baby sparrow in her hands, and the day a mute, traumatized teenager joined her wing.

There are very good reasons she's one of my mother's closest friends.

She sits down on the ground, keeping her eyes carefully averted from a four-year-old who's grappling with the enormity of what just arrived. I see the flicker of empathy in dark hawk eyes and the rapid calculus of an astute alpha. Kendra casually surveys the rest of the gathered wolves until she finds Ravi. "I believe this one's for you." She holds up a guitar case almost as battered as Kel's favorite duffle bag.

Ravi looks utterly terrified, and it's not the hawk scaring him.

Kelsey's eyes fly up, smelling a need bigger than her own.

I send a message through the pack ether, alpha to tiny pack medic, for her to help us ease him where he needs to go.

Her lips curve up.

Rio rolls his eyes.

I ignore him. I didn't set up this delivery. I'm just helping it land. Although I might have to get in line. A juvenile bear is on his feet, walking over to Kendra like he greets hawk royalty every day of the week. He grins at her and swoops up the guitar case.

She shoots me an amused look as he heads straight for his pack buddy.

I ignore her, too. She's got an absolutely deadly bite, but the juvenile hawks in her wing are some of the most empowered shifters I know. She won't find it at all surprising that pups are big players in this pack.

Reilly sets the guitar case down in Ravi's lap, his eyes shining. "I remember. You used to play while we were falling asleep at night. Really pretty songs with no words so we would have good dreams."

Kelsey's eyes light up.

Ravi turns a shade of green that makes my wolf wince. "I haven't played for a long time."

"It won't matter." Shelley shrugs as we all look at her. "Start with something easy. Something for the pups."

Smart wolf. One who's fighting the hard battle against some of her own scars and winning.

Ravi's fingers touch the case and jerk back again.

Kelsey makes a soft sound of distress.

Kendra, who is never a stupid hawk, opens the much smaller case and extracts a hot-pink baby guitar. "This one is yours, cutie. Next time I come, maybe you can play me a song."

Kelsey strokes the small instrument and its magic strings. They vibrate a little, and she murmurs back to them, an awed, incoherent song of pleasure. Then she looks up and offers Ravi a smile that would slay much bigger demons than any of the ones chasing him. "Will you show me how?"

His head nods. Shakes. Nods.

My wolf yips sharply. He can see the looming storm. A wolf who isn't ready for his pack to deliver any more of his dreams.

Lissa and Cori are on their feet, tuned in and frantic.

I catch Lissa's attention and put sharp request in my eyes. They're both so very important to Ravi's journey, but right now I need them to stand down. My wolf knows it, my human knows it, and whatever extra layer of instincts baby alphas are born with knows it absolutely. They set this in motion. Now they need to let claws and teeth have a turn. It's how wolves work. We guard the perimeter. They make what's inside it worth protecting.

Lissa wraps an arm around Cori's shoulders. Kel

joins them, using whatever submissive magic he has to ask them to hold steady and let the dominants of the pack do our small part.

Cori eases. A little.

Lissa stays with her, but my wolf knows that's a very temporary state. Not because she doesn't trust us. Because she stands that fiercely for those she loves.

Ebony plunks down beside Ravi. She doesn't grab him or sit on him or try to block his exits. She does something far more effective. She wraps strong fingers around the neck of his guitar. "If you leave, I will chase your ass down. Just so we're clear."

A growl has us all looking, astonished, at the bear it came from.

Reilly swallows hard, but he doesn't back down. "That's my job."

Ebony's lips twitch. "Fine. *He'll* chase you down."

Ravi's wolf winces.

So does mine. Ebony isn't using wolf dominance, but she's blasting a righteous version of the human kind.

I spare a quick look at Kelsey, but dominants throwing their weight around isn't bothering her at all. She's sitting quietly a few feet away, her head tilted like the hawk beside her, as Ravi's wolf tries to thread an impossibly skinny needle—the one that gets him out of this trap without leaving some of his self-loathing behind.

Kel's eyes are full of empathy. He knows just how hard that is to let go.

He doesn't step into the silence, though.

I have half a breath to think that it might be my turn

before Rio's looming shadow lands on Ravi's other side. He takes a seat and reaches out his hand, touching the road-weary curves of a guitar that's seen a lot of miles. When he speaks, he pitches his words so quietly I have to strain to hear them. "You have a choice. You can be the wolf you think you are, or you can be the wolf your little girl and your mate and your pack need you to be."

Kendra's eyebrows fly up. That's hardball, even for a hawk.

Rio isn't done. "Look at your pup. Look into her eyes and take this one step at a time and know that your pack has your back. But only you can take the first step."

Consent, freely given. Choice. Free will. Sentinels signed on to the Whistler Accord centuries before my mother wrote it.

Ravi vibrates like a string on the battered instrument in his lap.

Now it's my turn, since other than toddlers, we're fresh out of available pack dominants. I clear my throat so he knows where the next attack is coming from. "I ate all the berries."

He stares, confused.

My wolf whines.

I don't care. I'll use every embarrassing life lesson I've ever learned if it helps one of my wolves stay where he needs to be. "It's okay to be greedy sometimes. To take before you give."

Ravi makes the sound of a wolf who was planning on pouring himself out until the end of time and never taking a damn thing.

That's exactly the place submissives go when they're most wounded—and exactly the kind of shit teeth and claws are supposed to kill. "Your pack needs you. It needs your music. It needs you to find the place inside you that knows how to make songs that are heartfelt and real and good." I've never heard him play, but every wolf knows that place. I wink at a small wolf who knows it better than most. "And it looks like Kelsey would like some lessons."

She does her job and launches a moonbeam of a smile straight at a guy who has zero defenses left.

He closes his eyes and lays a hand on beat-up guitar strings. "I don't know if I remember any songs."

"I do." Cori, her eyes shimmering with emotion, sits down beside him. Ebony and Rio, smart wolves that they are, make like dust and get the heck out of the way. "There's one you wrote for me that day we snuck off together."

My wolf aches that there was only one.

She reaches out and strums the strings lightly. "We went to the ridge and watched the lightning and we got all wet, but you played it over and over for me, remember?"

Ravi's breath leaks out of him. "The one about how strong you are."

Her smile could power half the continent, and it's all pointed at one guy. "Yes. That one."

His smile is shaky as hell, but he finds it. "That's not exactly starting me off easy."

She snorts. "You're the best guitar player I've ever known. You don't need easy."

His hand brushes the strings again. They make a small sound this time. Every wolf in the pack leans in, resonating with a language as old as our DNA. "I don't know how to accept this."

Cori huffs out an amused breath. "We got you the ugliest one we could find. It has good sound, though. The guy who owns the store said so. He said it has miles and it's been through a lot, but it knows how to be happy."

There's only one mystic I know who runs a halfway house for beat-up instruments. If Milton says it's a good guitar, it's a great one.

Ravi's fingers seek the strings again, more intentionally this time. He hasn't picked the guitar up yet, but he plucks the strings one at a time. They all sing sweet and true until the last one. My wolf winces. He doesn't have fancy human words, but that one isn't right.

Kelsey scowls at the misbehaving string. Then she plucks at her own small guitar, making a face as the second and third one both crunch against every wolf's sense of what notes belong together.

Ravi smiles, and something inside him changes shape. "We have to tune them, sweetheart. Maybe Reilly can help. It's a big job for small hands."

A bear moves in, always willing to be helpful, and settles Kelsey in his lap. They both look up expectantly. Then their gazes stray, along with every set of eyes in the pack—drawn to the small hands reaching for the neck of Ravi's guitar.

Jade beams at her daddy and lands the knockout punch. "My help too."

LISSA

My wolf wriggles, so happy she can hardly stand it. My human is nearly swamped by the message landing, sharp as pups' teeth. Strings can be tuned. What matters is to pluck them.

I've been so very focused on the awkward landings of my pebbles—and missing all the healing, the strengthening of pack, the resilience that blooms as a string gets adjusted to true. It might even make the music that happens in the end better.

I wrap my arms around my knees as the full weight of that lesson lands, the one that began over a sink of soap bubbles and deepened when we walked out of the bank with a couple of sacks of shiny coins and sharpened when my best friend sent a berry box and I saw little-boy wonder in a grown man's eyes.

Imperfect gifts are still gifts.

My wolf snorts. This one will be a lot better once the music starts and I stop thinking so much.

I shake my head at her, amused. They don't even have both guitars tuned yet. And might not for a while if Jade keeps helping.

Ravi grins as his daughter turns another peg way out of whack. He plucks the string for her and she wrinkles her nose at the sound. "You have to turn it gently, monkey girl."

Reilly's much bigger hands make a delicate adjustment on Kelsey's guitar. She plucks the string like a pro and they both listen carefully. Then they move to the one beside it, listening for the chord the two make together. When those two meet with their joint approval, Kelsey plays the bottom string, looking at Ravi. A small wolf who knows that their notes need to agree.

He plays the same string on his own guitar and reaches to adjust his pegs. Kelsey holds up an imperious hand and shakes her head. Reilly murmurs something and makes minute adjustments to one of the pegs on the hot-pink guitar as she plucks and listens.

Matching Ravi. Insisting that he be the anchor. The home note. The one that shows the rest where they belong.

Jade wiggles her way into her daddy's lap, apparently done with thwarting his efforts to get his guitar in tune. He cuddles her in, wedging her between the guitar and his chest, and plays a pretty melody as his other hand effortlessly adjusts multiple strings.

Reilly stares in awe.

Kelsey elbows her bear, getting him back on task. Ravi plays a light tune that vibrates against Jade's chest, sending her off into giggles that somehow work their way into the song. Mellie climbs into the lap of her favorite hawk and adds some companionable owl hoots that have Kendra rolling her eyes in not entirely mock disgust.

Kelsey slides her finger up and down a string until she finds the note that matches Mellie's hoots.

Ravi responds with a very decent acoustic impression of a hawk's fierce cry. Kendra snorts, but her hands start tapping a beat on her knees.

That's a game I know. I grab some handy rocks and look around for my son, who loves rhythm. He's in Kel's lap, already swaying to the forming beat. Kel, who misses nothing, reaches for a couple of sturdy twigs. Myrna stuffs a pair of pants in a pot to muffle it some and hands over a makeshift drum.

Robbie grins. He's not the best musician in the pack, but he might be the most enthusiastic.

Kelsey studies Ravi's fingers fiercely as he walks her through some notes. She's a far better student than I ever was. He gets her going on a simple, three-note melody line, and then he starts playing fancy things underneath. Ones that don't sound fancy, because that's not the kind of man he's ever been, but Kendra's eyebrows fly up.

I smile. We might have more than jam to offer in exchange for hawk rides and guitar deliveries.

Jade wriggles out of Ravi's lap, a pup already dancing. Braden bounds to join her, their feet hitting the ground in time to Robbie's beat, which is remarkably steady. I look at Kel, and then I look closer, but it still takes me a minute to see his hands quietly squeezing a rhythm on my son's knees.

He glares at me when I flash him a hand sign in thanks.

I shake my head, but this, too, is part of today's sharp messages.

In the kind of pack we're working so very hard to become, there are always other hands and paws to help.

I sigh. I'm probably not done feeling guilty for the parts I got wrong. Again. I wasn't ready for Ravi's panic when the guitar arrived. I forgot just how hard it is to drink when you've been parched for six years. But as I listen to Kelsey's happy notes dancing with Ravi's rusty, creaky, gorgeous ones, and all the happy rocks and sticks and feet and hoots surrounding them, it's hard not to acknowledge the obvious.

My pack's got this.

Reilly is beaming as he helps Kelsey, and Kel is finding Robbie some sturdier sticks, and Ebony is making Rio dance, and none of it needs me to do anything except be happy.

A cheek nuzzles against my shoulder as Hayden slides in behind me. "That was really smart. And you picked the right place to shop."

I lean back against his chest, drinking in my alpha's affection and approval and remembering the guy who played a hot-pink child's guitar on video chat with us with as much care and pride as he played the fanciest instrument in his store. "He's going to put some student guitars aside for us. As we can find room in our budget."

A chuckle against my neck. "You and your magic spreadsheets."

I take a breath. The messages landing today have

mostly vanquished my guilt, but not my gratitude. "Thank you. You stopped him when he would have run."

He snorts. "I just added a few words to what was already a done deal."

"Your words come with alpha weight. They matter." Especially to our wolves.

He shrugs. "Your friend Bailey gave me a pretty good line to use."

She'll like that. She'll like it even more that he actually used it. I wiggle backward on the grass, snuggling in a little more firmly to his warmth. "She's going to be a major annoyance for a while. That's kind of how she rolls."

Arms wrap around my ribs, holding me close. "Big catcher's mitt, remember? It's all good."

My wolf sighs happily.

His goes all quiet and still—and suddenly smells like reticence.

"Shit." His arms loosen, waiting for my spine to engage before he very carefully lets me go. "I'm sorry, Lissa. I'm not thinking and I'm crossing lines." He scoots backward, his hand rubbing my back.

Soothing me like he does everyone in this pack.

Nudging me over to the other pups with his nose.

The sharp-edged lessons of this day drive my wolf to her feet—and a green-eyed human rises, too.

Both of them spitting mad.

25

LISSA

My wolf is really patient, until she isn't anymore and she's ready to bite someone's nose off just for breathing—and she's not the most furious part of me right now.

I crash to a halt in the trees. I've dragged Hayden far enough. Any farther and there will be dumbfounded sentries watching, and we probably only have two minutes before pups and inscrutable betas and a really annoying sentinel and a couple of reporters come to chase our asses down.

Because we're that kind of pack now.

My wolf growls and spins to face the man watching her with really cautious eyes. I glare at him with all the fierceness I can muster. It's a pretty impressive amount. "Why are you pulling away? From me? From Robbie? Why are you hurting your wolf?"

I don't know if any of those are the right questions,

but at least I'm not sitting quietly like some kind of scared bunny snack.

Hayden stares at me. His hand lifts slowly, reaching for me. To pet. To soothe.

My wolf nearly bites his hand off. "Don't. You keep trying to make me happy and safe and comfortable and it's doing something weird to your wolf and I want to know what."

His palms go up.

Good. He can hear the bomb ticking. He's not an entirely stupid wolf.

I make a grab for mine, because I think I'm maybe overreacting just a little, but she's not having it. She shakes me off like slowpoke fleas and growls again. She can smell what she's chasing, she just needs to hunt it down. "You pushed Robbie away. Yesterday when the pups were hanging out with you. You put him back with the others."

Guarded sadness touches his eyes. "Yes."

My wolf snarls. "Why?"

He turns around and kicks a tree. I stare, and then I stare some more, because his hands are fisted and he's cursing under his breath and most importantly, Hayden Scott is breaking his own rules and leaking dominance—and I suddenly know, deep in my bones, that this is his equivalent of Ravi ready to run for the hills.

A wolf teetering on the edge.

One who's got his back to me, a wild act of trust as he tries to get himself under control. I step forward and put a hand between his shoulder blades. Carefully, gingerly, and deeply aware of the irony.

His back turns to hot steel under my touch. "Just give me a second."

Oh, no. We've already gone down that road. My wolf snarls at him again, because apparently she's insane. "Talk to me, Hayden. Quit trying to be the tough guy who never makes anything harder for anyone else. Eat all the berries again and *talk to me.*"

That gets me an amused look, even though he's still fighting hard to control his wolf. His very dominant, very riled wolf.

My wolf snorts. She can handle him.

I shake my head. "I'm sorry. I think my wolf has lost her mind."

He sighs and steps into me, leaning his forehead into mine. "She knows this is all a big show from a dumbass who isn't doing a good job of being patient."

That word tries to set me off again, but I don't let it this time. I listen, instead. I listen and I hear and I let my wolf's nose guide me, because we're hunting something so very raw and important.

Something lost that needs to come home.

I lift my hands to his cheeks, cupping the face that brought kindness and compassion to my pack and has never asked for them in return. "You're backing away. That's different from being patient."

He swallows. "Not so different."

I run my thumbs over the scruff on his cheeks. "Explain."

He wraps his fingers around my wrists and sighs. "I'm your alpha, and your wolf needs that energy and connection from me. Which is not the same as... other things. But it's not always obvious where the lines are, especially when my wolf gets all happy because the music is playing and his pack is happy and he starts rolling around and wants to hold you while he does it."

Something centers, deep inside me.

I hold the face of the man who's gone so very still in front of me. The one who's tucked away so many of his wishes and needs and desires so that he doesn't make things harder for his pack. So that he doesn't pressure me. So that his fragile places stay hidden and he doesn't have to feel us as we see them.

A man who's made a good choice and a wrong one.

Because he's strong and wonderful and weak and imperfect.

Because he took a walk through the woods one day and his whole life changed and he made us promises and he intends to keep them.

Because he's still a small boy who misses his dad.

Because just like me, Hayden Scott isn't all the way home.

I look at him and I think of Ravi's panicked eyes. Of Bailey's annoyed, fierce ones. Of Shelley's brave, anguished ones as she robbed a bank and Miriam's wild ones as she took out her alpha at the knees. Of a bear, stepping up to what was asked of him, and two teenagers who went off on jobs far too big for them, and the look in a mother's eyes as she remembered a day so long ago that has never really ended.

I finally know what they've all been trying to show me.

This isn't about choosing Hayden. He isn't my destination.

It isn't about being ready, either.

It's about being willing.

HAYDEN

I just said big, important, probably inappropriate words to her, and she's not listening to them. She's listening to something else. Something deeper. Something that I'm pretty sure has just stripped me naked and I'm never going to be able to find my pants again.

She slides her hands down to my chest, her green eyes staring straight into mine. "Tell me the rest."

I'm literally not sure that I can.

I let my head dip down and land on her shoulder. "We all have history. Empty places. Jagged parts. A lot of mine are in the shape of my dad."

Her wolf croons against my ear.

I lean into that and try to find the strength to set down every alpha instinct I have, because that's not who she's asking to see. She wants to see Hayden Scott. "My mom thinks my highest dream is to be alpha. She's wrong."

Utter, sudden stillness.

I gather up all the pieces of small, broken boy and lay them in her hands. "Waiting for you is hard. Waiting for Robbie is even harder." I gulp air in and wheeze it back out. I'm not sure who's holding us upright, but it isn't me. "I'm not saying your son needs a father—but I need to be one."

Breath whooshes out of her, and the unit that we are gets dangerously wobbly.

I laugh, even though it makes all my jagged edges scrape against each other, and wrap my arms around her ribs. Around her precious, ferocious heart. "Is that so hard to believe?"

She shakes her head. Yes. No. Yes.

Confused, wondrous wolf. I hold her tight, because apparently that's all I can manage. "I watched Robbie swing on the rope at the falls for an hour and it nearly killed me. I remember my dad teaching me how to swing like that, and I didn't want to let go either." I just wanted to fly and fly and never have it end, but it did, and the small boy who lived through that ending doesn't know how to resist the pup with the big heart and the wild smile and that same desire to fly. "I don't know how to say these things to you without them becoming something that squeezes your choices."

She sighs and pushes back far enough to see my eyes. "Words are only pressure if I let them be. I needed to hear this from you."

I wince. "Dominant instincts aren't always the right

ones. And neither are really-fallible-guy ones, either. I'm sorry."

She just studies me. Listening one more time to something I didn't say.

LISSA

He'll take this all on himself if I let him. Silly wolf.

Home isn't a place you earn. It's a place you choose to be.

I run my hands into the hair at the nape of his neck. I tug gently, working my fingers against his scalp, getting a firm hold. Speaking to both parts of his soul.

His breath catches. He quivers under my touch, a wolf not entirely sure what he's just scented.

I take my time, even though I can hear the whispers and the crackles as our not remotely stealthy pack closes in around us. Even my very private human can't get twisted up about that, though. It's right that they're here. I choose this.

I choose home. I choose center.

I choose him. I choose me.

I tug on his hair again and his eyes turn deeper gold. His breath huffs out against my cheeks. I lift up on my toes, pulling our bellies together, our hearts.

My wolf snorts. That is not a belly.

My cheeks turn the color of fall leaves. There are pups watching.

She nuzzles against a yellow-gold wolf. Silly human. All the pups will see is life.

Hayden's throat closes on a whimper.

I brush my lips against his neck. Against the part of him that took so long to speak. Against his need to hold his secrets inside. My heartbeat thumps in my chest. My ears. My fingertips. I breathe in the scent of him, this very good man and magnificent, fallible wolf, and offer him the smell of decisions made in return.

His cheek rests against mine. Breathing. Hearing. Hoping.

My lips travel his jawline. Memorizing, ever so slowly seeking. My wolf isn't impatient at all anymore. Her tongue sneaks out, tasting him, laughing at the sandpaper of his scruff. A squeak from behind me, and Hayden's quiet chuckle in my ear.

I don't care. There's nothing but goodness here. Nothing that needs to be hidden.

His heart thumps against mine, fast, like we're running up the ridge lines. Telling me a story far different from his stillness.

I stretch up a little further and nip his earlobe.

He jerks, and the hardness pressed against me turns into a furnace. Something inside me revels. I seek his lips, and I'm not going slowly now. There will be time later to know all of him. Right now I have a promise to make and a promise to keep and I really hope he's not kidding about the size of his catcher's mitt. My lips find his, warm and sweet, and I push up further on my toes.

The statue that is Hayden Scott shatters. A growl rumbles up from his toes as his hands lift my hips.

My legs wrap around his waist, holding tight in the sudden storm of man and wolf and need. I meet his fierceness, because I don't need him to be gentle and I don't need him to be careful and I don't need him to be safe. I need him to be real. I nibble on his lip and nip harder when he laughs, delighting in this man who tastes like summer and sun berries and truth.

The kiss quiets, and the thundering of his heart morphs into a song of reverence.

My feet reach for the ground, but I don't let go of him.

His head dips to my shoulder again, and his soft exhale vibrates every atom of who I am. He stays there, his wolf and his soul having a conversation with mine. I run my hands through his hair and listen to his heart.

To the sound of home.

26

LISSA

It's just how I imagined it. Soft guitar playing by the river, the music traveling easily to ears that are settling down for sleep or talking quietly or finding a small moment of solitude wrapped in the gentle blanket of night.

My imagination totally failed me on the rest of it, though.

There's a man with yellow-gold eyes leaning against the tree beside me, our bellies full of pizza and our hearts full of something I'm still working to wrap my arms all the way around. Whatever it is, it's not going slowly. Which is probably something I should think about, but every time I try, my son licks Hayden's nose or Ravi starts playing a song about the winding roads that lead to home or someone feeds me pizza.

My pack, catching the pebble I've become.

I look over at the man whose music has been washing over us for hours. Cori is leaning against Ravi's knee as she talks to Eliza and Miriam. She's expressive and vibrant in a way I've never seen before. Having her mate back has allowed her to be three-dimensional again. The kind of dimensions that let her yell at him over breakfast and then kiss him silly after. Which the pups watched with avid glee and so did all the adults.

Wolves don't have a word for privacy.

I tip my head against Hayden's shoulder and sigh. He so very clearly wants me and my wolf is entirely gone over him and my human isn't far behind—and I totally get why Cori lost her temper this morning.

It's not choosing Hayden that's hard. It's choosing me. Owning who I want to be in my life and in my pack. Pebble thrower. Spreadsheet magician. Mom. Risk taker. Deep believer in my motley band of wolves and who we can be. After six years of stringent caution, it feels like jumping on a roller coaster blindfolded.

One that doesn't have any tracks.

I inhale and let it out slowly.

Hayden's fingers brush my arm. Not soothing, exactly. The touch of a fellow traveler who knows what it is to breathe into things that are fragile.

My wolf leans in and licks his neck. Just a small taste. Then I cuddle against his shoulder and let my eyes travel the river's edge. There are wolves on both sides. I mostly can't see the ones on the far bank, but I can sense them.

Some are the sentries, on some kind of rotation Ebony set up after a visit from Ghost.

Some aren't sentries.

I catch sight of Kennedy, perched in a tree. She grins at me, laughter and happiness and mischief in her eyes. I shake my head. The pebble she went off to toss hasn't even landed yet. Which doesn't feel nearly as scary as it did last week.

I reach for a small bowl of berries that keeps refilling as we empty it. Sun berries, from a stupidly big basket of them that showed up for Hayden this morning. With a note. *You can share these.*

Best friends can be really annoying.

I hope she's close enough to hear the music.

I look over at Kel, who's leaning against Shelley and Myrna and keeping a close eye on the woods. I could tell him there's no danger there, but I'm sure he already knows. So many wolves taking steps toward home. Toward happiness. Toward each other.

Ravi switches to a mournful melody, one with hints of something happier trying to sneak through. Kelsey lifts up her chin and howls from her spot on the leaf-floating log. She doesn't mirror the happy notes. She makes the mournful ones stronger. More urgent.

Rio snorts and tosses a pinecone at her head.

Ravi chuckles and does something to his song that makes it brighter.

Kelsey smiles at Rio, who rolls to his feet, picks her up, and dangles her upside down by her ankles. Making sure one very wise four-year-old doesn't grow up quite so darned fast.

Ravi catches her giggles with his fingers.

Cori reaches up and touches her hand to his cheek.

The man with his head tilted against mine exhales, a sound drenched in absolute pleasure.

My wolf sets her chin on her tail.

This. She chooses this.

HAYDEN

I let my fingers tangle gently with Lissa's. The tension that ran through her a moment ago has eased, but I say the words anyhow. I won't leave tricky things unsaid, not anymore. "We can take this at human speed." Lots of wolves do, especially if they've spent any time on the receiving end of my mother's lectures.

Which has always amused me. Pack legend says she took one look at my father and toppled like a giant, majestic, old-growth tree.

Lissa strokes the fuzzy white head currently occupying my lap.

There are all kinds of reasons to go slowly, and he's probably the very best of them. "We could go on some dates. Ones that aren't photographed and put up on ShifterNet as breaking news."

Her giggle rouses Robbie. He licks my knee and goes back to falling asleep.

My wolf's desire to be a good, upstanding, evolved citizen disintegrates. I sweep up all the dust I can reach and make one last, whimpering effort. "I know what you're feeling from me, and I can't do anything about that. But there are still choices."

"I know." She smiles up at me sweetly and my wolf rolls over and wriggles on his back. "I made them. I reserve the right to change my mind, and so should you, but I'm pretty sure you're stuck with me."

My wolf understands none of the words in that sentence. He only has one, and he says it every chance he gets.

Mine.

Neanderthal canine.

That doesn't even get a rise out of him. Probably because he thinks early humans were a lot smarter than the modern kind. Eat, sleep, hunt, love. It was a good era for teeth and claws.

I roll my eyes. It was a good era for scrambling to survive and watching too many pups die. He nuzzles into the spot at the crook of Lissa's neck that smells sweetest and utterly ignores me. I can't blame him. She smells really good.

Rio catches my eye and flashes a hand sign I really hope the pups don't learn. Which is all the feedback I'm getting from him. One big, black wolf has had suspiciously little to say about his alpha's current state of green-eyed dizziness. Not that I think he's going to object. The ripples of absolute rightness this is causing in the pack are hard to ignore.

Which shouldn't get to press on Lissa either, except she's being really clear with me. She chooses this. She chooses to be the beating heart, right at the center, and she'll take whatever tight squeezes and uncomfortable moments and lack of privacy that entails.

I get to choose whether or not I hold her cape.

My wolf snorts. He made that choice the moment he laid eyes on her.

Sometimes Neanderthal canines are really smart.

Something shifts slightly in the pack ether, and Lissa tips her chin up and kisses my cheek. "I'll be right back."

My heart squeezes as she walks away. I watch as she scoops up one of Mellie's toys, winks at Reilly, picks up a pitcher of water and refills the glass on the stump near Ravi's left hand. Collecting up strands of pack as she travels and leaving them better because she walked by.

She leaves me often, and my wolf is already learning to deal, because he likes how she feels when she's had space and time and freedom. And because the pups have taken to crawling into my lap when she goes, like they know that their big, bad alpha has some issues with the people he loves not making it back home again, and the solution for that is maple syrup and cuddles.

It's hard to disagree with them.

I stroke the fuzzy, white, snoring head in my lap.

A wolf steps just far enough out of the shadows that I can see her and vanishes again. I sigh. It's respect, of a sort, and the only kind I'm likely to get from that particular shifter for a while. And it's a request, even if it's a bossy one.

I look around for Kel and Ebony. The glowing lines of pack on the back of my eyelids tell me there are at least a dozen wolves inside the inner perimeter who aren't supposed to be here, and Bailey vouching for them isn't going to change my betas' need to track all of them.

I spy Lissa instead, watching me with eyes that make my human gulp and my wolf swoon. I smile back at her and let her see all that I want and need and wish for—and that I've got a good hold on her cape.

ADRIANNA

I stare at the two pictures I just got from my favorite bear.

In the first one, my son's ears are bright pink and the woman in his arms is kissing him silly and he looks absolutely dazzled.

In the other, he's leaning on a green-eyed wolf, looking like his entire world just tilted and gravity will never ever be the same again and he hasn't yet remembered how to breathe.

My fingers touch the screen, tracing the contours of Hayden's face. My heart reaches for the mate bond that is somehow still there and the man who's somehow at the end of it still. I don't bother to hide my tears—he's always thought they were the best part of me. "Look, James. Our boy has found his love."

His deep laugh resonates inside me. *It looks like she's found him.*

I smile. He's right, of course. She did find him, just as James once found me.

It's what hearts do.

Next up: Teenagers just might be taking over the pack. Or breaking it. Get Rebel, book three in the Ghost Mountain Wolf Shifters series.